AMUSE

By Karma Marie

This novel is a work of fiction. Names, characters, places, and events are either the product of the author's imagination or are used fictitiously.

No part of this book may be reproduced or transmitted in any form or by any electronic, or mechanical, means, including information stoprage and retrieval systems, without the express written permission from the author. The only exception is for brief quotes used for book reviews or press articles.

This book is dedicated to my wonderful mother, who has encouraged all my artistic endeavors, my family and many friends who encouraged and supported me and my most special friend Jon B. who I know is looking down from heaven shaking his head saying, "It's about damn time, Karma."

FOREWORD

I felt extremely honored when Karma asked me to write a foreword for her print release of Amuse. Who would have thought she would ask me to write anything for her, let alone a foreword. Then I thought, what should I write about?

I understand a foreword is a chance for another author to give their take on the story, which I loved. But I also would hate to give anything away. The temptation is there, still. I would love to regale you about my favorite scenes in the book or what comes to mind when Calli does something I am not quite fond of. However, I think you need to discover these things on your own first.

Instead I thought I would tell you a little about Karma. I like to consider her a very dear personal friend of mine. Well more than that really. She is one of the people I turn to when ideas are richochetting around in my head too fast for me to make sense of them. I think it takes a special kind of skill to be able to catch thoughts and themes and help decipher them without knowing the full underlying story. She has this skill, which makes her unique.

Enjoy the book, I know you will. And, when you get a chance to meet her in person, ask Karma about the long conversations about Calli's coming exploits. You will be amazed at what she has planned.

-John Harrison

PROLOGUE

Death comes in many forms; it can be sneaky and as subtle as a whisper or as large and clumsy as an explosion. Mine was both; Dragon. It stood 100 feet tall with razor sharp talons, large leathery wings and rows of teeth gnashing together, eager to rip through my flesh. Its destructive appetite was overwhelmingly apparent, yet it was controlled by an unseen master, hidden in shadows of intrigue and motivated by mystery.

Blood trailed from a gash in my head, stinging my eyes which were already blurred from smoke and heat. My dove white robes were stained crimson from additional wounds on my arms, legs and back; miraculously or perhaps not so much, my stomach was injury free. My left arm was broken, a result of the monster crushing me in its claws as it yanked me from a restless slumber.

The yells and screams from the camp below sounded like a dull roar as consciousness slipped away from me like water through a sieve. My last thought was of indifference; either option, whether life or death was no more appealing than the other. I was broken at last.

One

Endings, Beginnings and the In Between

I knew my life was over; at least life as I knew it, when I noticed David's silver Lexus sitting in the driveway of my parent's home. It was Saturday; a little past 10. My mother, brother and I had just finished brunch consisting more of champagne mimosas than actual food. Dad was tooling around in his shed, having been up since the crack of dawn and seemingly unaffected by the late-night partying.

We had been celebrating my parent's 25th wedding anniversary, most of which was spent showing off my 2-carat diamond engagement ring. David had been absent, having been called in to the office for a client crisis. I wasn't upset, it wasn't often he was called away and I enjoyed the quality time spent with my family. Ever since becoming involved almost a year ago, I hadn't much time to visit and he had at least remembered to sign the card on the gift from the two of us; a Caribbean cruise.

The plan today had been to meet at his office and then dinner at Fleur de Lys followed up with "Pippin" at the Orpheum Theater. Since I had canceled my lease on my loft in San Jose, quit my job and moved everything into storage I was sleeping on my parent's couch. David was bunking at a friend's. Later this week we were supposed to be moving into a condominium in the financial district of San Francisco. His company, Oly Management, had recently purchased the building across from their main office and was offering a gorgeous two-bedroom apartment with breathtaking views of the bay and the Golden Gate Bridge as an early wedding gift.

We were starting over together in a new place and for me a new job working with him in the recruiting department. We had well thought out and structured plans; nothing had been left to chance. Or had it? Obviously, those plans had changed. How did I know? Well, let's just say I had a kind of six sense about these things.

My heart plummeted into my stomach at a force even my optimistic nature couldn't stop. I was a fragile kite in the rough March wind, miles above the Earth. I could almost hear the metallic snip of the scissors of fate.

In dream fashion, time slowed, and I moved as if in deep water against swift currents. I slid the ring off my finger without looking at it and proceeded downstairs. I couldn't feel the steps beneath my feet, but the ring felt heavy in my hand like a grenade and I resisted the temptation to throw it and run. I startled him as I opened the door before he could knock. He knew I knew the moment he saw my face. Though I wouldn't let any tears betray me, I didn't have the talent of better women at hiding my pain. Raw and exposed, he read every page of my open book. "Calli, we need to talk," his voice sounded rough.

I placed the ring in his hand, turned back into the house and closed the door.

"No David, we don't." I leaned back against the door, sliding slowly to the cold tile floor. An eternity passed then I heard his footsteps fading, his car door shut, his car driving away and then I heard my brother coming down the stairs.

"You okay?" He asked with concern but not purpose. Charlie never pressured, he was just there. I shook my head 'no'. "You want to talk?" I shook my head 'no'. "Want to go to our spot?" I nodded and allowed him to pull me to my feet. "Can you tell me anything?" I held up my naked hand and he shook his head in quiet understanding.

Ten minutes later we were sitting on a rocky bank overlooking the Paradise Cut; a lower branch of the San Joaquin River smack dad in the middle of farmland. Northern California or NorCal as it was dubbed by its residents, didn't subscribe to the hype and glamour most tourists associated with the 'Golden State'.

Many would be surprised to learn that the home state of Hollywood was also the country's leading producer of fruits, vegetables, nuts and wines. Los Angeles was only five hours away, yet the closest I came to the glitz was watching the Academy Awards on TV at home. Though I did visit Disneyland once, and it was amazing.

Today we drove but growing up Charlie and I had ridden our bikes, well from our grandparent's house, as we hadn't been allowed to ride to or from our parent's house in town. We had designated this as our special spot where we felt our conversations were protected and private. It sat on property owned by a sweet couple who grew alfalfa and never minded us kids there; as long as we were careful.

Of course, we weren't so young anymore and neither were they, but she always popped her head out of the kitchen window when she saw us and called out, 'You be careful kids, don't get too close to the water.' We received no call today which left me feeling a little cold.

Our only company was a couple of beautiful blue gray Sandhill cranes that eyed us warily but otherwise remained where they were. They were a common sight that I never took for granted. The wildlife around here might not be exotic enough for most zoos, but I relished it; even the coyotes, though their howling at night made me nervous.

They never got too close to our grandparent's house, maybe because of all the windmills; there were probably close to fifty of every shape, size and color. Nana said they helped circulate the energy or something weird like that. She was a beautiful odd ball.

Most of the sounds out here were organic; none of the traffic and people noise of the city I had become accustomed to since moving from my parent's home in Taylor. The sky was cloudy, threatening to rain but gratefully there was little wind. The dull weather was comforting; if the sun had emerged I would have probably cursed it for mocking my gray mood with its light.

I pulled my cardigan tighter, more for comfort than for warmth. I had just thrown it over my pajamas, rather than grab a change of clothes from my suitcase in the den, unable to face either of my parents who were basking in the glow of their successful union.

Charlie sat with me in silence. I stared at the murky blue green water, counting the water lilies, while he fiddled with his cell phone. He was the only one in our family who truly understood me and knew what I needed; time and space.

When the oppressing weight on my chest had lifted enough I spoke.

"So, when do you go back to school?" I didn't recognize the tiny voice that came out of me.

"I'll head back tomorrow but I'm off in two weeks for Spring Break," he said this with a slight hint of sarcasm. Charlie was as far on the opposite spectrum of the MTV beach clad revelers as one could get. He was tall, pale, lanky, and moppy headed with thick glasses and a brain that ran at high speed and capable of multitasking. During any number of conversations with me I caught him solving complicated mathematical equations in his head. I, on the other hand couldn't even balance my checkbook.

"He left an envelope on the porch swing." Charlie never stayed on personal topics applying to him for very long.

He placed the thick parcel in my hands and waited for me to open it, which I did for his benefit only. I didn't care. My emotions were dull from soaking in David's bathwater. Inside was a letter, which I laid on the ground next to me, a check for a substantial amount of money as well as a large ornate key on a red silk cord and the engagement ring. I handed the letter to Charlie.

"I don't care the reasons; just tell me what's what and why." He unfolded the letter carefully, scanning it quietly. Then he folded it up and placed it back in the envelope.

"The check is to compensate for living expenses since you gave up your place and job. He says it's to help get you back on your feet." He looked at me with soft eyes. "Frankly I think you should invest it in a little company called My Tech, get super rich, invite him to a gala celebrating your good fortune then slap him in front of everyone with an overpriced salmon in a sparkly dog collar."

"The collar is on me or the fish?"

"Either or both. Future you can afford it." He nudged me with his shoulder and I offered him my one and only smile. "The ring he wants you to keep. Perhaps you could pawn it and invest it," he winked. I slipped the ring on my other hand for the mean time. "Okay, moving on he also included your spare storage key and a necklace you left behind."

"This isn't the storage key," I told him. I turned the envelope over and shook it. Nothing else fell out. "So, this must be the necklace." I slipped the silk cord over my head. The antique key slid beneath my shirt. Oddly, the extra weight of it made me feel lighter.

"Does it open anything?" He asked. I shrugged in response. "I don't know. I've never seen it before."

"Then how is it yours?" He asked. I shrugged.

"It isn't, not that I recall. But it's obviously not his and it probably doesn't open anything, just decorative; like those quirky ladies' necklaces they sell at Madeline's."

"Calli," my brother's voice was cautious, "is it possible? Do you think it belonged?" He didn't finish his thought, didn't' need to. I knew where this was heading.

The faint strains of a jazz band slithered through my mind and I'm suddenly back at the Oly Management Company Christmas party. I was decked out in a gorgeous red Vera Wang column dress that accentuated my curves, Jimmy Choo heels and about three months' rent in diamond jewelry. My normally out of control curly hair was smooth and swept up into a complicated up do. I was shocked every time I glimpsed my reflection; chestnut brown hair, pale skin, sheathed in sparkling blood red. I was eerily beautiful like a dark Cinderella. I hadn't known I could look so cosmopolitan.

I had giggled self-consciously all night, feeling like a child trying on Mommy's clothes though David had been grooming me for this event for months, gradually adding something extra to my wardrobe; a pair of heels here, a La Perla bustier there, I had even started getting my hair and nails done on a regular basis. Still, you could remodel the exterior but inside I was still the same awkward and careless tomboy.

David, on the other hand was looking like he stepped off the cover of GQ, sandy blond hair short but slightly tousled, black Armani tux, and black shirt with silver striped tie. He led me from one group of people to the next; making introductions I wouldn't remember, at a speed that made my head spin.

At one point he left me by a large ice sculpture to take care of some urgent business.

"Champagne," a waiter appeared with a tray of sparkling amber filled glasses.

"Thank you," He flashed me his nametag, "Dion." He smiled and left the tray on the table next to me with a wink. Somehow the one drink turned into four, liquid courage to overcome my social anxiety in a room full of strangers.

David never talked about the people at work and little more about work itself and I had never pressed for more details. The gist of my knowledge was this; they were a management company and he was one of their field reps. I searched the crowd for one familiar face but of course there was none. I was in the midst of a loud exuberant crowd of people, yet I felt woefully alone. I gave up my post and went searching for David.

The ball room was opulent and resplendent with so many golden accents it glittered. The history, I had read on a nearby pamphlet, had been just as intricate and possibly as embellished and I regretted not taking the time to appreciate it, feeling almost rude as I performed my perfunctory search.

I continued my search into the hall, performing the same investigation of the pool area. Which was equally enthralling with its multi colored lights both around and floating on the surface of the water and I was more than a little envious of the couples enjoying the fresh air, moonlight and overall romantic ambiance.

Luckily Dion was quick to offer me more fuel for my search and I was well beyond tipsy at this point. I ended up on an elevator that stopped at each and every floor. Oops! I laughed at the illuminated square of numbers, all of them save one; the 13th floor. For some drunken rationale I hit that button and made that my new destination.

The ride up I sang along to a Muzak version of a Carly Simon song while gripping the hand rail. By the time the doors opened on 13 I was feeling a little woozy and extremely nauseous. I raced into the first office I saw, which gratefully had an adjoining bathroom complete with shower and a closet full of toiletries and men's clothing.

After 'donating' my dinner and champagne, I rinsed my mouth with water and a generous swig of mouth wash. My reflection glared back at me miserably and chided me mentally for what exactly? Getting drunk or being here in the first place? I flushed with embarrassment. This wasn't me, this was me with David. I was like a lump of clay being shaped and molded by someone else's hands.

I suddenly came to the realization that this night was a very real interpretation of our relationship; out of my control and fast paced. I began to question everything and all my choices in life so far. Of course, all the questioning made me tired and motivated to get home, into my comfy pajamas and slide into my familiar bed. I heard David and hurried out into the hall, his voice was suddenly muffled.

I turned a corner and saw him talking animatedly inside an office with large glass windows with the door closed. I hesitated, nervous about the expression on his face, one he'd never worn for me; anger. I contemplated what to do next. Should I wait for him, go to him or leave all together?

The decision was made for me when I saw who he was talking to; She was tall, blonde and strong looking. Her physique contrasted greatly with the overtly feminine lines and frill of her pink cocktail dress. She moved toward him and threw her arms around his neck. I didn't stay to see more.

Somehow, I managed to climb into the limo and back to my apartment. The next morning, I awoke to find him sitting on my bed, smiling at me in that loving way I'd only known from him. He made me tea, which helped my hangover, breakfast in bed and then made love to me, his hands gentle, and his kisses soft.

While I lay there in blissful warmth, he proposed, and I said 'yes' because that's what I felt at that moment. That incident at the office party was the one and only blight on our idyllic relationship so I pushed it away and when it wouldn't stay put I explained it away; just a confused memory created through a cloud of alcohol and stress. 'It never happened' became my mantra until I no longer needed it. I shared none of this with Charlie and never would.

"No, he wasn't another Joe." My face was pinched from the taste of that sour memory. Joe was my boyfriend from college and he had very definitely cheated on me and hadn't even bothered to hide it. We hadn't discussed marriage, but we were definitely on that track. That is until he introduced me to 'the other woman' mere minutes before dinner with my parents. Actually, I think she was the hostess at the restaurant.

"Are you sure?" He asked again. The look I shot him was icy.

"I'm sure Charlie," I wasn't but I knew I didn't want to be a habit. Poor Calli, the victim, the left behind. "It doesn't matter. I don't care."

"But you quit your job and moved out of your apartment for him. How can you not want to know?"

"Easy," I said with a forced smile, "It's in the past, we're in the now and I have to move forward towards my future on my own, without him."

"Maybe you should read it," he started to open the letter again; I silenced him with a look.

"Does it contain the phrase, 'Surprise, this was all just a joke!'?" He shook his head somberly. "Then I'm done talking about it Charlie, please let's go." He helped me up and hugged me tight.

"What are you going to do?" he whispered. "I don't know," I whispered back. As we head to the car I swear the stupid cranes are eyeing me with pity.

When we arrived back to our parent's house, my grandmother and mother were sitting at the kitchen table talking very quietly. Honestly, the faint tick of the 'Home is where the heart is!' clock above the door was louder.

I steadied myself; in my family quiet equaled conspiracy. Sitting there together they looked more like sisters than mother and daughter, though there were strands of gray in my grandmother's chestnut hair. My mother and I were often mistaken as such, also. Women in my family retained a youthful quality. A gift when you're in your fifties but a curse when you're 19 trying to sneak into bars.

The chatter stopped abruptly when my brother and I walked in. Conspiracy! I gave him a stern look, but he shrugged and continued upstairs to his room. Our parents maintained his, even though he had an apartment near his college, Sacramento State. Mine had been relegated to a fitness room immediately after I moved out.

There was no pretense of me moving back in. I was the explorer, as kids I was the one covered in bandages or on crutches, always grinning through the mud and blood. My brother was the one who often stayed behind where he felt safe, close to our parents, especially our mother.

He once insisted I was the reason for my mother's premature delivery. He should know he was my womb mate. The fact he attended a school over an hour away was more a testament to their computer science program than his maturing bravery.

One thing was sure; though my renegade tendencies had softened much over the years I had neither the intention nor the desire to move back into this awkward space. It would be like wearing jeans from high school; tight, outdated and uncomfortable.

"Have a seat Calliope," my grandmother always insisted on using my full name, which I never used except on formal documents. I found it silly and antiquated, like a 1900's cartoon character in a long dress and twirling a parasol, possibly being courted by a man named Reginald. Their dates would consist of carriage rides, crumpets and tea and he would kiss the inside of her wrist only when no one was looking as to not offend anyone with his lusty tendencies.

I slowly slid into my seat, feeling more like a criminal about to be interrogated than an offspring of caring women. They glanced at my left hand but didn't comment, confirming my suspicion that Charlie had snitched. I'd let him hear it later.

I cherished my privacy and independence and hated intrusion from anyone, most of all family. He knew this. It was one of the reasons David's leaving hit so hard, it had been a long painful process of letting him inside all the walls I'd built up only to have him vacate without any notice. I was brave with many things; love wasn't one of them. I suddenly felt vulnerable and exposed like a cadaver ready for autopsy.

"What's up?" I asked, trying to sound light and failing miserably. I occupied myself with braiding a strand of hair.

"Your grandmother and I were discussing where you will be staying. I can't imagine the couch is comfortable long term and you know how your brother is about his room." The three of us nodded in agreement on this last point.

"I have money. I can get a new place." Problem solved, have a nice day, I'll be going now. The two of them looked at me with a mixture of pity and concern; my least favorite recipe.

"Where," my mother demanded. She was all business; the business of Calli.

"I don't know, yet? Maybe those apartments on Cypress, off of Main St."

"That neighborhood is kind of sketchy." The neighborhood was actually quite nice.

"Fine then I can move back to San Jose, maybe get my job back."

"You should really stay close to family right now." You should really stay close to me was what she was saying.

"I'll figure something out." I strained my feeble brain but nothing. I tried vainly to hide my desperation.

"Calli, you need a plan." I could finally hear the desperation she had been hiding.

"Jesus Mom," I slammed my hand down on the table, stinging my palm. "Can I have a moment to breathe?" Normally I would have been embarrassed by such an outburst but their timing, while logical to them was too soon for me. I envisioned them riding with me on the way to the hospital poking and prodding my open wound after ripping out my heart to show them the damage.

"You can stay with me." My grandmother offered.

"Only until we get your old room sorted out," my mother added firmly. She shot my grandmother a warning look.

I shook my head 'no'. Staying at my grandmother's? No way! So I could suffer more of this?

"Yes, the guest room is all ready for you!" Nana smiled wider. I shook my head 'no'. Goodbye privacy, self-respect, integrity and anything else that differentiates grownups from children.

"Ahh but you see I already had them move your stuff in from your storage." She slid David's spare storage key across the table to me. I shook my head in wonder then realized this was my Nana we were talking about. She was crafty, purposeful and highly motivated, not to mention bull headed. If she had been on the Titanic, the iceberg would have lost.

I nodded in defeat and sighed loudly to convey my disapproval. Don't get me wrong, I loved my Nana dearly, in fact, next to Charlie she was my closest confidant. However, last year, around the time I had started dating David a gap had been forming pushing us further and further apart. It was even more apparent when I thought to show her the antique key but hesitated, fearing she might take it away. It was a ridiculous feeling, though one I couldn't shake, and it illustrated just how far our relationship had degenerated. As much as I hated to admit it, perhaps moving in with her would be beneficial. Still I hated feeling as though I had no voice in the decision.

I wasn't sure I was capable of a better plan, as my brain was still thawing having been doused with a bucket full of ice cold reality, but my pride was still intact and therefore wounded.

"Fine," I mumbled grudgingly, "but only until I get back on my feet." The two female consorts smiled at their victory while I pouted.

After it was made clear my input was no longer necessary for their frenetic planning, I quietly excused myself, grabbing a cold bottle of Moet on my way upstairs. Charlie found me twenty minutes later riding the stationary bike in my old room.

"Trying to make a get away," he stayed in the doorway, probably for fear of his safety. I laughed at his joke a little more loudly than normal.

"If only that easy," my smile was strained.

"I see you're staying hydrated." He indicated the champagne bottle in my hand.

"What? It's technically leftovers from breakfast. It's still half full or empty, whichever way you choose to look at it. I don't know how to look at it myself except when it's gone I know I will be much happier." I forced another smile and pedaled faster towards my unseen destination.

"I think you've had enough Sis," he gently pried the bottle from my hands, which wasn't difficult even for him. He caught me as I fell off my perch and hugged me for a moment. The warmth felt alien in my chilled and numb state.

He led me carefully down the hall and into his room, which I hadn't seen the inside of since my brash intrusion when I was 10; my parents had been locked out since he was five.

Charlie didn't value privacy for the sake of secrecy, he was just fearful of anyone disturbing his experiments, his scientific equipment and his overall sense of order. After I was tucked in securely in his bed, he closed the door quietly and left me alone with his unnecessary but greatly appreciated apology which offered the promise of deep and dream free sleep.

Two

To Grandmother's House We Go

The hangover the next morning helped explain away my malcontent of the day's upcoming event; moving into my grandparent's house. My scowling, grumpy, defensive attitude was lovingly washed over by my caring parents and grandmother and the subsequent guilt left a sour taste in my mouth that surpassed that of the alcohol.

Added to that was the fact that Charlie had already returned to Sacramento before I had awakened and had a chance to thank him. I felt like an infected patient who was contaminating those attempting to treat me. This was only the first day of a long battle; casualties must be kept to a minimum!

I struggled through smiles, hugs and countless variations of 'thank you' before climbing into my small Toyota and driving 'home'. Nana's place was an old bleached white wooden two-story farmhouse situated near the water about a quarter of a mile from mine and Charlie's spot.

It was neighbored by a small ranch with horses, goats and a cow on one side and an open field on the other. Usually tomatoes were grown there but over the years the farmer had tested out other crops like soy and corn. Of course, country neighbors were not as convenient as in the city; it was a long jog to the Walker's ranch not a step from your door to ask for a cup of sugar.

I wasn't sure if the space and remoteness would be an aid in healing or a hindrance; a grim reminder of how alone I was now. One thing was for sure, it was definitely slower paced; I waved politely to a passing farmer on a tractor blaring John Denver on a portable radio.

Being so near to my parent's home in town, a short 15-minute drive meant that while I stayed here I would be under even more scrutiny than ever; like an ant under a magnifying glass. I tried not to panic, feeling that smothering baby blanket wrap tighter around my nerve as I recalled their enthusiastic conversations.

"You'll be so close!" My mother had exclaimed over breakfast with me and my father. Close for what? I didn't know but my proximity seemed to make them happy. I suspected she had already taken on writing a life list for me; a habit she was teased about behind her back.

My mother made lists for everything, as though she could commence order in the Universe merely by applying pen to paper. I pondered what she thought should be on mine but quickly shuttled the thoughts away; I had enough to deal with at the moment, like having an elderly roommate.

I took a deep breath and walked into my grandmother's house for the first time ever feeling like a resident rather than a visitor. It was weird.

Don't get me wrong, over the years we had stayed many a night, weekend and even weeks with our grandparents but it always felt borrowed or rented; like a hotel room. Now my mail would be addressed here. I felt simultaneously blessed and saddened by that thought.

It wouldn't be all bad though; as much as my mother's place was granite and stainless steel, my grandmother's, was antiques and lace. I found it quaint and charming. Growing up everything seemed more special because it had a history, whether you knew it or not. Though usually Pops would tell a most excellent tale concerning the acquisition of say the grandfather clock in the hallway (stolen from pirates!) or the china set on display in the large oak hutch (a gift from the queen of France ooh la la).

While Charlie always concentrated on the age and wear and tear of furniture in the house and how it needed to be replaced, lamenting about a crack or a tear while I would sometimes come up with my own stories of how the piece was damaged and therefore most valuable.

She showed me my room, which was upstairs down the hall from hers. It was more than familiar to me; it had been the guest room since our grandfather had passed, before that it was his study. I had so many great memories of my grandfather sitting at his large mahogany desk tinkering on his fishing lures while telling outrageous stories. Whenever we visited I made him promise to wake me early, so I wouldn't miss out on any excursions. We always invited Charlie to go fishing with us but he always answered, 'maybe next time.' He never made it out before Pops died.

I strained to find something in the room to connect me to him, but all was left was the striped wallpaper, everything else had been moved to the cellar. The double bed with the simple white headboard and matching dresser were purchased within the past two years and the full-length mirror on a stand was unfamiliar all together. It reeked of newness, causing my nose to crinkle and my heart to ache. I stowed my luggage in the closet and took a hot shower; the numbness of the day slowly began to wear off.

When she asked about dinner I passed and crawled into bed, quietly crying myself to sleep while I cradled my pillow. I felt pathetic and small in the strange and lonely darkness, afraid of becoming so empty I might wither and float away into oblivion. Dawn couldn't come soon enough with its golden rays that poured through the gaps in my window curtains. I made a resolve, much like I did with any challenge in life; I purged myself and was ready to move on...without my fiancé and love of my life. Damn. I spent the next twenty minutes crying in the privacy of the shower. It didn't feel good, but it sure felt appropriate.

My first full day as new resident was the hardest. I awoke that morning feeling raw, bruised and emotionally exhausted. I zombie marched down the stairs and into the kitchen for a hot cup of coffee with a side of sanity. My grandmother had coffee waiting for me but was all out of the other it seemed.

"I thought today we could go to this interesting place I frequent that sells magic potions, herbs and other trinkets."

"Magic potions," I asked clarifying what had to be faulty hearing on my part. She nodded vigorously.

"Herbs and trinkets, yes, but not voodoo. I'm not sure if you're into that but she doesn't carry it. I personally am not a fan but to each their own." She shrugged as casually as though comparing musical styles.

"Not a voodoo practitioner but sure I can Google where to get supplies if I ever convert. So, are you going to buy magic potions?" I asked her slowly, waiting for her trade mark laugh when she's pulling your leg. She didn't laugh.

"I wasn't planning on it this trip, but you know how it is; you go for one thing and end up coming home with an armload."

"Does Mom know you're a witch?" I teased. She raised an eyebrow.

"She's made that mistake before but no."

"Um, okay." I forced a smile and after finishing my coffee went upstairs to get dressed. I chose comfortable yoga pants, t-shirt and tennis shoes, as I wasn't sure what appropriate attire for spell shopping was. I thought I should be prepared to run in case anything tried to eat me. Nana shook her head as I headed down the stairs.

"Something a little more respectful and somber please Calliope." She was dressed in a wine-colored skirt, emerald green draping top with short sleeves and a braided belt. I headed back to my room of boxes and dug until I found some black slacks and a crimson top. "Oh, that is perfect, thank you," she exclaimed when I came into the kitchen. She handed me a travel mug of coffee and motioned me towards the door. "I'm driving!"

It wasn't too long after we passed through the Altamont that I suspected our destination. "Nana, where are we going?"

"I told you, we're going shopping."

"Yes, but where?"

"In the city," she responded coyly.

"In the San Francisco city," I asked a little louder than necessary.

"Well of course, where else would you shop for magic?" "I guess that makes sense in crazy town, but you do realize that San Francisco is still a sore spot for me."

"The city?"

"Well, not technically the city but what it represents or more specifically, what it represented."

"Commerce, tourism, sea lions, the 49ers and the Giants?"

"What?"

"I'm sorry dear, I don't think I understand. Explain to me how the Giants hurt you."

"They didn't."

"Oh good, cause I'm a Posey fan."

"David and I were going to move there. Being there will make me sad." I felt like I was communicating with a 3-yr. old.

"Honey, I thought it might be difficult for you that is why I'm driving."

"You didn't think that walking would be a problem for me or standing?"

"I would hope not; goodness knows I can't carry you." Her tone and demeanor were complete seriousness. "Look Calli, I understand that something you thought you wanted badly didn't work out, but you can't hide from an entire city, you shouldn't want to, especially San Francisco. That's just a crime against human nature. There are too many wonderful things in life to be spoiled by one rotten one." I started to respond, and she eyed me sharply. "We wouldn't be going if it wasn't important and if you're worried you'll run into him don't. Tourists don't go where we're headed."

"Okay," I said as politely as I could manage and gazed out my window for the remainder of the trip. Of course, everything she said made sense but what ever happened to the grieving process. If this is how she handles day 2 then I should be courted and married to some new guy by day 10. Would I even have a choice in the suitor or would I be forced on some hybrid reality/dating show? The one positive was at least I knew he wouldn't be a voodoo master.

Try as I may it was impossible to keep up my sour disposition once the San Francisco – Oakland Bay Bridge was in sight. I couldn't help but smile, it had been a source of delight and excitement for as long as I could remember; as a child I practically climbed out the window to get the best view of the water. We parked in a seemingly normal garage near Fisherman's Wharf then took two trolleys, disembarking on Grant St. and then weaving our way through Chinatown toward Waverly Street.

"Nana, I thought you said we were going off the beaten path." It was hard to get more tourist attraction than San Francisco's famed Chinatown. Not that I minded; I found it beautiful and enchanting, creating this overwhelming feeling like I'd been transported to another world. The streets were lined with colorful signs, banners and lanterns with elegant Chinese scroll and the shops were filled with everything from the exotic like Buddha statues to the practical, toothpaste and shampoo. I marveled at everything as though it was my first time though my steps followed her knowingly.

"You'll see." She smiled and led me to Waverly Place.

"The Tin How Temple," I scrunched my face in confusion. "There's no store in there."

"So many questions Calliope just come." I threw up my hands in defeat and followed her up the stairs to the top floor.

Tin How Temple was founded in 1852 by Chinese immigrants and was dedicated to the goddess Mazu. It was small but just as respectable as any gargantuan tribute. We made our donations then headed out to the balcony, taking a moment to take in the ruby colored lanterns above. Though it was a weekday, there was still quite a crowd and I heard murmured conversations in various languages I couldn't comprehend. A young Asian woman wearing Nike tennis shoes and a white track suit with green piping and a ponytail pulled Nana into a tight hug.

"My friend, I wasn't expecting you until the Harvest Moon," she raised an eyebrow. My grandmother shrugged. "Something came up," she said casually though I saw a flicker of concern cross the woman's face. She recovered quickly and turned a beaming smile towards me. It's hard to explain but I felt relaxed and confident in her presence. "Is this your granddaughter," she asked Nana while eyeing me intently.

"Yes, Guan Yin I would like you to meet Calliope."

"Guan Yin," I smiled at her, "I like your name." She shrugged her shoulders and beamed back.

"I like yours, too." She took my hands in hers and stared deeply into my eyes. They seemed to sparkle, and I was mesmerized. "So much sadness for one so young, the sun will shine again once you call upon it," she whispered just loud enough for me to hear. She then turned to my grandmother, breaking the spell, and motioned to the far-right corner of the balcony. "Come, let's see what I have for you today."

A staircase led upstairs towards the roof. I quickly scanned my memory for any sighting or mention of this before in my visits. I came up with none. Also curious was none of the other tourists seemed to take notice of us or this additional route. My grandmother grabbed my hand and urged me to follow.

The temple was on the uppermost floor, yet here we were entering a large smoky shop with aisles upon aisles of wooden shelves. The first thing I noticed was the smell, an intoxicating blend that brought to mind waterfalls, mountains and moonlight. My grandmother ushered me forward, allowing little time to inspect the contents on the shelves.

"Is this new? How long has this been here?" I found myself having to force the words out, my mind slow and wandering. By the time she answered I found I didn't care.

"I've been here awhile," Guan Yin smiled up at me while she handed Nana a small wrapped package.

"I never noticed this before," I navigated through the shop as though being pulled by an invisible force. There was a room hidden by a curtain that seemed to be my destination. As I turned the last corner I was suddenly face to face with Guan Yin.

"You never noticed because you never truly looked," she beamed at me and gently placed a small pin about the size of a quarter into my hand. The adornment was comprised of many gold rings overlapping one another, creating a flower type pattern. "You are a well of infinite courage; draw on it when you need it most. You will not fail." She winked at me and closed my hand as my grandmother approached. I took her meaning and slipped it into my pocket. We said our goodbyes and I whispered a thank you.

The ride home was more torturous than the trip there. As the miles increased the spell of San Francisco weakened and I gradually slipped back into my pity pool. By the time we pulled into the drive my emotions were wrinkled and pruney.

My grandmother hadn't needed her long years of intimate experience to know that I was, metaphorically speaking; lying on the floor. I had been there once or twice, literally and physically, but gratefully she wasn't home at the time and therefore blissfully unaware. Left alone in private, or at least with private thoughts I found myself opening and reopening the wounds of David's memory.

Any time I wasn't preoccupied with something else I was dragging the sharp blade of agony over the freshly healed memories. The pain became a temporary connection that I could cling to, like a dinghy while feeling adrift in an ocean of uncertainty. It was a sad, sick cycle. Luckily, she saw this coming and tried to keep me as busy as much as possible, while slyly sneaking in golden nuggets of possibility.

"Say I saw this amazing program the other night on the African Savannah. The video footage was spectacular. Can you imagine people do that for a living," she mentioned one morning while we were dusting her enormous collection of books. Another time it was, "Check out this advertisement in the paper, 'Johansen Art Exhibit March 12th at 7 pm' we should go to this!" Or the most flamboyant, "My friend Rebecca says she's moving to Costa Rica, how exciting would that be?"

I would nod and get back to the task at hand but some of those comments would take root and perhaps if fed a proper diet of hope and faith they would grow and blossom. Slowly her patience, love and understanding started to work their magic. I was by no means near cured but by the sixth day I was feeling an emotion I hadn't had access to since David's abrupt breakup; cautious optimism. It was like a weak glimmer of light amidst an ocean of fog and I aimed my heart towards it. Saturday came and brought its wicked baggage, but I managed through to Sunday, which in my book was a day for newer if not new beginnings.

That night we ate dinner outside. My grandparents had a deck that wasn't tall, yet still gave a clear view of the water. Pops had built it himself, a little over a year after they had bought the farmhouse. When they had first toured the property, Nana had mentioned how perfect it was though a deck 'sure would be swell'.

It took him two summers to get it done and included help from family, friends, random laborers and the occasional neighbor. It was his pride and joy and looked new even now thanks to timely coats of weatherproofing and it was so smooth you could walk across it barefoot without fear of splinters.

The table was a large and heavy wooden item with no history that I could remember being told. It had solid rectangle top, strong legs and was stained a dark green. Six matching chairs surrounded it; they were stained red, yellow and blue. The dinnerware was of various colors, patterns and styles; as if orphans of box sets had been collected. The table runner was woven from a type of flowering vine, which still bore fresh and fragrant blooms and little candles resting in delicate glass bowls added a sparkle of light and movement. The end result was a magical festive ambiance that coaxed forth a reluctant smile. I hadn't known if she had done this for me or if this was always the norm but I appreciated it either way.

The nature scene was surreal; tall elm trees swaying in the slight breeze like dancers, the rain during the previous night leant a different quality to the air, the sunset reflecting off the water and casting everything in a ruby orange light and the occasional playful otters splashing. Strains of Chopin's 'Fantasie Impromptu' from an old record player floated through an open window. I laughed as she 'conducted' with her fork.

She wasn't trying to entertain; she just did, as was her nature. Our conversation was light and cheerful, mostly reminiscing about various family events and funny anecdotes. I appreciated that she didn't force talk about David but there were far too many stories of me falling off roofs, out of trees, in the water and even on the way into the emergency room.

As a child I had an exuberant spirit that couldn't be contained, like an eagle yearning for the open sky. It was something I eventually outgrew in my latter years, which culminated in me taking a safe job in advertising sales for the San Jose Mercury News rather than pursuing my dream of international photo journalism. It was coffee runs, endless phone calls and overtime spent at a desk versus war zones, volcanic eruptions and archaeological discoveries.

"Do you remember when you made that rope swing for the tree overlooking the water?" She grinned like a child opening birthday gifts. I nodded and winced; the pain of the memory so very fresh in my mind.

"I think I more clearly remember falling, roughly into the water on the very first swing. I got banged up on the way down, actually bounced off its roots." I shook my head in disbelief, as though remembering someone else's story.

"You always loved trying what others thought was impossible. Didn't you get into an argument with Charlie over schematics?" The few wrinkles Nana possessed were the corners of her eyes, probably from all the smiling.

"Yes, I did. Wasn't the first time, either, man he was quite the brainiac at 11, wasn't he?"

"Oh yes, you two were, well still are, quite the pair." She spoke with regard as though proud. She could have been complementing me on a school art project or test grade, rather than our character. I smiled, pleased, none the less.

"He kept telling me the projection was all wrong, something about rope length and 10 points of safety concerns." "You didn't let that stop you; you were so fiery and strong willed."

"I think you mean stubborn and bullheaded. If scars were medals, I'd be a well decorated general." Nana laughed slightly then became solemn. "I miss that about you; that spark. It was a very special quality and I wish your mother wouldn't have extinguished it." She had a faraway look in her eyes.

"Mom had nothing to do with it. I turned 18; I became an adult and had to start taking responsibilities. Sure, she seemed to relax more but it was all me. I enjoyed my childhood, but I don't miss it, I mean, not in the way of wanting to recreate anything from it."

"Actually, you were 16, but interesting choice of words," she murmured. I shot her a funny look. "I wonder perhaps if there aren't some things you miss; activities that didn't involve injury, necessarily." I gave it some thought and shrugged, my memory well empty, my bucket dry. We went back to eating, my mind whirling with curiosity. This was a strange conversation even for her.

"So, what did she mean by 'sorting out my old room'," I asked casually though I was very interested in the answer. My plans were to do my required time, just enough to appease my family, most notably my mother and grandmother then I would get my own place, like nature intended. Nana laughed.

"She's worried about you; she wants you home with her. If that room had been empty, she would never have let you come here. However, she is having a hard time moving that exercise equipment." She shook her head in mock sympathy. Yes, I said mock sympathy, when you've known a woman as long as I have you learn to read her. "She can't sell it and can't manage to get any movers over there to take it to the garage. So, I guess you'll have to stay here longer with me." There it was, I knew something was up. I didn't fault her intentions, she had to be lonely here and my mother had my dad.

Also, though my grandmother was strange, I did feel more free and capable here. She not only allowed me to be who I wanted but encouraged it. Maybe she went a little further than I felt comfortable with, but I applied the brakes when appropriate. At my mother's I'd be more of an employee following her direction. Don't get me wrong, I loved my mother, but we had very different visions for my life. If losing David had taught me anything it was to evaluate who I was and where I was going. I feared becoming a passenger on a train holding someone else's ticket.

"Figure out who you are Calliope," she said as though reading my mind. Her words burrowed deep and took root, nudging something that almost came into focus. She smiled and stood, "well wasn't that a lovely dinner, thank you for joining me." I cleared the table and did the dishes, so she could putter around the backyard. She said she wanted to enjoy it as long as 'the sun still favored it with its golden light'. My grandmother had a magical green thumb that resulted in a lush green retreat that could grace the cover of any Better Homes and Gardens magazine.

A flagstone path led away from the deck, twisting and turning at what seemed odd angles; however, from above it was a well-planned maze created by walls of various shrubs, bushes, trees and flowers and punctuated in the center with a tall laurel tree with a bench that curved around its trunk. At the opposite end from the deck, near the back fence, was a large stone fountain containing a beautiful bathing mermaid.

As a child one of my favorite spots was on a blanket on the grass positioned where I could gaze up at her. She was a silent friend, but we shared many secrets from desired adventures to life's ambitions and even talk about boys. I thought I heard my grandmother laughing and humming and then most definitely talking while she sat on the bench under the tree. I suspected she was conversing with Pops who had passed away ten years prior.

I gave her some privacy and cuddled up on the couch with my latest book, a paperback; The Dark One Rises. I couldn't remember when or where I picked it up or why I was so fascinated with it. My preferred genre was gritty action fiction, like Ian Fleming or John Grisham, not romance in a fantasy setting. Considering what I had been through with David I should have been repulsed not intrigued and yet I couldn't seem to get enough. So much so that my hand was beginning to cramp and my eyes blur.

"Hey kiddo, I'm heading to bed now, goodnight." My grandmother's voice startled me, the book slipped to the floor. The thud was alarmingly loud in contrast to the quiet of the sleeping house.

"Already?" I picked the book up off the floor, unsure of which page I had last read. She chuckled and shook her head; her ponytail bobbing and green eyes sparkling.

"It's after eleven dear," she smiled and patted me on the shoulder, "that must be some book!" I rubbed my neck, suddenly aware of how stiff and sore it was. Though by her reasoning I had been reading straight for over four hours. How on earth had I not finished this thin little paperback yet?

"Eleven? Wow, I'm sorry I didn't realize." I stammered my excuse as though I were fourteen again on a school night. I managed to stretch my legs, though the muscles protested. Then I stretched my arms, they were much more complacent.

"It happens to the best of us, what's it about?" She took a seat beside me on the couch. I scrunched up my face in thought. The plot, scenery, location, essentially all details save for the main character evaded me like minnows in a stream.

"Well, um it's about this man and he goes to this place and meets this woman." Wow, it sounded as stupid out loud as it looked in my head. She gave me an odd look that morphed into a warm smile.

"Wow, complicated plot! Is he handsome?"

"Yes, extremely," I replied enthusiastically. She eyed me with interest and I blushed. Why was I acting so foolish about a fictional character; practically giddy and bursting to rave about his traits, talents and accomplishments. I bit my tongue hard; the metallic taste of blood grounded me back into reality.

Nana got up and walked over to the shelf and retrieved a heavy leather-bound book. She stared at it fondly for a moment and then handed it to me. It felt even weightier than it looked. "I've always been a fan of the old stories," she said with reverence and a twinkle in her eyes. "Why don't you give this one a try?" The worn cover bore the title, 'The Odyssey'. It smelled of age and importance.

"I remember this," I smiled fondly; "I used to devour all your mythology books; I loved the magic and action. I haven't read any in years."

"That's right." My grandmother's eyes shone with excitement. "Hey kiddo, since you're not tied down to a job right now!" Her voice was loud and boisterous.

"Nana, some people might see that as a matter of concern not a positive opportunity," I chuckled.

"Well those people don't have any vision or the chance to win a trip for two to Greece!" I sat up straighter. Now this was interesting.

"I'm listening," She took a seat next to me and started gesturing wildly with her hands.

"You know how long I've wanted to go there and your grandfather well he wouldn't go and the time for traveling will be here soon and..."

"Alright, spit it out woman," I teased her gently. "How do we win this?"

"Oh, sorry dear, it's a game show and it's about Greek mythology and the winner wins the trip." She waited for my answer.

"I'll have to check my schedule. Oh, look it just opened up. Sure, I'll be your teammate Nana. When is it?" I was really looking forward to this. Greece was a long way from California and David, by default.

"I'll have to check on that and get back to you."

"Okay, where is the show? Burbank? Because that's where I think Price Is Right and all those other game shows are televised. We wouldn't even need to fly; it's like a five-hour car trip although, flying might be more fun."

"I'll check on that, too." She quickly stood and kissed me lightly on the head. "I'll let you know, but in the meantime, brush up on as much as you can. Goodnight."

"Goodnight Nana." Her excitement was infectious, and I found myself eagerly digging through kitchen drawers for a notebook and pen. I wasn't going to tell her but if we were training for a competition then I would be reading more for info than for pleasure; in which case, I would be sneaking on the internet as much as possible. She didn't have that service, so I would have to visit the coffee shop in town.

My grandmother had odd opinions about technology; it was as if she was plucked from another time and transplanted here. My parents had it, but I didn't want to involve them, unsure how my mother would react to a trip overseas. I read a few pages before bed, just to get started, I didn't remember falling asleep.

The next morning found me camped out next to the automatic coffee maker as it began to percolate. My eyes were swollen and raw and my entire body ached. I felt as though I'd competed in one of those triathlons and boot camp followed up with a nice game of rugby. Nana bound into the kitchen like she was walking on springs, grinning and humming. "How did you sleep my dear?" She asked while handing me a mug from the cabinet.

I mumbled a response and she gave me a knowing look. "I wasn't crying, I've been having some crazy dreams over the past few days," I gave up on standing and slid a chair over collapsing on the seat. "I tossed and turned all night."

She tilted my chin towards the light from the window and recoiled slightly. While she was busy in the pantry, I risked a look at my reflection on the toaster. I looked like I survived a bout with Mike Tyson.

"What's in these dreams?" She asked casually, I blushed, thankful she couldn't see me.

"I don't remember," I lied. She came out of the pantry eyeing me suspiciously I stared at the coffee maker willing it to brew faster. There were some things beyond sharing with your parents, let alone grandparents.

"Why don't you get comfortable on the couch and I'll fix you a cup." I mumbled thanks and stumbled into the den. Unlike the firm and conservative style of the couch in the formal living room, this one was soft and inviting.

"Here you go dear," she handed me a steaming mug. I smelled it and looked at her quizzically. "Oh, it's my special tea, you'll like it better than the coffee, trust me." I drank half of the sweet beverage and then felt my mind slowly shutting down as my body relaxed. My last thoughts were of blue flames.

I awoke calm and well rested and headed into the kitchen. The newspaper was lying on the counter and I perused the cover page while I mixed some creamer into my coffee. Before I had drunk half my cup I had casually read to the events section, skipping over the less interesting topics.

"Hey Nana," I called out unsure if she was even in the house, "there's a showing of 'Jason and the Argonauts' tonight at the Grand." The Grand was a quaint old theater downtown that played the classics. "Oh wait, it doesn't start until Friday." I sighed disappointed. Oh well it was only two days away. 'No wait, today would be Thursday.' I argued with myself. I checked the date on the newspaper; Friday! Wait, I had slept for two days? What the hell was in that tea?

I intended on having a serious discussion with my grandmother about the dangers of drugging her one and only granddaughter. Not that I missed anything relatively important in those two days, but shouldn't I have been warned first? On the bright side, my sleep was dream free, restful and the shadows under my eyes were gone and my energy had returned but still I didn't like the trickery.

I went searching for her all through the house and garden and then checked the carport. Her beat up Toyota pickup was gone; meaning she probably went to town.

I decided intervention would have to wait so I might as well get to work on setting up my room. However long or short my visit, I wasn't one for living out of suitcases. I cringed when I saw the wall of boxes and considered just leaving them there. Then again, with nothing to do I'd return to my David torture. I could almost hear the imaginary knife sharpening up for another round of rehash the past. Unpacking it was!

I spent most the morning sorting; having decided that perhaps it was time to lighten the load. Nana's Greece trip got me thinking; Now that David was gone, as well as my job and apartment; I would be free to travel the world. Not right away of course but after I saved up a little money. These thoughts inspired and motivated me, and I excitedly got to work paring down my wardrobe and other possessions; all the while dreaming of exotic locales and locations.

I made three boxes; Keep, Sell and Gift. The Gift box was for family; whatever they didn't want would go into the Sell box. The Keep box was for anything I didn't want to part with but wouldn't be using right away. By lunch time they were full and ready to go. I took a glass of sweet tea out to the deck to relax.

"She's got no quarrel with me," I followed my grandmother's voice to her vegetable and herb garden. It occupied the furthest corner of the yard and was bordered with the white picket fence on its west and north sides and wire mesh on the east and south. "And no right here even if she did."

"Nana," I called out nervously. It bothered me to hear she was having trouble with someone. She stood up and there was a flurry of black feathers as a startled bird took flight.

"Yes dear," her smile was forced.

"You okay? I overheard your phone call," I didn't see a phone in her hand, but she couldn't have been talking to the bird, could she?"

"Oh, I'm fine," she lied.

"What's wrong?" I asked her, shielding my eyes from the surprisingly bright sun. Though it was already technically spring, our weather had a way of a menopausal woman; hot and then cold and oftentimes blustery.

"Oh, it's just my plants aren't doing well, especially my chamomile." She stood and dusted her khaki pants. She looked almost 'normal' in her blue flannel gardening shirt and floppy hat.

"Are they getting enough water?" I asked, simplistic in my knowledge of anything dealing with horticulture. Even the hardiest of plants suffered at my hands. Calli the plant killer.

"Yes, it's not that or sunshine," she glared at the ground like it was an enemy, "it's the soil!" She grabbed a hoe and hacked at it angrily. Whoa! I decide it's a bad time to bring up her 'special tea' and a really great time to bring her inside for lunch.

We dined on tuna sandwiches and sliced veggies because that was pretty much the extent of my culinary abilities. I could follow recipes but failed to acquire my mother's talent of creating delicacies using whatever odd items were found in the cabinet. I called her the Foodie Alchemist and teased her about getting her own cooking show. Charlie even filmed a test segment, but she had hated being in front of the camera; baking, not acting was her forte.

Neither of us suggested dining outside, instead we ate in the den. It was my favorite room in the house because with all the photos of family, it never felt lonely. It was the perfect size for company, without feeling cramped, yet it never felt cavernous when it was just you. It contained the comfy couch which formed an "L" shape along the left and back wall, a short but long coffee table made of knotty pine, a flat screen TV, which was the only TV in the house, a DVD player and a shelf of movies, mostly black and white classics.

Even though there was a light fixture on the ceiling, a floor lamp was near the chaise section of the couch to offer light for reading. The bottom shelf of the coffee table was home to the favorite collection of books. I was happy to see that Pops' favorite western series hadn't been boxed up and stored away. Pictures were hung all around the room in what appeared to be random order at first sight but if you paid attention, they told a story. I had spent many hours following those tales and elaborating with outlandish details of my own. That was the one connection we all shared; our family could sure spin a yarn!

Another great aspect of the room was it also allowed for a nice segue into safe conversations about family members who weren't waging war on their gardens or drugging their granddaughters.

"How is Aunt Cathy?" I asked after glancing at a photo of her and my mother when they were in their teens. They were straddling identical red Schwinn bicycles and wearing matching dresses and grins. They looked like twins, but my mother was a couple years older. "I haven't seen her in forever." Actually, it had been almost four years.

Last we hung out, we were doing shots at Haven Acres for my 21st birthday. Charlie had opted out that year, preferring to hide out in his lab. Maybe he was afraid that birthday margaritas coupled with dance music and general merriment would infect his hard drive and corrupt his operating system.

Our aunt was unperturbed, and Charlie had her all to himself the next day. She patiently spent hours listening to him talk excitedly about his experiments and then presented him with his very own cake (carrot) and a check to further fund his research. She always knew exactly what each of us needed.

Illuminated thoughts of Aunt Cat (my nickname for her that was never ever uttered in front of my grandmother) and how amazing it would be to have her sitting with us now, flooded my being. She had this effect on people, regardless of whether they were young or old, male or female, it didn't matter. It was as though a star had yearned for a human existence, possessing an ethereal quality you couldn't decipher and didn't care to.

I basked in these happy thoughts while I could, eager to squeeze out every drop just like those last few rays of sunlight you try to catch before they're gone on a swimming day. Such was her power to create such joyous sublimity with a mere memory of her presence. There was a slight shift in Nana's expression and then back to normal.

"Catherine is in India," she responded quietly. I waited for more details but was offered none. It wasn't unusual for Aunt Cathy to travel; she was the 'me' I longed to be, however, it was unusual for Nana to hold back. Once, when Aunt Cathy went to Africa for a week, she gushed about it for months. Oh, how she had reveled in the stories she recounted. Poor Nana, she had loved to travel but had loved her homebody husband even more. No wonder she wanted to win this trip to Greece. She continued to sit quietly.

"Oh, how thrilling," I smiled politely. My mind was buzzing with questions that I didn't dare ask at the moment. Was there some kind of disagreement going on between them? What was Aunt Cat doing in India? Why hadn't I seen her over the past few years? Even more, why hadn't I at least talked to her?

"Yes." My grandmother, woman of many words, looked like she spent all her energy on that solitary one. I took the hint that this particular discussion was over, but I was going to mention it to my mother. Surely, she would know what was going on between her mother and little sister.

After her curt response Nana took the dishes to the kitchen while I went back to my task at hand. As much as I dreaded it, left to all my thoughts undistracted was sure to drive me even crazier than before. I sequestered myself to my room until almost dinner time, feeling worn out but that I had made it my space as much as possible in only one day.

Almost symbolically, the very last item from the very last box was my camera. My camera was my pride and joy; a Canon EOS 70D. It was meant for bigger and faster things like volcanic eruptions or the running of the bulls in Pamplona. Sadly, the most exciting thing I had captured was my parent's Yorkie Roxy chasing a butterfly around the backyard.

The battery was near full and I slipped the strap over my neck. An idea for a photo collage documenting my new life had inspired me. It would be a nice transition into working on a professional portfolio. Where had that thought come from? My room was on the second floor facing the front yard, the long gravel driveway flanked by windmills and further out, Dry Creek Dr. I snapped some shots of both the road beyond from the doorway, as well as leaning out as far as I could to isolate the strip of gravel.

The room was small so next I focused on the French doors that opened out onto a large bleached wood balcony that surrounded the entire second floor. Stairs led down from the balcony to the backyard. As a child I was a princess waiting on this balcony for my prince to slay the dragon that kept me prisoner and set me free or I was a brave fighter or pirate, who would rush down to battle; usually with one of the neighbor kids or a cousin, as Charlie was usually more interested in bugs or safer indoor activities.

I really wanted to include him so one time we made him king. It was the perfect role, so we thought; it required him to sit on the throne and send us on quests and reward us on our return with a grand feast of milk and peanut butter cookies.

However, Charlie feared sending us on quests wrongly and throwing the entire kingdom into peril, turmoil and eventual demise so he refused. When he finally did engage, he was the 'keeper of scrolls and knowledge'. Somewhere was a drawer full of pages of the history of 'our world' as well as documentation of the amazing feats of Calli the Great.

The cool breeze beckoned me out and I found myself retracing the steps of my youth; around the balcony, to the stairs, racing past the garden, through the back gate and almost to the water. I stopped suddenly and automatically turned to my left. The weeping willow tree, illuminated with the glow of sunset as its backdrop, was a very real and solid childhood memory. It was situated on a rise of the bank, several feet above the water; the very same from my rope swing accident. I took several more shots before grinning and hurrying under its branches, searching for signs of my childhood.

It felt like I was embracing an old friend. And in a way, I was. This is where I camped and dreamed; this was my secret place. Well secret except from Charlie, this was the only place he'd agree to play with me, where he would for a short time act like a kid and not a NASA scientist in training. Sometimes we'd sneak out at night and tell scary stories by flashlight, the long covering branches a natural tent and I'd be the one who got scared and Charlie would interject funny details until we forgot how afraid we were and roll around laughing till our sides hurt.

The willow tree was also where all our special trinkets were kept hidden from others in buried treasure chests or hanging from high limbs; I was the climber and Charlie would toss the 'booty' up to me. Our treasure was usually cheap costume jewelry, various old metal tools, shiny rocks and anything else of interest we found.

Once Charlie found and old simple brass door knob and insisted we put it in a box and bury it so no one else could find it. He said a goat told him it was very important and very powerful and only for us to use. I remember we spent countless summer nights seriously trying to guess what door it went to and where it might lead.

Funny, how everything and anything in our youth could be magical in the midst of so much ordinary. We sure loved our stories and to believe that amidst the dairies, farms and alfalfa fields there were fairies, ghosts and two kids who had special magical powers.

In the fading light it was hard to see if anything remained, so I knelt in the soft dirt and felt blindly around the edges of the trunk. Before long, my hand connected with something solid and possibly wooden. At that exact moment I heard a growl. I froze, not sure of what I heard or that I heard anything for sure. Nana owned no pets, not even a goldfish, let alone a dog. And the chance of one of the neighbor's pets getting in through the fence was unheard of on this side of the property. Coyotes weren't strangers around here, but they tended to shy away from houses. Anyways, what I thought I heard didn't even sound like a dog; it sounded bigger, deeper and scarier.

The hairs on my body stood and I tried to coax them down with arguments of disbelief. It was just my imagination, kid's stories revisited, nothing more. If it was indeed a sound it was probably thunder. I grabbed hold of the object, about the size of a cigar box and tucked it under my arm. I couldn't wait to open it and explore its contents. I felt a twinge of guilt, perhaps I should wait for Charlie to come home for break? Okay, I would bring it in but not open it until he was with me.

Maybe we could make it a mini celebration; some appetizers, a bottle of wine, maybe a few words spoken and photos to commemorate the event... The growling sounded again, this time louder. I couldn't detect which direction it was coming from only that I was sure this time it wasn't my imagination. Instantly I was transformed into that scared 12year-old little girl, but with no Charlie to save me with his humor.

I searched for the flashlight, hoping it too had been left out here but even if I could find it in the dark it wouldn't work after all these years would it? I decided my best option was to run and anyways I didn't think I needed to see what I was running from; actually; that was most definitely preferred. I turned my back to the rough trunk and slowly rose as far as the lower branches would allow and turned toward the direction of the house.

Simultaneously a flash from the camera and a snarl, mere inches away from my face and I bolted, tree limbs lashing at my face as I made it out from the cover of the tree and into open land. The sun had set; leaving everything around me in deep darkness, save for strange misty white fog that rolled in slowly but deliberately from the water. It was so bright it seemed unearthly and dangerous.

My mind screamed at an unseen terror. I ran along the muddy bank until I saw the reflective post of the steps leading up to the back fence. At least that's what I thought I had seen but too late I learned I was wrong as I turned to the right and stepped into a gopher hole.

I slammed to the ground, jarring my teeth and jamming the box into my ribs. My ankle screamed but I forced myself to sit up and then half standing. Somehow, I managed to hobble up to the back fence. I threw myself into the yard and slammed the little gate shut behind me. It was only a little white picket fence, cute and covered with ivy but somehow, I felt safe enough on this side to take a rest and breathe.

My lungs burned, and perspiration drenched my hair and clothes, stinging my arms and face where I had been scratched by the branches.

Down by the bank I spotted red eyes staring up at me and then they were gone. I eased myself up, shaken and rattled and very tenderly started heading towards the house when I heard a familiar commotion behind me. A sigh of relief escaped as I saw a slow-moving boat, red lights glowing on the stern, engine chugging erratically.

I laughed and then cried from the pain. Eventually I managed inside, after first hiding my treasure box under the deck steps for safe keeping. Childish, I know but feeling like I needed   to

Three

Dream a Little Dream

I adjusted the bandage on my ankle and scrunched my nose. The smell was strong and stringent as my grandmother had soaked it thoroughly in Witch Hazel before wrapping it. She had expressed concern that I was by the river, so I modified my story a bit and told her I never made it down to the bank because I tripped on one of the loose paving stones near the rose bushes which were safely within the confines of the back yard. She seemed to buy it and relaxed a bit.

I was offended by her concern; did she think I was gonna fall into the river? She applied some thick salve to one of many scratches on my arm; it stung like hell. Then again, maybe she had a point. My reflection in the dresser mirror, though gruesome, would have shocked only David.

By the time we had met I had outgrown much of my tomboy tendencies. Right now, I looked like an oversized version of my 12-year-old self. The difference being I hadn't tried anything daring, on the contrary it had been a leisurely stroll down memory lane. I tried to imagine me, the now me, attempting any of the crazy stunts I had lived through in my youth. It wasn't pretty. I chuckled to myself and she looked at me funny.

"Sorry, I was just remembering how when we were little, I wanted to learn how to sword fight and Charlie wanted to learn I guess whatever was not sword fighting or any other risky activity."

"Well everyone should learn proper swordsmanship, even Charlie," her tone matter of fact. "Here's your tea," She set the steaming mug on my nightstand. I lifted it to my lips, pretended to sip and smiled.

"Thank you, Nana. I'm sorry about dinner." She waved me away with a hand and picked up my dirty plate. Thanks to my injury we feasted on sandwiches and soup; I, having insisted on taking up all the cooking due to my newfound awareness of Nana's experimenting with herbs and tonics on her guinea pig granddaughter.

Once she was gone I hobbled quickly across the room, well quickly for my condition and tossed the tea out the open window. The outside was alive and enticing me with its siren's song. I resisted the urge and made myself go to bed, counting on a sneaky old lady checking on her handiwork later. If I didn't think she was doing it to help me I'd be furious; one slip of the hand, I'd be a ghost.

Sometimes the way people showed they cared didn't always make sense. Thoughts of David tried to rise, but I beat them down deep, adjusted my pillows, lay back and closed my eyes. The dream started almost immediately.

"Come to me," his silky voice beckoned. I slid out of bed and stumbled to the floor; my head barely missing the dresser. I slammed my hands down in frustration and shifted to sitting. I've had flying dreams before and I can't manage walking across the room? I scrunched up my face and attempt flight; I didn't budge an inch and succeeded in only getting a headache.

In desperation I tried crawling. It was a slow process, but I made it through the French doors and across the balcony. However, once I got to the stairs I was stumped. I leaned against the rough wood railing and began to whimper.

"I can't make it, I'm hurt." I whispered quietly to the air. I knew he could hear me, just as I could hear him though I felt he was far away. I wasn't sure where he lived but I knew not only was it a great distance, but I had to take a certain route to get to him and it didn't include the interstate.

"I'll send someone for you," he told me gently. "Just stay where you are."

"Why can't you come and get me?" I whined. Apparently in my dreams I'm a crybaby.

"I don't have permission yet."

"I give you permission."

"I'm sorry my lovely, but that's not how it works."

"Maybe I shouldn't go. Seems like a lot of trouble and I am injured."

"You don't want to see me? It's been so long." His voice was slow and seductive.

"I don't know," my confidence wavered. He knew I was bluffing.

"I need to see you," he placed strong emphasis on the word 'need'. "Tonight is a special night for us."

"Who are you sending for me?"

"Someone trustworthy," his voice soothed, "He should be there now."

I looked around the yard but neither saw nor heard anyone approaching. A shooting star streaked brilliantly across the sky causing me to gasp but my joy was short lived. I was still stranded on the balcony like a ship run aground on the rocks.

"No one's here," I pouted.

"Look again." I glanced once more around the garden and noticed a golden orb of light traveling quickly. Within seconds I was bathed in its warm glow or rather his glow. A man stood before me, in golden robes and sandals. He was young, muscular and gorgeous. I lost the capacity of speech for a moment as he helped me to standing. I hobbled a little and he nodded at my foot.

"He'll take care of that," he lifted me gently and turned, "do you have your key?" I reached inside my nightgown and verified it was safely around my neck. I nodded and, in a flash, we were before a door.

"This is the only way you can travel to him for now; keep that safe."

"How else," I began to ask but he motioned for me to get a move on. I took out the key, inserted it into the rusty metal door and turned the handle clockwise until I heard a click. The door slowly opened revealing a softly illuminated tunnel carved into the earth. It traveled down, though it didn't appear too steep.

I replaced the necklace around my neck and we were off; moving so fast everything was a blur. When we stopped I studied him; winged sandals, staff with two snakes intertwined superhuman speed and gasped as recognition hit me.

"You're Her..." He silenced me with a look. "But how?"

"Careful, names have power. I understand your questions and your need for answers, but you will have to be patient, your world and the places in between are not the places to be having these discussions." He smiled at me to show me he wasn't angry.

"Thank you for coming to get me," I grinned at him, "whoever you are."

"My pleasure," he winked then we were off again. I couldn't say the experience was entirely unpleasant, but I was glad when we began to slow down as my nose was assaulted by the strong smell of sulfur. It was dim and smoky and I had the familiar oppressing sensation of being deep underground. I was excited to see HIM though, so my panic was short lived.

The tunnel abruptly opened into an enormous cavern, dimly lit by torches that lined the walls horizontally and vertically. How far up the walls went I had no clue as the light wasn't strong enough to illuminate but a few feet on either side. My eyes took forever to adjust, so I was grateful he was carrying me.

"There," I pointed eagerly to a line of people pushing and shoving. They were moving towards the bank of a velvet black river where a dark hooded figure waited. I was surprised when we bypassed the line and straight onto the large ornate wooden boat.

Many hands holding gold coins forced their way toward the figure but it raised a skeletal hand and forced them back. My companion and I alone were allowed on the boat. He set me gently on the hard wooden bench.

"Usually I have to wait and come with the others. Tonight I feel so V.I.P. like a celebrity or royalty."

"Well you are of sorts and as I'm sure you can tell he's been in a hurry to meet with you again." He chuckled. I prayed he couldn't see my flushed face in the dim lighting. The boat moved so quickly and quietly through the water I imagined we were hovering over instead and I glanced repeatedly over the side to verify. I didn't stare long however, as the water was so dark that nothing could be seen and therefore at the mercy of my imagination. Added to the cryptic ambiance, were more flickering torches on the walls along the waterway and they caused shadows to dance about eerily.

Under normal circumstances I would be shaking like a leaf but soon I would see HIM and that soothed my fears. Not to mention I was aware this was just a dream; nothing really happened in dreams, well unless you were in a Wes Carpenter film. Yikes!

I quickly turned my attention back to my chaperone and my mood lightened. The bank loomed before us. Further out I could just make out the gate in the distance but not the guard dog I knew lurked beyond. I had only seen him (I assumed it was a he) once before, when I had wandered the wrong way. That was quite enough for me. He was, dare I say, deformed? He also looked hungry and extremely vicious though he hadn't given me much notice.

"Is there anything more you can tell me?" My question caught him off guard. His face was full of thought then he started to speak but hesitated. I had no time to inquire further as our boat banked and the ferryman motioned for us to move along. My chaperone carried me passed more lines of people to the furthest section of the gate, where it merged into the cavern wall. He knocked on the iron bars and they began to twist and turn serpentine like until there was an opening large enough for the two of us to walk through. "Clever," I remarked.

This area had even more torches of an eerie hue of orange. A strange cat like figure perched on a ledge, swished its forked tail. I saw it only briefly as in a flash we were gone and standing on the familiar steps of a beautiful stone castle surrounded by a lake of fire. He sat me before the door and tipped his hat.

"Thank you, Hermes," I winked. He vanished as the door opened and I was finally reunited with HIM; looking perfectly glorious in dark flowing robes that simulated fire dancing atop black water. The fabric clung to his powerful frame where his muscles bulged. His face was strong and defined with full lips outlined with a roguish but defined moustache and goatee, soft black curly hair and intense blue eyes that flickered like flames.

It could have been my imagination but I swore his face lit up when he saw me. Suddenly I felt oddly out of place in my flannel nightgown but he seemed not to care. He lifted me easily and carried me into a brighter antechamber containing a red velvet couch, gold wardrobe and matching vanity with a large ornate mirror. After gently setting me on the couch he clapped loudly, summoning three strange little creatures with long snout like faces, beady eyes, small bat like wings and claws for hands and feet.

They were clothed in matching tunics that were badly scorched and covered in ash. As if reading my mind, he grabbed one by the scruff of their neck and admonished them in a foreign tongue, as he fingered the material angrily. He then threw it roughly to the ground and turned to smile at me. The creature reacted indifferently and eagerly took its place near the vanity.

"I apologize for the lack of manners of Grub, Stub and Mud. They aren't used to company of the likes of yours." He leaned over, took my hand and kissed it gently. An ache ran through my body but as always, he never offered more than a soft caress or a light kiss on the hand or cheek. Is this what dating as a Puritan was like? As though reading my mind again, he leaned in close and planted a soft kiss on my lips. My body went limp and he chuckled. "They'll help you get dressed in something more appropriate for the occasion."

As he spoke two of them pulled open the wardrobe revealing hangers full of rich vibrant fabric. They each took a dress and brought it over to the couch. They were long and ornate, replications of a fashion no doubt worn in the 17th or 18th century by ladies of the court. The first was a rich garnet with full skirt, blousy sleeves and gold ruffles, the second was onyx with a silver harlequin pattern and the third was emerald green with golden flowers embroidered on the bodice and sleeves tipped in delicate gold lace.

"They're beautiful," I remarked breathlessly. He smiled and bowed.

"I'll return when you're ready for me, just ring that bell." He motioned to a large brass bell on the table next to the couch that surely wasn't there before. The creatures eyed me awaiting command but the thought of having those claws anywhere on my exposed flesh made my skin crawl. As soon as he left I shooed them away.

Getting dressed with a sprained ankle was difficult as is, but getting dressed in an elaborate weighty costume was damn near impossible. I finally just draped it on the couch and crawled inside and once dressed I limped over to the vanity, which contained a hairbrush, various hair adornments and jewelry. I skipped over the jewelry and focused only on my hair; pinning up the sides with elaborate golden combs, exposing my neck and allowing the rest to cascade down my back.

I took my place back on the couch and rang the bell. He was there in an instant, dressed in a black tuxedo with tails, an emerald green tie and shiny black shoes. I was rendered speechless. He lifted me and carried me through the hall and into an enormous ballroom which was brightly illuminated with multicolor flames, up marble steps to the large dais located on the farthest wall.

"We match," I gestured to his tie. "How did you know I'd pick this dress?" He smiled as he set me on a soft ornate cushion atop a golden bench. It was as large as a bed and the moment the thought occurred to me I felt the intense longing again. I quickly tried to regain my composure.

"Why did you pick that dress out of the many?" He asked in response.

"I thought you might like it because," I flushed scarlet and couldn't speak. He lightly tilted my chin up towards his face.

"Because it matches your eyes," he finished for me.

"Yes," I mumbled softly. He sat beside me and clapped his hands. The lights dimmed and dark figures slowly marched into the room to Mozart's "Requiem". They circled the room and then paused dramatically before beginning a macabre waltz. My breath caught and he leaned in close to me.

"Are you afraid?" He whispered, his breath near my ear stirred my entire body.

"No, I'm fascinated," I whispered back, afraid of breaking the spell.

For the next hour I was equal parts mesmerized and aroused. It was a beautiful blend of music and movement. I felt swept away on the dark currents of the Styx, floating further and further away until he grasped my hand in his and brought me back to him. His grip was firm but not too tight and very warm; causing the rest of my body to grow jealous of his attention.

"You don't want to miss this," he smiled at me knowingly, pulling me back from my carnal thoughts once again. I was by no means a prude but still shocked at my very Lady Chatterly impulses. I pushed these erotic thoughts aside as best I could and focused on the space before us.

Suddenly the room was alive with color as the lights brightened to reveal exotic masked dancers; hundreds of creatures were represented, both realistic and mythological, from cats, birds and leopards to dragons, unicorns and animals I was unable to name.

One dancer wore a full white dress with black stripes and a hat in the shape of a zebra's head. Another wore a more slender dress with scales of varying shades of purple and green. The sleeves continued to her hands, her nails were long and wicked and the train flowed behind her several feet. It was amazing that no one had stepped on it. Her face was framed with the same scales and her lids were painted to resemble something reptilian. Shivers ran down my spine each time she closed her eyes.

The male dancers were dressed in similar tuxes with accessories that matched their dance partners; some had actual tails, spikes along their sleeves, animal skin ties (hopefully faux!) and cummerbunds or more daring appendages. The partner of a flamingo had a bright pink feather jutting from his kerchief pocket and matching feathered vest (tame) while a rhinoceros's mate had a horned cod piece, which would make it hard to dance I suspected, at least for their partner. I was very curious to spot the unicorn after seeing that!

There was a blur of feathers, fur, scales and skin as Tchaikovsky's 'Sleeping Beauty' began to play and the dancers moved in eerie unison, their dresses and capes flaring out behind them. I looked for the source of music and he pointed up towards the ceiling; there floating amongst the lights was a spectral orchestra. It consisted of a dozen ghastly ghouls from various centuries playing violins, flutes, oboes, bassoons, trombones and even a piano. The musicians never skipped a beat playing several selections from Vivaldi to Beethoven to Liszt and Dvorak. I was a guest at an undead Louis XIV ball and was soon giddy and breathless, my senses overloaded.

"Would you like to dance," he whispered in my ear, eyeing my movement in my seat. I looked down at my swollen and shoeless foot and frowned.

"Your feet will never touch the ground my goddess," again he lifted me into his arms and carried me onto the dance floor, the crowd parted. Schubert's 'Death and the Maiden' began and he propelled us around the room, chuckling at his little joke.

"Very witty," I mused. We swayed and twirled gracefully, true to his word my feet never touched the floor. I felt light as a feather and my spirit even lighter.

"Are you enjoying yourself," he sounded most interested in my answer.

"Of course it's beautiful and amazing and brilliant," I blushed, "I always enjoy my time with you." I couldn't remember how many times but it felt like multiple.

"I'm very glad you like it." I wasn't aware he was capable of pulling off bashful but here he was acting timid and awkward.

"Was this all for me?" I asked hesitantly. My awkwardness had never left.

"Yes."

"What is the occasion?" There had to be a reason, right? I wasn't used to showy gifts or effort without cause. I waited patiently for an answer. He grinned again and twirled me around.

"You are here and we are together," was his simple yet powerful reply. A new tune began, Chopin's 'Nocturne' a shy love song that lured me along windy trails through a lush green forest into a wild grassy meadow where my beloved waited for me at midnight. We spun, floating first only inches, then feet until we were all alone high above the crowd. Then swayed between elaborate chandeliers almost close enough to touch the glass dome ceiling that boasted twinkling lights that mimicked the stars.

"Hade…" my words were cut off by a passionate kiss. He pulled away and once more I found it hard to breathe.

"Careful my dear, names have power. Though, you already control me through and through." He took my hand in his and placed it on his chest. "You alone own my heart." I stared into his eyes until I felt the soft cushion below me. I heard the familiar notes of Clair de Lune but a quick glance around the room showed me we were otherwise alone. The dancers must have exited the room during our dance. The lights grew dimmer and he was kneeling before me on the floor.

"Let's make it official, shall we?" He took my hand and gently slid a blackened gold ring onto my finger. "Would you do me the honor?"

"You've got to be kidding me." I stammered, feeling equal parts mesmerized and foolish. So this is what my subconscious throws at me; a proposal from the lord of the underworld? Sick, Calli, sick. I laughed and inspected the markings on the ring more closely; impressive details for a dream. The smile faded from my face, startled by his pained expression. He sat beside me and stared at his hands. "What's wrong?"

"It's not exactly the response I was hoping from my new wife." His voice faltered a little and I actually felt guilty; an odd emotional response for a dream. I had an internal discussion with myself; the pressing concern was when I awoke I needed to seek out some serious therapy, possibly dragging Nana along but while I was here I might as well play it out and enjoy it while I could, right? Here was just a dream; no harm, no foul.

Here I could wear elegant dresses, waltz and laugh without the weight of David's memory. Here was happiness, something still desired in the real world but not yet attained, on lay a way until some unknown date in the future when its purchase would be paid in full with a light heart and boundless optimism and faith. Here was what I wanted and needed, for now at least.

"Wait, wife," I asked him suddenly, "I thought you were proposing marriage not actually doing it." Not that technicality mattered in this instance but my brain always wanted to process things accordingly. It was an annoying habit I longed to be cured of.

"We are far past that point my dear, don't you think? However, if you don't wish it so." I pulled him close and crushed his mouth with mine, abandoning all reason and letting myself go with the moment. It was liberating! After the pain of the past week any form of physical interaction was comforting even if only enjoyed within the confines of my mind. When I pulled back he was smiling, which made me happy.

"So, we're married now? That's interesting." He grabbed me and flipped me back on the cushion, leaning over me with a hungry look in his eyes.

"Not quite, first we have to consummate it. If you will allow me?"

The sensations leading up to the actual deed were overwhelming alone and yet minor in comparison; like little tremors before a volcanic eruption. At first he did little more than kiss me, occasionally brushing his hand along my bare shoulder or along the top of my bodice which was so daringly low my nipples all but jumped out and yelled, 'surprise!'

As the music became more dramatic, a selection from Rachmaninov, he became more assertive, his grip firmer, yet still gentle. No matter how quickly his hands passed along my body he took great care with my injured ankle. Before removing my dress, he burrowed underneath; slowly making a blazing hot path of wet kisses that traveled the full length of both thighs yet stopping before reaching a critical juncture.

I was left in a panting state that begged me to practically rip his clothes off of his body, which I did at the earliest convenience. Seeing him in his naked state had me torn between pushing him away so I could stare at him fully and pulling him closer so I could feel his hard solid form, so I divided my attentions equally. He lay there patiently, never taking his eyes off of me. I felt adored and wanted; feelings I hadn't experienced for a while and definitely never with this amount of intensity. It was though he was entering my very soul.

"My turn," he spoke feverishly. I anticipated a quick undressing but somehow he found a way to draw it out. First the dress then the hoop, slowly removed as my eyes begged him to hurry. He was even slower removing the petticoat and this was much harder for me as his fingers grazed my bare skin leaving a trail of flames. After each piece of clothing he would take a long pause to drink me in and then kiss me hard.

Eventually, though I don't know how I bore it, there was a tidy pile of silk on the floor. I lay there naked, weak and hungry. He then surprised me by lifting me into his arms and carrying me out on the dance floor. Though no one was here that I could see and of course this was a dream I still felt conscious of being naked in such an open space. Again we floated towards the ceiling, spinning slowly, his hands on my waist while his lips sought out every inch of flesh.

I gasped loudly as his mouth found my breasts and bit my nipples. One hand slid between my legs causing me to moan loudly. I grabbed his hair and crushed his lips with mine, biting his lower lip. Somehow, while still airborne, he managed to twist my legs around his waist and entered me. Call me Mt. Vesuvius. After what seemed like an eternity of bliss that was over much too quickly we lay spent on the couch, hands intertwined, his head lying on my chest.

"I love this sound," he smiled up at me, "especially when it does this" he ran his fingers lightly along my bare stomach, my heart raced. I frowned at him. "What's wrong my love?"

"Nothing, I just wish I could affect you as easily as you do me. It's child's play for you." He chuckled and pulled me in for a sweet kiss.

"This," he demonstrated by stroking me in more daring places, "is nothing to how you stir me." He took my hand and dragged it up his leg, paused a moment near his groin but then continued onward up to his chest. He held my hand in place over his heart and the room became brighter as the flames intensified. "I wish to someday stir you in the same way." The room dimmed once more and he held me tight and we drifted off to a deep sleep, my response unspoken and unnecessary.

I awoke the next morning feeling woozy but surprisingly light hearted. I grasped for the remnants of my dream but they floated away like petals on a breeze. I remembered vaguely a few things; dancing, sex and some tricky memory that flitted in and out of my reach. I finally gave up and stretched, light bouncing off the ring on my finger. I felt happy, relaxed and married? Wait, what? I examined the ring more closely and more details slowly revealed themselves; Hades, a marriage ceremony and hasty honeymoon.

I hid my hand behind my pillow then pulled it out again, expecting it to have faded away in the morning light with the rest of the visions. It was still very present and very solid. It would have to go in a drawer for now. I made to slide it off my finger but it wouldn't budge. I reevaluated my surroundings, perhaps I was still dreaming; nope, not so lucky. I sighed and put my head in my hands. My problems with David suddenly seemed small, normal and manageable.

Four

Brotherly Love

I didn't see Nana for three days, during which she communicated with me through various letters, post it's and chalk board messages like 'Spaghetti in the fridge', 'Gone out, don't wait up' or the strangest of all, 'Don't eat the pigeon liver in the glass jar'. She signed each and every one with 'Love you so much, Nana'. This did little to ease my mind.

I tried talking to my mom but she seemed almost bored with it; 'Your grandmother is a free spirit and comes and goes as she pleases. Everything is fine.' So I would wait for Charlie to come home for Spring Break; relying on his in-twin-ition.

"Hey sis," he called to me from the driveway. He eyed me curiously when I came out with my purse. "Let me guess," he winced, "we're going somewhere?"

"Yep," I jumped into the passenger seat. He sighed and got back in the car.

"But I just got here," he whined. I pointed at the steering wheel. "Drive." We drove to Haven Acres, a homey little bar and grill right on the water. It was a hop skip and a jump from home yet still comfortably anonymous, and as far off the beaten path one could get while still being considered local; essentially private.

The crowd was casual and preoccupied with darts and games of pool, the music on the jukebox consisted of mostly classic rock and country. We got a couple beers from a cute bartender with a nose ring and an obvious eye for Charlie. He of course was oblivious, even when she said, 'Let me know if you need anything else handsome,' so I would have to revisit our previous talks about the birds and the bees and remind him which was he.

We walked out past the deck that formed an 'L' shape along the back and side and down the ramp to the floating boat dock. We sat, our feet dangling over the water, beers in hand.

"So," Charlie started, "What really happened with you and David?" I'm immediately thrown; my intention was to discuss Nana, not my failed engagement. I wasn't prepared for how intense and fresh the pain still was. Perhaps stuffing everything inside and not dealing with it was a bad idea, like feeding a hungry monster that would eventually become so large it would eventually consume me.

"No, Charlie, I'm not ready to. There's other stuff going on." He shifted to face me. I stared at my hands on my lap, but all I could focus on was the bandaged ring. I chose a point on the horizon to focus on instead. The sun was low in the sky, not quite setting; casting everything in a burnt orange glow. "The other day at Nana's..." I was interrupted by him grasping my hand firmly.

"No Calli, no dodging this one, not now." I tried to pull away but his grip was strong. "I've known you all my life and I can see what this is doing to you. If you don't let it out, then you'll make yourself sick." As though a switch has turned on inside, I began spilling.

"It began a couple months ago; I was on my way to meet David, and was admiring the light refracting off my ring; little rainbows. I glanced out the window and saw birds; they were flying in a backwards formation, in the wrong direction." My brother merely nodded, waiting patiently for me to continue. "A couple weeks later we were leaving Johan's Bakery, after a wedding cake tasting." His eyebrows rose.

"I know it sounds sudden but it wasn't, he's very much in demand so you have to book him two years in advance. Anyways, I heard a commotion on the veranda. No one else seemed to notice but I couldn't ignore it. I followed the noise until I found a white crow hopping around. Well it wasn't really white, a container of flour had spilled on it somehow and it was trying to shake it off so it was this creepy half white, half black creature squawking. Then it looked right at me or rather through me and spread its wings then flew just inches over my head."

Charlie squeezed my hand. "Look Calli, I know with Nana and sometimes with Mom or Aunt Cathy, they get a little weird and superstitious but I don't think these things meant anything, if you saw them for what they were at all. You were on the train, not paying attention so maybe you were wrong and even if you weren't what made you think it had to do with you?" I started to speak and he stopped me. "Yes, the crow at the bakery, I know but it sounds more comical than creepy and again why are you choosing to see signs in these?"

"Why do you sound upset with me, like I did something wrong?"

"Well didn't you?"

"What? What could I?"

"You ended a relationship based on ridiculous coincidences seen as signs from the Universe. You're supposed to be the tough one, the reckless one, the one who is always brave and you let a bunch of birds scare you off?" His voice cracked; Charlie wasn't used to being assertive. Tears were filling my eyes making everything blurry.

"More things started happening," I continued, "a few days later, more frequent like a build up to something big. I thought about talking to David about postponing the engagement especially after I was taking yet another tour of another apartment.

The realtor stepped out to answer a call so I wandered around by myself. I was in the master bedroom, decorating in my head; this is where the dresser would go, the nightstands, the bed and then I heard it; a sound that was a mixture of panic and intense pain. Kind of like a cat's wail but different somehow. It was coming from the fireplace. I called for the realtor but he didn't hear me, well not at first.

I walked a little closer, the sound growing more intense. I felt strange, as though it was inside me, trying to claw its way out. Soot started falling from the flu and I was suddenly so scared I wanted to run away, not wanting to see the hideous creature making its way into the room. My mind had created a hundred different monsters by this time, each one worse than the one before. But I was frozen and couldn't speak."Charlie yelped in pain from my hand crushing his, I released it but continued on.

"Suddenly this crow stuck its head out, eyes large and searching. It flew out towards me but was caught in some kind of wire so it twisted in the air a couple feet. There was a puddle of blood on the floor from where the wire sliced into its body but it kept struggling as though nothing, not even death, would keep it from reaching me. Its eyes bulged as the wire cut into its neck. I don't remember screaming but that's how the realtor found me.

The bird was practically decapitated but still making noise and still contorting. He had the maintenance man take care of it. They were puzzled, said the chimneys were specially screened so that animals couldn't get in." I glanced at Charlie, who was practically wheezing at this point.

"I'm sorry Calli; I can understand why you did it now. You must have been terrified."

"Did what? I didn't do anything Charlie. Actually I'm surprised you think that, after all you're the one who read the letter. Why would you think it was my doing?"

"He didn't say what happened; only that he regretted the situation and decision. It sounded as though it wasn't his idea."

"It wasn't mine, even after all that I'd seen. That night I was resolved not to let anything come between me and him, not another person, not the Universe and especially not some stupid birds. I knew it was coming but I wasn't the one who surrendered. If he hadn't let me go, I'd still be with him today." He hugged me tightly and I wiped away a tear.

"So what did you want to talk to me about? That is if you're still up for talking and can forgive me for being a horrible twin and insensitive jerk." I pulled back and smiled at him.

"You're always looking out for me, even if I don't agree with it. I appreciate it so much."

"Good, cause I love you big sis." I laughed and punched him in the arm.

"Love you too, little bro." He winced, it wasn't an act.

"So what's life like living with the swinging senior?"

"That's what I wanted to talk to you about. She's been acting weirder than usual. She's pushing all these books on me, has been disappearing for days on end and she yelled at me over that ugly ivy all over the fence."

"Sounds like menopause." Charlie offered in literally 30 seconds; Sound prognosis from the great Dr. Charles.

"Gee thanks, could you give it a little more thought or I don't know, maybe come over and help me figure it out?"

"Maybe she's having an affair."

"She's widowed, so technically single; so no scandalous affair. Not to mention I don't think she's over Pops yet."

"Maybe she's shy." I gave him a shocked look in response, dripping with extra helpings of sarcasm. Nana, or Thalia Thorn as she was named, had been a successful Vegas show girl in her youth. Story had it that our grandfather, William Thorne, while on furlough, fell in love with her during one of her shows and stayed a whole week trying to woo her. He said he told her it was fate because they practically had the same name. She joked later at their wedding reception that her wedding gift from the groom was the letter 'e', but she was hoping for an 'o' on the honeymoon.

He must have done something right; they conceived my mother soon after. Thinking about my grandfather reminded me of my obligation to take care of my grandmother. Something he asked of me during the last days of his life when he was battling cancer. Whatever I had to do to help her I would.

"Um I forgot to mention I've been hearing her talk to herself or at least she's talking to someone or something when she thinks no one is around."

"You think maybe she's going senile?" I cringed hearing the word spoken out loud.

"I hope not, but."

"But what?" His face was soft but his body was tense. Preparing for the worst I suspected.

"The other day she was screaming and hitting the ground because her plants weren't growing." His face told me even this was a lot more than he expected. "Not to mention she lied to me about a play after I caught her acting up a storm in the backyard for an audience of no one; unless you count Calypso."

"Who is that exactly?" He scrunched his face in thought.

"The stone mermaid in the fountain. How could you not remember her name, it's so similar to mine?"

"Well maybe that's why you remembered it. I only remember she had nice boobs." I smacked him with a look. "Well all that sounds not good so what do you want me to do?"

"Move in?"

"Okay." He said calmly.

"Just like that," I hoped my suspicion wasn't obvious but my brother wasn't the bunking at other people's house type. He had his room at our parents and had expected to be staying there.

"Yep," his face was calm with no hint of sarcasm.

"I had a long winded and moving argument to convince you to stay. I literally spent hours."

"Hours?" He raised his eyebrows.

"Okay at least 15 to 20 minutes working on it. I even perfected fake crying."

"Perfected?" I shrugged in response. "Well, as enjoyable as that sounds, it's unnecessary, I'm here." He really was and I was beyond grateful. Things always seemed more manageable, no matter how difficult with my brother around. He was a calming presence that reduced the static of my mind. My own personal rabbit ears.

"Thanks lil bro."

"Don't mention it. I think if you hadn't asked, Mom would have. So where is Nana?"

"She should be home soon. I think she went to brunch or bingo or to taxidermy class. I saw her at breakfast."

"Please tell me you're being sarcastic," his face scrunched in disgust.

"Wish I could but at least she's not dealing with anything sharp or flammable. At least that I know of."

"Was she always this weird?" This was a valid question.

"I don't know, maybe she just seemed more quirky and fun when we weren't the ones responsible for taking care of her." I linked my arm in his and headed up the ramp back to the bar. I handed him my empty glass and smiled. "I think you should go refill these solo if you know what I mean." He didn't so I had to take the direct approach. "I believe the bartender likes you, maybe you should ask her for her number."

"Her I.Q. number?" Charlie wavered, empty glasses in hand. I smacked him hard on the shoulder.

"She's cute and she seems nice, go ask her out and get me another beer."

"Wow, didn't take you long to revert back to your old self did it?" I punched him harder and he finally left. Though I had to agree all the softening up David had initiated was beginning to wear off. I smiled to myself proudly as otters splashed in the water.

A John Mayer song was playing on the jukebox and I closed my eyes and smiled. It tugged at a memory but I couldn't quite place it. I shrugged to no one and realized I didn't have my purse. I ran back down the ramp to the dock and that's when I noticed that familiar eerie mist rolling in. It wasn't unusual for fog in the Central Valley, especially near the water but it seemed strangely timed and rhythmic, not to mention it was only 6pm.

My intuition screamed at me to get as far away from it as fast as possible and it took every ounce of self-control to walk slowly towards the ramp up instead of running hysterically. By the time I made it to the point I believed the ramp connected to the dock towards my left, the mist was thick and up to my knees; it felt cold, thick and slimy. Just as I stepped to my left to walk up the ramp my foot connected with something loose. It pitched upward and knocked me into the water.

I screamed for Charlie but soon my mouth was full of the Delta as I became entangled in weeds or rope below the dock. To make matters worse I felt myself being pulled further under, stronger than a current, perhaps some sort of pump. My childish imagination conceived terrible monsters with long tentacles hungering for a snack. I struggled but only managed to exhaust myself. My body went limp and I felt myself sinking.

This was it, I was dying. Images flashed of my parents, grandparents, aunts, uncles, pets and then Charlie. My brother was half of me and I him. How would he cope? Who would take care of him? Suddenly I went from quiet passing to pissed off.

I desperately kicked out and connected with hard wood and was able to propel myself above water long enough to grab hold of a metal stair that extended into the water. With all my strength I climbed up onto the deck and untangled my captor; weeds. Somehow, I managed to standing and didn't stop running until I was well past the ramp and on dry land.

"You were right, Michelle is nice and surprisingly bright for someone with facial jewelry," Charlie stopped midsentence as he noticed me shivering, dripping wet. "I suppose you don't want this now," he set the beers on a table and immediately removed his jacket and wrapped it around me. "Calli, what happened? It's not 6th grade all over again is it?"

"I fell in the water," words were punctuated with the loud chattering of my teeth. "I couldn't see with the fog."

"What fog?" Exasperated I turned and motioned towards the water. It was clear enough to see across to the opposite bank. Nana's sanity suddenly took a backseat to my own, which now felt in the driver's seat. Crazy car coming through! Charlie eyed me suspiciously the entire drive back. I had weathered similar looks before in the past but never from my brother. I hated it. It was like I was failing as a sister without knowing how or why. Even with the heater on full blast I shivered but it wasn't just from the cold.

My hold on reality was tenuous at best. I felt like I was caught in the middle of some cosmic storm, unable to navigate my own way. Charlie left me to my thoughts, probably involved with his own until making it inside. I was grateful when I was able to take a hot shower and dress in my warmest pajamas but felt vulnerable alone. I assessed myself quickly; I had reinjured my ankle but I was otherwise unhurt. I think scared was the appropriate condition. It didn't help that my accident happened after sharing my creepy story with Charlie. I sighed and limped downstairs.

"Are you sure you are alright?" Charlie wouldn't stop nagging, though I had to admit if roles had been reversed I would have been far worse. Growing up I took risks with my own actions but mothered him to no end. I was his big sister after all.

"I'm fine, just shook me up. You know how I am about water." I eased onto a stool at the island.

"Since when," his face scrunched up in thought.

"Since forever," I reminded him.

"Really? I don't remember that. What about the fog you thought…"?

"I did. Charlie you know how it is around here near the water." He started to speak and I silenced him with a look. He was like a rogue investigator, relentlessly searching for answers. I knew he wouldn't let go but hoped he'd at least shut up for a while. I knew what I saw and what wasn't there after which should have been and knew he was right to a point but I felt I needed a victory no matter how miniscule or accurate. "If you're still staying let's get you settled, unless you want to share Nana's bed."

Shortly after, with a little work we had the den set up for Charlie's stay, though it was obvious he wasn't comfortable. The sectional made out into a bed but the mattress was thin, you could feel the bars underneath, so I found a couple of comforters and folded them, stacking them on top of the mattress, under the sheet. It was lumpy but soft. He tested it out and gave me a less than enthusiastic thumbs up.

"Seriously, you can have my room," I offered for the fifteenth time.

"No, I like it here, really. I don't care for your location facing the road, so very not Feng Shui." He was being sweet. Not that my brother couldn't be nice to his sister, but he was worried about me and that was awkward for us both.

"Alright, it's yours if you change your mind." I frowned at the darkness outside and headed to the kitchen. Nana had left shortly after breakfast.

"I'll make dinner if you come keep me company." He took chicken out of the refrigerator while I took a seat at the table.

"You sure you can handle it?" I asked mockingly. "That food is raw; I think you have to cook it."

"I know my way around a kitchen, even if that is news to you." He winked.

"It is." I said with genuine surprise. "Just be careful, I don't want you to lose a finger."

"Speaking of fingers, what happened to yours? Is that from the fall?" He motioned toward my bandaged ring finger.

"Long weird and crazy story and unbelievable even." I managed to laugh in spite of myself.

"More so than tonight," he rummaged through the cabinet for a baking dish. Popped his head up for directions and then continued his search in the one I pointed at which was left of the oven.

"Oh so much more!" I nodded when he pulled out a large glass dish. He set it on the island and prepared the chicken; some olive oil, garlic powder and a few other spices I couldn't make out from across the room. I had to say I was impressed.

"Okay, I trust I can fix dinner and carry on a conversation, so spill." He danced the chicken around the pan and I laughed. It felt good.

"Short version," I ran through it quickly, "is I had a dream that someone put a ring on my finger and the next day I was wearing it."

"Where did it come from?" He asked giving the bird a massage.

"I don't know. I've looked around the house for a jewelry box or vanity or something but it's a mystery." With Nana gone, the searching had gone faster. When she was here it was very stop and go, afterwards however, I still hadn't any luck. I conducted a thorough inspection of every single bathroom (there were 3; a guest bathroom and master bathroom upstairs and a half bath downstairs), her bedroom, closet, dressers. No jewelry box whatsoever. Apparently the woman had an aversion to jewelry.

"And I'm guessing by the bandage that you didn't ask her." I shook my head no.

"She's been acting so stressed out; I didn't want to be the one to push her over the edge. I mean I don't know whose it is or where it came from but I have this overwhelming feeling that it's kind of a big deal. What if it is something really precious to her like something from Pops or I don't know, just what if it makes her upset?" Would she hack me to bits with her garden hoe? Charlie peeled some baby potatoes and placed them in the pan.

"Well if you're worried about it, why not just take it off and put it somewhere safe in the mean time? Better yet, you could leave it somewhere in her room for her to find and maybe she'll think she misplaced it." He placed the chicken in the oven.

"Those are really good ideas," I smiled nervously.

"But?"

"It's stuck; it won't come off. Believe me I've been trying!"

"Let me see it," He washed his hands, dried them then sat next to me at the table. He carefully unpeeled the band aid and gasped. My finger was swollen and purple though the ring was snug but not too tight.

"Wow, guess you weren't kidding. Are you okay?" I sighed.

"Yeah, it's just a little sore now," I stared out the window and studied the clouds on the horizon, they were getting darker. Probably would rain soon. I wished Nana would hurry up and get home. "You know I tried everything; lotion, baby oil, olive oil..."

"Motor oil?" I frowned at him. "You know; I think I've seen this before." He had my finger and the ring as close as possible to his face. He squinted hard.

"Where?" I studied the ring, not for the first time, hoping it would spark a recollection. Nothing. Not even a flicker.

"I don't know," He finally conceded.

"When?" That would be helpful, right?

"I'm not sure but I want to say it was when we were kids, like really young."

"I did find our old treasure box, under the tree. Do you think it could have come from there?" He shrugged and gently laid my hand on the table and fished out his cell phone. After taking a couple photos of the ring he finally spoke again.

"So what was your dream about?" I jerked my hand back suddenly and shooed him back to the task of dinner. He walked backwards toward the counter, eyeing me the entire way. The aroma from the oven was surprisingly delightful.

"Nothing that would help us to figure it out," I mumbled. He located a bottle of white zin in the fridge and poured himself a glass. I shook my head 'no', as he gestured to offer me the same, and instead held up the bottle of cabernet on the table in response. He grabbed a second glass then joined me back at the table. I quickly filled it and took a gulp.

"Calli, it doesn't help to hide things. I'm here to help and I'm your twin remember; we tell each other everything."

"Well, I guess there's a first time then because it's private." I limped to the sink, washed my hands and gathered vegetables from the refrigerator for salad.

"Oh, I get it." He grinned.

"Get what?"

"It's either a dream about you doing something super embarrassing or a sex dream. My money is on sex dream."

"What," I stammered, "Please, that's ridiculous."

"No, what's ridiculous is that your face matches that tomato in your hand." I didn't even bother to verify. Instead I focused on chopping it to little bits.

"Think what you want," I threw at him.

"Look, just tell me the parts that don't have sex, if there are any!" He chuckled loudly; I smacked him with a hand towel. "Seriously, there could be a clue you're missing. Sometimes you need an objective third party."

"Fine," I returned to my seat at the table. "But know that I hate you right now" I forced myself to talk but stared at my hands. "In the dreams I'm dancing with Hades."

"Interesting, so a date with the devil." He took a long sip.

"He's not the devil, this is Greek mythology not Christianity and he's really not that bad; he's charming and sweet and intelligent."

"Whoa, you're pretty protective of your new boyfriend. Interesting. Ok, so where do you meet? Does he come here? Does he sit in the living room with Nana while she threatens him if he breaks curfew while you get dolled up?"

"You're having way too much fun with this."

"I'm sorry; let me get into serious detective mode. Where do you have dinner? Please don't say Olive Garden."

"Funny. Actually, I go to the Underworld, he said he didn't have permission to come here."

"Wait, the God of the Underworld has to get permission to visit Northern California? Does he have an expired visa?"

"Cute."

"Hey everything matters, except gross my sister is having sex stuff. Give me a notebook or something and a pen." I found a pad and pen near the kitchen phone and handed them to him. He began writing notes.

"Okay, so we have Hades and the Underworld and he can't come here without permission. What else do you remember?"

"It's kind of fuzzy like being drunk but I remember the boat and the castle and all those poor souls waiting in line to be judged."

"So you go to sleep and end up there?"

"Actually I go to sleep and walk to a door." I stand up suddenly and pull out the key that's hanging around my neck. "Actually, I think the dreams started when I got this."

"I thought that was just a necklace," he asked. I shrugged in response. I didn't think it could open anything but how big of a leap do you have to take with a key necklace in a dream really? "Okay," he wrote some more. "So this ring means you're going steady? Engaged?"

"Married," Oh my God it sounded silly! I felt like I was back in 3rd grade; Bobby Sherman slipped the rubber band from his rolled up award on my pointer finger and said I had to kiss him. I ended up in the principal's office; I kissed him with my fist.

"You are married to Hades. Isn't he already married? You didn't tell me he was Mormon."

"Go ahead and say it Charlie," I looked down at my hands as a tear slid down my cheek.

"Hey I'm sorry sis; I'm not going to say anything." He handed me the notepad. I looked down at it and laughed. There were no notes, just one sentence. 'Calli, you are crazy.' I laughed because it felt better than the alternative.

Charlie and I stayed up late drinking wine on the back porch. Nana was still gone.

"Aren't you worried? I mean she's an old lady," Charlie asked while he rocked on the porch swing.

"She's not that old...well maybe in years but not physically. Besides she's very independent, she was gone for three days, no phone call."

"Maybe we should get her a cell phone." He held his glass out for more wine; I refilled both our glasses and laughed.

"She acts like they scare her. You know her and technology."

"The call is coming from your grandkids," he said in his creepiest voice.

"Stop, you're freaking me out and I'll have nightmares."

"So I'm guessing there was no prenup with this marriage or it would have been a nightmare, get it?" He leaned forward and nearly toppled off the swing. He threw out his arms to steady himself. He didn't spill any wine as his glass was near empty. I didn't offer to refill it.

"Very funny," I golf clapped. "Did you guys elope in Vegas?" He downed the last gulp of wine.

"Ha ha, you're a real comedian tonight aren't you?" He waved his empty glass at me and I shook my head 'no'.

"Was Elvis there? Was he the one who married you?" He attempted another sip, noticed it was empty and waved it again I shook my head 'no'.

"Yeah and Jimmy Hoffa was my maid of honor," I offered in return.

"That's stupid, that doesn't make any sense at all," his voice started slurring until I couldn't understand what he was saying.

"I think it's time for you to go to bed. I think you're drunk." I took his glass, which he reluctantly relinquished and only after he attempted yet another sip. He refused to give me his hands to help him stand.

"I'm fine." He said more to the air around him than to me.

"You're not coming inside?" I took a couple steps towards the door.

"No, I'm gonna sleep right here...when I'm ready, which I'm not." He grabbed onto the arm of the swing as if he thought I was going to drag him inside. I didn't think I needed to, if worse came to worse I'd grab one of the sleeping bags out of the hall closet and wrap him up. The nights here got cold still in March but not deathly so.

"What are you going to do out here all alone?" I rubbed my arms briskly. The cold was starting to bother me.

"I'm gonna watch the stars, there's animals up there and they do tricks and shows then maybe I'll go on a double date with you and your boyfriend if that's okay? I don't want to piss him off. I don't want him throwing lightning bolts at me or anything. I like my hair. Do you like my hair?" I stifled a giggle, Charlie was big on accuracy and hated to be 'incorrect' I wish I had thought to record him with my phone.

"Okay, it's gonna get cold, though." It was already too cold for me. The chilly breeze was nipping at my exposed flesh herding me back into the warmth of the house. I didn't argue.

"Whatever, I'm just as tough as you." He flung his right arm out at a weird angle and swished it around. Nana was right, he needed sword fighting lessons.

"Sure you are, good night." I walked five steps and was almost knocked over as he ran past me.

"I'm not sleeping outside, that's stupid." He dove onto the couch missing the coffee table by inches.

"Be careful okay?"

"Good night Calli." He curled up in a ball, cuddling one of the throw pillows. Luckily the bed was already made up so I wouldn't have to move him much.

"Good night Charlie. I love you." I closed and locked the sliding back door and wrapped a blue and gold quilt over my little brother.

"I love you too Calli...and Elvis, you too I love." He was snoring before I made it to the stairs. Even though the house was quiet and I still wasn't used to being so far from town, having someone else there well, having Charlie there made me feel safer, more secure and relieved. I was asleep as soon as my head hit the pillow.

"Come to me my darling," my husband's voice whispered to me. After the evenings events I was not receptive, quite the contrary, I wanted almost nothing to do with him. I say 'almost' because there was a tiny carnal bit that wouldn't allow me to commit 100% to that stance. Sadly, I knew that bit was my Achilles heel and put to the test my resolve would crumble like the proverbial cookie.

The image of a fortune cookie quickly came to mind; brittle, empty but containing a message. What the hell did that mean? I shrugged off any attempt to make sense as that would require precious energy better spent fueling my spirited resistance. 'Viva la leave me alone!'

"Go away, you're not real and I'm in no mood for indulging my crazy tonight." I attempted to sound tough but didn't even manage to sound authentic. He laughed.

"What pray tell, could have caused you to want to send me away so callously? Another suitor?" It was my turn to laugh.

"Oh well you know me and Poseidon thought we'd give it a go."

"My brother? That is so unlike you? It's very much him but not your type." He sounded serious.

"I can't handle one of you, let alone two. No, I just hate feeling crazy and this, all this is crazy. I hate it because just hearing your voice is so soothing and comforting. It's far too tempting to give in to my imagination."

"I like yours too but even more I love seeing you and touching you, especially touching you." My body tingled and I sighed loudly. "Isn't there anything that could change your mind? What if I were real?"

"That's even crazier than you not being real I think."

"Why don't we strike a deal? If I come to you and prove I'm real will you come back with me?" His voice purred and my body fought with my mind.

"Sure, Okay," I sighed and rolled over once more. I hugged my pillow tightly and let sleep recapture me. Just as I was falling I felt a light touch brush my hair off my face then soft lips first on my cheek then my lips. "You came?" I asked smiling, my eyes shut tight. I couldn't bear opening them and destroying the fantasy. I felt the blanket lift away and then he was leaning next to me on the bed.

"My sweet, sweet wife, open your eyes." His voice was soft yet commanding and reluctantly I did so. He was really there, looking magnificent in his dark robes, blue eyes flashing and a grin that made me blush. He leaned closer and kissed me passionately and I threw my arms around his neck and pulled him closer. When he pulled away he was laughing quietly.

"I missed you, too." I moved over on the bed and motioned for him to join me. I didn't have the energy to fight it and just hoped it was a vivid dream and not my final collapse into dementia. "I'm so glad you came." He sat down, took my hand and frowned at the bandage. "I'm just keeping it our secret a little longer." This answer seemed to please him.

"We must go now." He pulled me towards him.

"We can't stay here?" I eyed him seductively. "I mean we have a bed, it's big enough for the both of us and would save a lot of time and effort." I took his hand and sucked on his finger. He closed his eyes and moaned. After a moment he slowly pulled it away and tilted my chin.

"It's not safe here."

"Of course it's safe here. My grandmother is down the hall, but she'll never even know you were here." I batted my eyes.

"She is not my concern; there could be problems, dangerous problems." His face indicated more than his words. A chill ran down my spine.

"What kind of problems?" My voice was pitched and I was gripping the sheets in fear. It seemed irrational but I couldn't help myself, my primal urge of fight or flight was overriding my mind. I was like a gazelle that couldn't see the lion hiding in the grass but knew it was there.

"Things that I can't explain now but I will later, I promise. We must hurry." I panicked and leapt off the bed, intending to run out of the room towards the hall but the sudden weight on my still healing ankle caused me to stumble. He gently pulled me back and held me tight.

"Shhh, it's okay. I don't mean it's dangerous right now but if I stay here with you I will attract danger. You don't want that do you?" I shook my head 'no' and after sliding my feet into my comfy slippers allowed him to lift me up into his arms and carry me out of the room onto the balcony.

"Will we be attacked?" I whispered as quiet as possible. My eyes darted around the yard and I hated the openness of our surroundings feeling like a giant bull's eye was painted on my back.

"No, we will be fine; I promise you are safe with me." His words calmed me and my body relaxed. I couldn't tell the time but the moon hung high in the sky. I shivered slightly and he wrapped me tighter, shielding me from the wind which had grown stronger since I'd been out. His body heat radiating and warming me wherever our bodies made contact.

Once we were down the stairs he set me down on the cool wet grass and stared out towards the water, listening intently as I held my breath. As soon as he was satisfied he picked me up once more and carried me to the cellar door. With no kids around to get hurt it wasn't locked, just latched.

He easily opened the door with a wave of his hand and carried me down the stone steps into the cramped and musty space. Across the room was a dusty shelf full of old tools and cobwebs. He pushed it aside revealing a large metal door. It was set deep into the wall so that the oddly mismatched door knob didn't jut out. If you had looked from the side, you wouldn't know there was anything unusual there.

I took my key from around my neck, twisted it clockwise until it clicked, turned the knob and pushed open the door. He set me down as he closed the door behind us. The tunnel or rather tunnels this time, stretched far before us.

"Interesting," he mused, though I couldn't figure why.

"Which way do we go? I don't remember there being more than one tunnel before." I looked up at his face instinctively, it was pensive. He noticed me and relaxed a little.

"There wasn't because before you had only one destination in mind. Tell me my lovely, where do you want to go?"

"With you of course," I laughed.

"Yes, but where? You must lead the way." He hesitated before the two routes.

"I don't understand."

"You will." He said his voiced drenched in melancholy.

He lifted me into his arms once more and waited for me to point to the tunnel to the left, the new tunnel. I don't know why I chose this; it wasn't a conscious decision but rather an automatic one. Like when someone asks you to say the first word that comes to mind. I clung tightly to him as I awaited our destination, colored with equal parts curiosity and apprehension.

We travelled uphill for what seemed like an hour but he never tired of carrying me and I never tired of being carried. I studied his face in the dim torch light; that of a perfect marble statue. He sighed as I reached up with one finger and traced his jaw and then his lips, amazed at their warmth. Eventually he stopped and set me down once more and motioned for me to wait while he slowly peeked behind a curtain of foliage. I heard him gasp and then he turned, picked me up and carried me outside.

The first thing I noticed was the air. It was sweet with an array of scents I couldn't quite place but all equally pleasant. Though it was dark here as well, I was warm enough in my nightgown. My eyes slowly adjusted to the moonlight, revealing a wide grassy meadow surrounded by tall dark mountains and a cluster of trees. It created a walled in effect though not constricting.

"Where are we?" I whispered.

"You don't know?" He eyed me with interest. I shook my head.

"No, but it's beautiful," I sighed. He set me gently on the grass and instructed me to lie down. He reached down slowly and took my injured ankle in his hand and kissed it softly. Warmth emanated from his lips and traveled throughout my foot, as well as the rest of my body most notably my female parts. I moaned quietly in anticipation.

"That should feel better," he smiled. I waited for him to seduce me once more but instead he helped me to my feet. There was no pain when I tested my weight. I smiled fascinated.

"I apologize my dear, I could have, should have done that sooner but I must confess I really enjoyed carrying you." I reached up on my toes and kissed him quickly.

"I really enjoyed you carrying me." I took his hand and urged him to follow as I explored the outer rim of the meadow. One side was part of a hill, where we had emerged from the tunnel. It was rocky with strange vines with purple flowers splayed across. It continued further than I could see, winding towards the north where it eventually grew into the elevated mountains.

A grove of olive trees formed a wall from east to west, imparting a Dali-esque quality to the environment with their twisted trunks and branches. They reminded me of taffy that had been stretched and turned and then plied to resemble actual trees, more decorative than purposeful yet they indeed yielded fruit.

To the south was more open meadow and the remains of a wall of some sort, short and broken in many spots. I was drawn and he followed. Upon closer inspection the wall appeared to be some sort of bench chiseled out of polished gray granite, though large enough and wide enough for several people, not just a couple looking to get cozy. It was stately with various symbols etched into the base of the seat. I couldn't see them clearly but could feel them when I rubbed my hand across. The back was broken and lying a few feet away at an angle, which looked odd.

Seems it would have just fallen straight down if it had fallen apart due to age. It was nearly covered in some sort of blooming plant, almost as though the ground was trying to hide it, to sweep it under the rug. A new assessment told me the bench had been destroyed. By who or why I didn't care to know. Not that I wasn't curious, but my intuition told me it was better left alone. That thought was affirmed when I noticed he refused to look at it. I wondered if there was a story there and if he'd ever share it.

The distinct sounds of water coaxed me out of my thoughts and past the bench and down a gentle green slope of soft grass. I discovered a large pool, not quite the size of a lake being fed by a stream that originated somewhere up in the mountains. I sat on the soft grassy bank and dipped my toes in its cool depths. He gently pulled me away.

"You must be careful. You never know what is living in there." I laughed softly at him. What could possibly be dangerous in this tranquil and beautiful setting? As though reading my mind, the pool transformed as several water lilies began to bloom, glowing in the moonlight. They floated in a lazy circle and I leaned forwards to touch them but he locked me in his arms. After a while I gave up and allowed him to hold me, stroke my hair and kiss my forehead. As I lay there he hummed; a sad tune of love found and love lost that ended with a happy reunion.

"That was beautiful, what was it?" I dabbed at the uninvited tears in my eyes.

"Your lullaby," he said into my hair. His voice conveyed so much emotion with those two little words. Again I was curious but apprehensive.

"You surprise me," I whispered. He lifted me once more though I didn't need him to and carried me back towards the meadow. "This place," I said and he stopped to look at me intently, "I like it, I'm glad we came."

His face relaxed and he gave me a smile. As we reached the mouth of the tunnel, I stopped him.

"I expected horses, is that strange?"

"There are many things here for you to explore another time my dear." Then we plunged back into darkness.

"Are they amazing?"

"You have no idea." He lit the torches with a wave of his hand, shadows danced erratically on the walls. As we traveled downward, my heart yearned to return outside. He must have noticed this because he stopped when we arrived back at the door, rather than continuing down the main tunnel, to his home. I smiled at him gently and motioned for him to continue.

As much as I yearned for the smell of the breeze through the blossoms, the twinkling stars above and the soft cushioned earth, I couldn't bear the thought of not being with him. Stronger than the yearning of my flesh, it was a new stirring, one he had been longing for; my heart.

The trip with Hermes had been quicker than on my own but it was nothing compared to traveling with Hades. We literally stepped out of the tunnel and into his bedroom. "I had this specially decorated for you, do you like it?" He set me down upon the softest rug I had ever felt. I slipped off my shoes, my toes wiggled delighted. The lighting was dim but a pure white, instead of the drab orange of the torches and provided by a giant crystal chandelier.

The grand wardrobe, vanity and dresser were smoke gray wood with iridescent quartz tops. The walls were draped with rich amethyst silk that shimmered in the breeze through the open window. Wait, breeze?

"Smells like the ocean," I looked at him quizzically.

"I had it imported for you."

"Air, you had air imported?" My face lit up.

"Well, I know it can feel a little confining here so I hope it helps." I closed my eyes and breathed in the briny essence. It was mesmerizing. "This is what I think you'll like the most." He took my hand and led me up three steps to a large canopy bed. It too was constructed of quartz, with four large posts that curved into arches on each side which were draped with more silk. I smiled coyly at him.

"Oh of course, this has got to be my favorite." I dove and pulled him down with me on top of the softest bed I'd ever laid on. "Oh my, it's like resting on clouds." I sighed loudly as my body floated blissfully.

"Watch this," he grabbed a tassel and pulled, revealing an opening in the canopy above where there appeared to be no ceiling, just pitch black. He was giddy like a boy showing off a new toy. I started to speak but he silenced me with a kiss. "Keep watching." He smiled expectantly. I tilted my head back and slowly lights began to emerge like stars. As I continued to gaze patterns became visible.

"Are those the constellations?" It brought back memories of elementary school field trips. I had always enjoyed them but never pursued more knowledge on the subject. Lucky for me, I didn't need to. I had a knowledgeable astronomer lying next to me.

"That large one there is Pegasus, the one to the left is Andromeda and the one above and slightly to the left is Cassiopeia." He spoke with casual authority.

"That's incredible," I smiled as they shifted, new patterns rearranging. "Alright, which are those?"

"Hydra is on the left, directly right of that is Canis Minor and below is Monoceros." The stars shifted once more. "Cepheus..." I cut him off with a kiss.

"Thank you, the astronomy lesson can continue another time. Right now I'm interested in anatomy." My voice was a purr.

"My, so much different from the timid woman I started wooing so long ago," he eyed me intently. I slid off my pajama bottoms and then my underwear, tossing them on the floor.

"Yes well you've given me a taste and I want more." I found the place where his robes opened and tugged hard revealing his chiseled flesh and then straddled him. I slowly and purposefully unbuttoned the pajama top, his eyes never wavering, then slid it off and tossed it onto the pile. I leaned across him for a moment, bare skin touching bare skin. The combination of his heat on my front and the cool breeze on my back was exhilarating.

"Don't you want to kiss and explore each other awhile first?" He whispered. I shook my head and ran my hands along his shoulders down his chest and past his stomach until I found what I wanted. He moaned softly and then I was on top and he was inside of me. I rocked back and forth as waves of ecstasy threatened to overtake me.

"My turn," his voice was husky as he flipped me over, pulled my legs high and wrapped them around his waist. Whatever pleasure I felt before was magnified with him on top. I begged him to stop then screamed until he continued. When he exploded inside me I thought I would be carried away and when my turn came I was, to a heavenly floating space.

Spent and giddy, I draped myself across him while he stroked my hair.

"I love you," he whispered softly.

"I love you, too," I whispered back. As I drifted off to sleep I felt something wet land on my shoulder."

Five

Do You Mind?

The next morning, I woke up sore, extremely hungry and my heart was so light it felt like it would float right out of my chest. I tried to recall any dreams from the night before but my mind was clouded. Swirling around my brain were bits and pieces but nothing connecting; stars, water lilies, olives and a meadow. Of course, Hades was present, though I also couldn't remember any specific details, just an overwhelming emotion; love.

When I went down to the kitchen I immediately noticed the empty wine bottles on the counter and sighed knowingly, glad for some explanation. Charlie was snoring on his stomach with one arm and leg on the floor. I tried to shift him to a more comfortable position but failed so I set the coffee maker to brew and took a quick shower.

I lathered up I noticed there were parts of my body that were tender, most notably my breasts and my southern region. I observed my hands suspiciously as though they were perpetrators. After towel drying my hair I dressed in some comfy cotton pants and a t-shirt. I couldn't find my slippers so I put on some thick socks and padded downstairs.

Hey early bird," Charlie rubbed his eyes as he walked out the sliding patio door. I took a sip of coffee and shook my head.

It's almost 9:30, I'm on my second cup." He slumped in the seat across from me and took my mug.

Hey that's mine," I said but not before he took a big gulp.

Fine, keep it, I'll make another." He was lucky I was in a good mood. I took my coffee very seriously.

"I se you already had breakfast," he waved his hand at a plate of crumbs.

No, no, I wanted to wait for you that was just a snack. I was starving, still am." I frowned, "I think I'm a stress eater."

"Are you stressing about Nana, the ring, David, starting a new career, how best to invest your 'severance check' or where to honeymoon?" I gave him a dark look as I headed back inside.

"I see you leave your funny button on all night." I called out from the kitchen window.

"Of course, I'm an animal, I'm always on."

"Do me a favor and check in Nana's room and see if she's back please."

"Do me a favor and turn off the jackhammer in my head," he growled on his way to her room. He returned a moment later. "Nope, still gone. Should we call the cops or CSI or something?"

"Okay, first off, CSI is for crime scenes, we don't have a crime scene just a grandmother who doesn't care enough to call or check in. I do think we should call Mom."

"I'll call her," he offered. I handed him the kitchen phone. It was old, yellowed white and attached to the wall with a long curly cord that plugged into a base that had a keypad. We both had cell phones but there was some sort of weird interference that made the signal wacky; either a call wouldn't go through or it would but you would hear irritating squelching sounds and once I overheard two women discussing the sordid details of some randy neighbors. I did the respectful thing and hung up, almost immediately.

My first week here I had tried several locations on the property to find reception until I almost fell off the balcony; standing on the railing, one hand gripping the roof and the other extended out like some misplaced Cellini statue. Now my cell was pretty much a glorified phone book and watch, except when I went into town, which was almost never. Charlie slid a business card over to me.

"Who is Dr. Monroe?" I asked after glancing but not picking it up.

"Your new psychologist," he said hopeful. He flashed me his 'don't be mad at your little brother' smile.

"Where did you get this?" I glanced at it curiously, refusing to touch it.

"I got it from my CPA. Well not mine yet, Dad's CPA. Okay, from a guy in the same office."

"So many questions; why are you carrying this around and why are you giving it to me?" I tried to tone down the annoyance in my voice but I had enough to deal with at the moment and I didn't like thunder clouds shadowing my sunny disposition.

"Well there was a time I felt I needed some help."

"But you decided you didn't?"

"No, well maybe a little but I was worried it would hinder my intellect if someone was rooting around in there."

He gestured with the phone in his hand, smacking himself in the forehead in the process. He grimaced and rubbed at it with his free hand.

"You aren't confusing a psychologist with a brain surgeon are you?" I asked, ignoring his not so sleight of hand.

"Listen Calli, the mind is a delicate and highly complex organ and who knows what damage they could inadvertently cause with reckless questioning and snooping or worse yet, implanting. Besides, it wasn't anything major, I just couldn't sleep without the light on."

"Okay. And you think I need it?"

"Oh yes."

"What about the threat of my hindered intellect?" He answered with a snigger.

"You want me to go to someone referred from Dad's office?"

"Actually, Dad's CPA's office, to clarify." I motioned to hit him. "Why does it matter? It's no different than picking someone at random from the phone book."

"Exactly, that is why I would want to carefully and thoughtfully evaluate the right person. This is my brain we're talking about. Even if you don't regard it so highly I don't want to go to some hack." I sipped my coffee more for something to do than refreshment.

"Fine, don't call him but I think you should call someone. This is serious Calli, you could get hurt." He leaned on the counter, already wrapped up in the cord.

"I already got hurt. Remember? You were there." I stared at the cup in my hands, feeling my good mood loosed like air from a deflating balloon. I sagged into the kitchen chair.

"I know I'm sorry but I'm speaking of physically getting hurt Calli."

"You want me to see a shrink because I'm clumsy? What are you worried about Charlie?" I quickly regretted the question.

"After I went to check on Nana I took a look around your room. The balcony door was open and I found these," he reached under the kitchen table and pulled out my slippers, they were muddy and wet. He set them back on the floor when I refused to look at them.

"Where," I asked somehow already knowing.

"By the back stairs," he stared at the floor unable to look me in the eye. "I think you've been sleepwalking."

"That's ridiculous," I said, my voice wavering under the weight of the truth. "No," I shook my head. "I could have worn them yesterday morning and forgot."

"Where," his gaze challenged and my mind scrambled.

"Watering the front garden, you have to step into the bed to get the hose." There was no conviction in my words.

"Alright, let's go check," he headed towards the front door. I stayed in the kitchen, staring at my cup of coffee but unable to drink it. The stress was now making me nauseous. He returned quickly and headed for the backyard. This time I followed him.

"What are you looking for," I asked, again not wanting to hear the answer. I felt threatened and on the verge of discover like a spy vainly trying to hold closed my bag of secrets that was splitting at the seams.

"Tracks," His eyes widened and he ran back to the balcony stairs, turned and walked slowly forward while checking the grass for evidence. I sat on the swing in defiance but the rocking motion made me sick and curiosity was getting the best of me so I followed him. There was nothing of note in the grass so he focused on the softer dirt next to the house. He pointed to something about five feet from the stairs next to the part of the house that faced the water.

"That is just mushed dirt; it could have been from anything, maybe a bag of fertilizer. It doesn't look like footprints, I'm sorry Charlie. Let's go make breakfast, better yet, I'll take you to Elaine's. How does that sound?"

"After," He moved past the deck to the section of house shaded by the tall elm. "And I want to go to Emerald Isle. They make the best potatoes O'Brien." He stopped and studied the area that hid the river from view. The ground was wet near the tree and especially near the house, next to the weathered cellar doors. He took my slipper and held it next to a depression in the mud. He looked around curiously.

"What?"

"I can't find footprints leading anywhere else. I'm wondering if you went into the cellar."

"What? I've never been down there; I don't even think I could open the door?" He stepped back and motioned for me to try. I glared at him and almost stormed away but again, curiosity grabbed me by the hand. I leaned over, grasped the metal handle and pulled. The door creaked in protest but it opened easily enough.

"I've heard that sound before, maybe even last night."

"Stop it Charlie, now you're just making shit up!"

"Am I Calli? So far we found muddy shoes that match muddy footprints. I'm going inside and see what else there is." He disappeared down the stairs. "Ayyy," his voice screeched. I screamed and almost fell down the stairs running to him. I found him, or rather collided with him. He was standing in front of an old painting leaning against the wall; it was ghastly in both technique and subject.

"You asshole! I almost broke my neck!" I punched him hard in the arm and busied myself with steadying my breathing.

"I'm sorry," he yelled back, "It scared me, like truly scared me. She's got worms for hair! You know those are the one insect I truly despise!" I ignored him and the painting and glanced around for a light switch. The sunlight from outside was filtered and only lit a small square of the floor. When I couldn't find a switch or chain I opened the second door giving us a little more light.

The cellar wasn't ominous in the least. It appeared to be fairly modern just underutilized and therefore dusty and full of webs. I found an old sheet and threw it over the painting to sedate Charlie. He checked a tall wooden shelf against one wall for a flashlight.

"There are fingerprints on here."

"Are they yours?" I called over to him as I peeked into boxes stacked near the wall closest to me on the opposite side. All they seemed to contain were books, some old clothes and some tennis shoes.

"No, Calli they aren't," he chided back. "Wait, maybe they are, I don't know." We finally gave up and went inside, opting for oatmeal and toast; neither was up for a road trip. We didn't talk anymore about dreams, sleepwalking or much of anything save his conversation with our mother. "She said not to worry; Nana will come home when she's ready but..."

"What?" I asked him as I dried the last dish and put it in the cabinet.

"She asked me what today's date was."

"Check her calendar on the fridge, you never know. Maybe she has a Gaelic festival or Scandinavian candle making scheduled. I'm going to go lie down." I desperately needed to be alone. I was scared and confused and more scared. I sat down on my bed with a notebook intent on purging my overwhelmed mind, instead I ran to the bathroom and purged my stomach. Something told me the stress was only going to get worse.

Try as I might to argue, Charlie's words rang true deep down inside. I eyed the French doors with animosity, as though they were silent accomplices in the crime against me. Around four o'clock, Charlie knocked on my door. "Hey sis, I got something to cheer you up."

"Flowers," I mumbled into my pillow.

"No."

"Candy," my stomach growled.

"No."

"Hmmm, there is one thing that would really cheer me up but you couldn't possibly know what that is or how to get them." I sat up a little on my bed and wiped my hair out of my face. I had slept hard.

"Actually, I think I might."

"No!" I struggled to smile.

"Yes! Playoff tickets for round two, whatever that means but they're actually from Dad. I'm just the messenger." I flew off the bed, threw open the door and nearly knocked him over with my hug. He regained his balance and handed me two tickets.

"You're coming with me!" I told him with a wide grin.

"No." He waved his hands in front of him

"Yes!"

"But I don't even like hockey," he pouted as I shut my door and started to dress.

Six

Get the Puck Out

"You know that glass is pretty thick," I called over to Charlie who was wincing in his seat like a scared little girl for the umpteenth time. "You're starting to embarrass me little brother." He glared at me and pouted. I sighed exasperated, I could get his non-interest in playing sports but going so far as not to enjoy watching them, especially live and most importantly, hockey?! That was just absurd.

"Why do we have to sit so close?" I was worried his high pitched whine would crack the glass. Again, he missed the point. Somehow the fates had smiled on us for we had not only scored playoff tickets to my favorite local team, the Port Town Thunder but in the coveted glass section of 105. You couldn't get any closer unless you were a player or referee.

"Because we're damn lucky! These seats are never available; you have to be a season ticket holder. We attack this goal twice!" I bounced in my seat. "Wow I haven't been to a game in ages. This is so freaking cool!" I pounded my fist on the glass, he cringed. "Let's go Thunder!"

"Why can't you be like other girls?" He feigned disgust. I stuck my tongue out.

"I could ask you the same thing," I smirked and pointed to a couple 10-year-old female fans seated a couple rows behind us. They were dressed in matching black and yellow jerseys and cheering loudly.

"I'm going up to the snack bar where it's safe." He started to stand and I pulled him back into his seat.

"You can't leave until there's a stoppage of play and for the millionth time, no one ever gets hurt in the stands." As soon as the words came out of my mouth Charlie got his stoppage of play as the puck hurtled into the stands and hit Thor, the Viking mascot who was rousing the fans in the upper level. As soon as the whistle blew Charlie ran up the stairs with an athletic flair I wasn't aware he possessed.

"Penalty on Las Vegas #13 Lo Kee," the announcer's voice boomed over the loudspeaker. The crowd was in an uproar, out for blood and riled up. Thor shook it off; his costume consisted of thick foam and attempted to move the crowd into a cheer, exaggerating his wellness by disco dancing.

Distracted, I didn't see what happened next but I heard it; the sound of two trains colliding at high speed. The arena exploded with applause as Thunder fans jumped to their feet.

"Penalty on Port Town #1 Joe Roth," you could hear the smile in the announcer's voice. Number 13 lay sprawled out on the ice, inside Vegas's goal, helmetless and dazed. He shrugged off the medic and his coach and jumped to his feet. He had a strange countenance about him, very exotic even for a sport comprised of mostly foreigners. As bearded as the other players were his face was bare, save for a long red goatee and very angular face, almost elfish; well the movie depictions of elves, not like I had ever seen one in person. His eyes were the strangest, like liquid pools of inky black depths that continued into infinity.

He pointed at Roth with his stick then skated to the penalty box. Roth took a couple bows and waved to the stands before allowing the refs to lead him to his spot in the box next to Kee. On the jumbo screen they flipped between shots of Kee and Roth, eliciting boos and cheers respectively. Roth's attention seemed to be fixed intently on a spot to his right.

"Do you know him," one of the girls asked me with intense interest. I shook my head no. "I moved away so I haven't been keeping up the players."

"He's staring right at you," they giggled. I shook my head 'no'; he definitely wasn't looking at me. She pointed to my image on the screen. I risked a glance in his direction; he was most definitely looking at me. After a while, Kee joined him in this strange reverse spectator sport. His gaze was curious while Roth looked as though seeing a familiar acquaintance or friend. I tried to ignore it but I could feel the intensity of their gazes on me.

Thankfully play started soon after with only a minute left before the period break. As the players exited the rink Roth waved to me and grinned. I spent the next twenty minutes fielding questions from my neighbors. I suspected some were secretly wondering if we were somehow related as I was dressed plainly in a t-shirt and jeans with my unruly curly hair pulled back into a pony tail; not exactly hot model girlfriend material.

"You missed a great game," I scolded Charlie on our way through the parking lot. I suspected he had hidden out in the lounge for the remainder. I was about to fill him in on the odd events after his departure; the next two periods Kee and Roth spent beating each other up and watching the game from the penalty box, though they glanced my way repeatedly.

"Hallo mooie jonge dame," a man's voice called out across the parking lot. I turned and saw a Viking in a Calvin Klein suit. He was tall and muscular with a coppery beard and long hair that hung past his shoulders."Excuse me lady please."

"Hey Charlie, come have a beer," a group of men converged around a car two aisles over. They wore slacks and matching white shirts and lanyards.

"Friends of yours," I asked.

"The stat guys, we bonded over numbers."

"Of course," I laughed.

"Friend of yours," he eyed the Viking who was making his way over to us.

"Not really sure what that is," I answered honestly. "I think he's one of the players." Charlie gave me a 'no shit' look and left to join his new buddies.

"I'll be right here if you need me," the humorous statement hung in the air long after he was gone.

"Hello, fair maiden," Viking's grin was electric and made up for his cheesy salutation.

"Hello."

"It is a nice night tonight, is it not?"

"Yes, it's lovely. I'm sorry but who are you?"

"They call me Roth, Joe Roth."

"Oh, the brawler," he appreciated the compliment, "good game out there."

"Thanks, it wasn't the fiercest battle but it was good fun!"

"My name is Calli." I held out my hand for a shake. He grabbed it eagerly and kissed it, his lips lingering a little too long to be considered platonic. I blushed when I noticed an audience had gathered.

"It was nice to meet you and again, good game. I have to get going, have a nice night." I had my fill of the spotlight for one night.

"Calli, might you call on me some time?" I tried not to giggle at his odd turn of phrase.

"Uh, sure, I guess." He pulled out a marker and wrote on the inside of my wrist. "Your accent doesn't sound Canadian."

"No, much further north," he winked. I thanked him and hurried over to Charlie. Roth climbed into a Jeep and sped through the parking lot, heavy metal music blaring. I spent the ride back home pondering the night's strange events while Charlie recounted with enthusiasm his time spent with the statisticians.

"So now you're a hockey fan?" my voice accusing.

"Well now it makes more sense, it's not all about the hitting and fighting." He smiled at me as though sharing a secret. I laughed.

"You know that's the main draw for a lot of the fans."

"Barbaric," he snorted. This brought me back to Joe Roth. Unusual things had been happening since David broke up with me. At least this time I hadn't been injured or nearly drowned. I added that to my blessings list.

He was also very hunky and awkwardly charming. My mind lingered on his hand holding mine, it was large and strong and his lips made me quiver at the mere memory. Heat surged into my face and I was grateful for the dim Interior of the car. Very quickly my lust was replaced with overwhelming guilt. I became angered at my invisible accuser; I was single after all! As I pondered this new emotion I realized I was spinning my 'wedding ring' with my free hand. Well wasn't that great?

"Want a glass of wine?" I asked as we settled into the kitchen.

Nana had a nice large island that we used more for meals than the actual dining room table. It was less formal, cozier. He pulled up a stool and gestured flippantly with his hand.

"Oui garcon." I found a step stool and pulled a nice red down from the top of the cabinet. I didn't recognize the brand and it looked old. I hesitated, thinking maybe it was a rare vintage Nana was saving but Charlie grabbed it out of my hand and had it open before I could protest.

"C'est la vie," I sighed.

"What?"

"I was thinking maybe she didn't want us to drink that but too late now."

"Well then she should be home to supervise, don't you think." I shrugged.

"What's that," he grabbed my wrist and flipped it over. The word 'THOR' was scrawled below my palm in black permanent ink. "He autographed your hand, so fan girl of you Calli, I'm shocked." I pulled my hand away and swatted him lightly.

"He must have gotten hit hard, that's not his name, its Roth and there's not even a phone number."

"Wait, you thought he was giving you his number?" He snickered. I was disappointed and found myself wishing he'd given me more than that.

"Oh no, how are you going to see him again? They go on the road for the next three games."

"Okay, first of all, you're starting to freak me out with your newfound interest in the sport, well any sport for that matter and secondly, you can trust when I say that I will not be seeing him again ever," though various parts of me wished very differently.

"That's too bad, probably wouldn't be a bad thing," I almost choked on my sip of wine, embarrassed he was reading my dirty thoughts. My mind had been running through a play by play of my own game. He scored every time he was in my zone, the game went into overtime and was rife with misconduct penalties of hooking, charging and roughing.

"How is that?" I grabbed a towel and dabbed at my now damp shirt a little rougher than necessary as though I was attempting to stamp out fires.

"Well, it doesn't have to be him but I think you need to get with someone. Nothing serious, just fun, I think it would do you good."

"When did you become so cavalier about sex?" He shrugged.

"At least get out with me some more, like I don't know, maybe Haven Acres? Possibly this Friday night?"

"Sure you don't mind helping me out like that?" I eyed him knowingly. I was actually pleased he had a romantic interest.

"What are brothers for?" He waved his hands gallantly. I smiled and then sighed.

"I don't know Charlie, I just don't feel like doing anything remotely risky, physically or otherwise."

"Wow, what happened to you?" he immediately cringed and added, "I mean obviously there was the David thing but I'm talking about before him. Since being back here I'm reminded of earlier days and you were a lot spunkier." He refilled both our glasses. I sat across from him and scrunched my face.

"Nana mentioned something like that too, she blamed Mom," my voice full of skepticism. I found it difficult to blame my mother for something as enormous and all-encompassing as responsible life planning. It wasn't like I suffered from a severe phobia resulting from her forcing me to walk a tight rope or tossing me into the ocean without a floatation device. For instance, I had a healthy and reasonable fear of spiders because of the spiders themselves and not due to any maternal influence.

"Hmmm I guess it could make sense. Like a form of hypnosis, you hear 'don't touch that', 'don't get too close', and 'don't mix any chemicals in your bedroom without a trained professional present' enough times and eventually it sticks. She wasn't like Nana; she didn't support you having your form of fun." My eyebrow rose. "Well I'm sure she gave you similar yet slightly different warnings but I heard them too."

"So I grew up. Isn't that what you were harping on me about our entire childhood?"

"That was just me being Charlie, reacting to you being Calli. You had a carefree spirit and laughed so much. I was scared for you and sometimes indirectly myself but I was also jealous. You had a courage that I didn't possess. I wouldn't want you any other way." I reached over and squeezed is hand.

"Thanks lil brother, that's sweet and means a lot."

"Look, I know you've been through a lot recently but maybe it's time for some serious soul searching. Find out who you really are, I mean you seemed to lose yourself with David. I barely recognized you." He took a long sip of wine waiting for my response.

"You know I have been thinking a lot about all that lately. I mean I was dumped by my fiancé, who I met only one year prior, I quit a job, sitting at a desk selling advertising and I was living a short hour away from Mom and Dad."

"Hey I take offense to that last one."

"Do you really?"

"No," his shoulders sagged. "Hey at least you don't still have your room at Mom and Dad's."

"Seriously," I stretched my arms out.

"Oh."

"You're right, though, I shouldn't be mourning a man and a life that I really didn't want. And I hate that I am scared all the time, seriously the first week I was here I about killed myself running from the willow tree and the sound of a boat!"

"Camp Archimedes, you went there without me?" He sounded like a wounded child. Sudden illumination spurred my lagging brain.

"That reminds me, by the tree I found an old wooden box. I was waiting for you to get here to open it. It's under the stairs to the deck." I followed him outside and smiled to myself as he gleefully excavated the 'treasure chest' and placed it on the outside table as though it contained actual treasure. He grinned at me and I frowned.

"What's wrong now?" He sounded annoyed. I made a silent promise to try to be more cheerful around him. He was sacrificing so much personal comfort for me that the least I could do is outwardly show him I appreciated it.

"It's nothing big, I just remembered something else; I lost my camera. Wow, that was weeks ago, how did I forget about that? I'll have to look for it tomorrow when it's light."

"You've been under a lot of stress what with the wedding and Nana going crazy. Here, I promise this will help. Let's open it together." I stood opposite him and placed my index finger under the box lid, he did the same on his side. With his other hand he imitated a drum roll. Then we flipped it open.

Seven

Hands off My Booty

As simple and informal as our proceedings were the actual contents of the box were astonishingly not. Charlie's first find was an iron dagger. He studied it intently in the moonlight. Unsheathed it was wickedly sharp, so definitely not a toy. It bore a twisted vine pattern on the hilt and sheath and appeared to be ancient, though anything left outside for more than a summer around here appeared that way to me.

"I don't recall putting this in the box, do you?" He looked unsettled.

"No," I shared his discomfort. It was a feeling of being violated, though nothing had been taken, boundaries had been crossed, privacy had been compromised. "Turn on the deck light," I urged him.

"This is pretty dangerous looking." He set the dagger aside and motioned for me to inventory the next item, it was something hard wrapped in a piece of beautiful red silk that appeared to have been cut from a larger cloth. An intricate gold pattern was woven throughout. I opened it carefully, fearful of what it might contain after seeing the dagger. A brilliant stone that resembled a ruby dazzled in my hand. It was the size of a small egg.

"Charlie, quick turn the light off." I threw the contents back in the box and hurried for the door, locking it behind us.

"What's wrong?" He asked as I closed all the blinds and poured another glass of wine. I motioned to the box sitting on the kitchen island as though it were a contaminate I wanted to distance myself from.

"We didn't put that stuff there. Someone else did. Doesn't that scare you, at least a little?" My voice rose in pitch.

"Maybe it was Pops or Nana," he shrugged. I flashed him a look.

"No, what, why? No, Charlie, someone else, a stranger hid those things on our property, maybe the people in that boat. The boat people. This could be dangerous, what if they're art relics? This is a huge stone, possibly a real ruby and that dagger looks really old. We haven't played out there in years, it was a perfect hiding spot for us, so why not anyone else?" I tried to sit but wound up pacing almost sloshing my drink on my grandmother's favorite throw rug.

"I don't buy it, who would know enough about who lived here and whether they would get caught or obviously their stuff found by us?"

"Someone who knows Nana but didn't know we would be here. If it was the boat people they could easily bank and do whatever without anyone in the house knowing, especially Nana." Charlie exhaled loudly and shook his head.

"Boat people? It sounds a little too fantastic, my money's on Nana. Now let's see what else is in here." He pulled out a weathered leather satchel, untied the cord and tipped it upside down. A brilliant gold necklace with a strange circular pendant fell loudly causing us both to jump. Charlie inspected it a moment then stuffed it back inside.

"Anything else in there," I asked hoping we were through. I felt extremely uneasy even with Charlie's theory.

"No, that's it." He proceeded to place everything back in the box. As he wrapped the ruby he stopped and waved me over.

"Look here, there's a symbol stitched into the cloth." I leaned in closer.

"Looks Chinese," I shrugged. "Take a picture. Maybe we can look it up online." Charlie added it to his phone gallery.

"It's definitely an eclectic bunch of items," he mused. "Maybe we should have them examined by a professional."

"And if they were stolen?" I reminded him.

"We didn't steal them." His voice was full of reason.

"We can't prove that." Mine was fraught with frantic.

"Well what do you want to do with it?" He threw his hands in the air in defeat.

"We can't put it back outside I guess, so maybe under that loose floorboard under my bed for now." I hated having the items so close but also didn't want them too far away, either. We headed upstairs, Charlie with a long flat head screwdriver and a hammer. I tucked the side of the comforter back and pointed to a plank of wood that looked similar to the rest of the floor except for a slight notch on one end. Charlie stuck the screwdriver into the notch and pushed down on the handle. When the plank was lifted enough, he stuck the claw end of the hammer underneath and pried it open the rest of the way.

I exhaled a long breath when he finally removed it. Much to my relief, the hidden space under the floor was empty. Good, I didn't think I could handle any more surprises. Charlie was right about me going through a lot lately, but oddly enough none of it involved David. I felt like a character in a paranormal horror film. A common theme in those was the sudden acquisition of a strange object. I inspected the key around my neck but it didn't feel evil and to be honest had provided me with the only good experiences of late. In fact, just looking at it made me tingle all over. Maybe it was best to chalk it up to hypersensitivity after a distraught situation and feeling out of place in an old environment. Oh, and lots of clumsiness.

A little after midnight we got a pleasant surprise; our grandmother had returned.

"Oh good, I was hoping you were awake." Charlie and I stared mouths gaping from the couch in the den. We had been watching a Bruce Willis movie marathon. "Nice to see you Charlie, your mother told me you were in town. How was the drive down? How's your ankle doing Calliope?"

"Good." Charlie responded in a daze.

"Good." I mimicked his reply. Nana shuffled into the kitchen, she was wearing blue jeans, cowboy chaps, boots and a long sleeve shirt, her hair was in a single braid down her back. We followed. "No hat," I asked.

"Kept falling off," she replied nonchalantly. "A lovely lady friend of mine gives riding lessons, I didn't need them, obviously I know how to ride, but I didn't want to be rude and it didn't hurt to sharpen my skills for when we go to Greece.

I'm going to check on my garden, I'll be right back." I waved and she stopped short. "What on earth did you do to your hand?"

I almost fainted thinking she meant the ring; perhaps the bandage had fallen off. A quick peek proved it was still there.

"Is that marker on your wrist? Heaven's child there's a pen and paper right there for notes." She slipped out the back door before we could respond.

"That's weird," was Charlie's take on the situation. I laughed.

"Weirdly normal, hell that's the first thing she's said and done that's made any sense."

"You're kidding, right?"

"Wish I was. No, wait, I don't. I like that Nana's quirky, she's true to her nature."

"I guess. So why do you still have that guy's name, do you like him?" He reached for my hand and I pulled it away.

"No," I tried to be mature but stuck my tongue out instinctively. "I've tried everything it won't come off. It's like this damn ring. I guess I'm a magnet for the strange and unusual."

"More like glue. Hey, do you mind if we don't finish the movie? I think I'm going to call it a night? I'm working on something incorporating Einstein's time dilation factor theory."

"Okay but only because this isn't Die Hard and only if you tell me why," I teased.

"I just did," his tone was serious as he quickly kissed the top of my head and waited patiently as I left his room. "What's this about you going to Greece?"

"So much you still don't know lil bro. I'll fill you in tomorrow." Soon after the door to the den closed I heard talking, laughing and most definitely the word Michelle. I smiled to myself; my brother used science to lie to his big sister about calling a girl. I was finally rubbing off on him. I patted myself on the back and sat waiting for Nana.

Bored, I started putting away the clean dishes and when that was done I straightened the canisters on the counter and the salt and pepper shakers on the table. With nothing left to do I grabbed the pen and pad from next to the telephone and started making a list of all the strange occurrences over the past few weeks. I had high hopes that getting them on paper would take away their paralyzing stranglehold over me.

It definitely couldn't hurt. It looked like this...
My Crazy List
David's sudden break up (It counts!)
Strange key
Weird sex dreams about Hades
Feeling like I was being attacked near our tree
Feeling like I was being attacked on the dock and in the water
Finding a box full of real treasure in our boring treasure hiding spot
Waking up with a ring on my finger (Duh! Can't forget that one!)
Being...

The last one was left unfinished as Nana hurried in from the back door, panic stricken and out of breath.

"Are you okay," I tried to put my arms around her but she was moving too fast.

"I need to call Catherine, excuse me."

"What's wrong?"

"Um, it's a gardening thing, you wouldn't understand." Dumbstruck I went back to my list. Crossed out Being and added 'Nana acting overly crazy about her garden again'. The next morning Nana was gone again. Charlie was pushing to tell her about the box when she returned but I was hesitant considering her frantic state. I was worried about her craziness over that garden of hers so much that I wondered if she was growing pot.

It was legal to grow marijuana if you were selling to dispensaries for medicinal purposes. You had to have a medical card to buy it. However, there was a danger involved from criminals who wanted the crops. Neither of us knew what it looked like in person. Charlie looked it up online and we compared the picture to the various plants. We found one that was similar but it had pink flowers.

It was time to call Aunt Cat and get some information. Unfortunately, her number was disconnected.

"She moves around so much she probably changed it," Charlie suggested. It made sense. She had lived in practically every state here in the U.S. and several countries. Now she was in India, for how long I had no idea. She was an antiquities dealer and thus traveled for her job. That was it, a solution to one of if not two of our problems!

"We need to talk to Aunt Cat," I exclaimed loudly. Charlie rolled his eyes dramatically.

"Yes, I believe we just established that."

"No, I don't mean just about Nana and last night but about the box of treasure."

"That's right, she knows that stuff, she could be our professional and probably wouldn't rat us out to the cops."

"Probably?" I gave my brother an uncomfortable look.

"Eh, you never know. Hey, maybe she can tell you about that ring on your finger, too."

I glanced at the very real embodiment of my failing sanity and sighed loudly. Now that Nana was back I needed to hide it again. I wondered if she would question why I was wearing a bandage for this long but the alternative would be harder to explain. I headed into the bathroom and within minutes the charade was reestablished. At least I needn't be concerned about her gleaning more of the situation.

Worried about further delving into delusion, I had been taking Nana's sleep aid, though careful to use as little as possible. I hadn't had any dreams and subsequently no more sleepwalking.

"Yeah, hopefully she can," I motioned to Charlie when I reentered the room, "But we need to get ahold of her first. Call Mom, she's got to have her number or at least know how to get in touch." I paced in the kitchen, aware I was most likely wearing a trench into the honey wood floors while I waited for Charlie's response.

He had taken to talking in the den because my pacing was 'too loud' for him to hear Mom. It was nearing half an hour when he finally emerged.

"I got nothing." He slumped into a kitchen chair looking like a defeated warrior.

"How could you get nothing; you've been on the phone for hours!"

"Okay, first calm down, no need to yell and second, it was a fraction of that long."

"What did you guys talk about if not Aunt Cat?"

"Mom's the master of misdirection, I asked for Aunt Cat's number and she changed the subject while she was looking for it. She asked about school, about you and next thing I know she's saying she has to run but will call when she finds it."

"Where? Oregon?" I threw my hands up frustrated.

"I don't know. So what's for breakfast?" He pulled open the fridge and started digging. I pulled him out and shut the door.

"You're giving up already," I asked. He shrugged.

"I'm hungry and stumped, what do you want from me?"

"Look, we're two intelligent people," he raised his eyebrows, "hey, I'm not illiterate and you're twice as smart as most humans so together it evens out."

"But I'm hungry." He gave me his best puppy dog eyes.

"I know me too," I confessed as my stomach growled. "Look, we're probably too close to the problem here, let's go eat somewhere, how 'bout Annie's? We can still brainstorm. Who knows maybe something will come to us."

Annie's was a quaint diner on 2nd St. that had been a favorite spot growing up. Pops would take us at least once during a visit, twice if we were lucky. Charlie ordered a Denver omelet while I seemed to order everything else breakfast related. The waitress eyed me curiously before leaving the table.

"Are we expecting company," Charlie asked. He looked towards the entrance expectantly.

"No, it's all for me. I've been so stressed I haven't been keeping much down so I'm starving all the time." I threw in a look that said change the subject. When the waitress brought our coffee I focused on the process of adding the sugar and creamer a little too intently. "Can't you just look it up online," I asked him finally, breaking the silence with my cross words.

I didn't need to look up to know that I had wounded him. I was startled with my overwhelming frustration; my nerves were tangled and jumbled and my mind wouldn't stop buzzing. What the hell was wrong with me? I imagined my anger was a camp fire and doused it with a big bucket of cooling calm, inhaling deeply a couple times before feeling comfortable enough to speak.

"Oh my God, I'm so sorry. I really don't know where that came from." I risked a look at his face, aware that I would start bawling the moment I saw his pained expression but wasn't prepared for what he wore; amusement. He was practically laughing at me. I started fuming again and he held up his hands in defense.

"Hey, it's okay. Look, I did go online and I didn't find anything, that's why I didn't say anything." He tried to hide his smirk but failed, nearly laughing out loud. The waitress brought our plates, which took a while my eyes being bigger than my stomach, and I waited until she was done before I spoke.

"Why are you laughing," I started to ask but then answered my own question, "wait, you're enjoying all this, aren't you?" His long pause confirmed my suspicions.

"Maybe a little; it's fun. We're trying to solve a mystery or mysteries rather. You should enjoy it too," he unrolled his napkin and removed his knife and fork, "doesn't it remind you of when we were kids?" His eyes were sparkling and his face was illuminated. In some reversal of fortune, we had traded hats, he was becoming more carefree and dare I say, reckless? While I was yearning for order, calm and quiet. Eww, I was becoming our mother.

I focused on my food, taking little bites of everything, my thoughts bouncing between when and how I had become such a bore, such a tight ass and how on Earth was I going to finish all this food? When I had finished the four links of sausage, two eggs, half my plate of French toast and a bowl of fruit I was able to concentrate as my emotions via my stomach were mollified.

"So, how do we find Aunt Cat?" I scrunched up my face in intense thought but nothing came forth. "I thought about calling hotels but Nana didn't mention a city so I wouldn't even know where to start."

"She may be using an alias, anyways," Charlie offered. My gaze bore into him, demanding elaboration. "Well, she deals with priceless artifacts; there are some unsavory types out there that would probably want to get their hands on them."

"I guess so," I nodded then nearly bolted out of my seat, "Do you think she's alright? What if that's why we can't get ahold of her. She could be hurt or...or worse." My heart was racing and my breathing jagged. Charlie reached across the table, full of calm and laid his hands on mine.

"Calm down Calli, think about it; neither Nana nor Mom could hide that from us." The nightmarish scenarios in my mind of my aunt being bound and gagged while being robbed and possibly tortured clashed with the rationale of my brother. The latter won out and my breathing returned to normal. He was right, well to a point.

"That's only if they knew something happened," I reminded him. The panic prepared to rise again.

"But they know everything," he responded in a matter of fact kind of way. I didn't laugh at him or chide him for his joke. He was right. My mother, grandmother and aunt had an unusual connection that bordered on the supernatural. If she was hurt or the other thing I couldn't even think let alone say, they would know and subsequently so would we. Something nagged at me but I couldn't quite grasp it.

"What if she isn't hurt or whatever but she could be in some kind of trouble."

"I guess, if it weren't too substantial they could maybe hide that." He shrugged then pulled out his phone and dialed. I gave him an annoyed look. What a time to call your girlfriend!

"Seriously Charlie?" He put his finger to his lips and gave me a stern look. I rolled my eyes and focused on my coffee.

"Mom," he spoke rapidly into the phone, "Oh thank goodness I got a hold of you. I've been trying to get through." He took a sip of coffee while my mother was probably responding. "No, I'm fine. It's Calli. No Mom, she's not hurt she ran off. To India, can you believe that? I don't know, she had that determined look in her eyes and muttered something about going to look for Aunt Cat. She thinks you and Nana are hiding something." Another sip, "I know, I tried to reason with her."

I sat squirming in my seat, desperately needing the ladies room but not wanting to leave. I had a new found appreciation of my brother and his thespian skills that I had previously believed to be nonexistent. Collecting dust on a shelf next to his unused athletic skills.

"Wait, you found it? Oh good because I think I found her. She stopped for gas. Hey look text me the number, I'm gonna try and talk some sense into her, love you bye." He hung up the phone with a smug look that could only be appreciated for a few seconds before I had to run from the table. Several minutes later I returned feeling much lighter.

"Sorry, you were about to tell me what that was all about," I flagged the waitress over for a coffee refill. Charlie gave me an exasperated look. "What? I like coffee."

"Leverage," he offered. My face registered my confusion. "Mom would lose it if you left town, let alone the country so I played on that and she gave me what we wanted." He held up his phone to show me the text message from our mother with our Aunt Cat's contact number.

"Where do you think that is?" I asked looking at the foreign area code.

"Not India," Charlie snorted.

"Why do you say that?" I was prepared for some logical theory.

"Because Nana wouldn't say India if that's where Aunt Cathy was. She doesn't want us to know. She's probably in Houston."

"That number isn't American Charlie," I reminded him. Boy he was getting sloppy.

"Fine. Australia then maybe or Brazil. I'm just saying it won't be India."

We waited until we were home to call, preferring the privacy of the house to the busy diner. Before we left I got a couple of to go boxes for my leftover food. I ate half of it on the way home. I was concerned that by the time we got through all this I would be too big to fit through the door. I vowed to start walking every day figuring in the very least it would keep me away from the food.

Of course we couldn't call from inside the house or even within the fence due to the crazy interference so we stopped at the end of the driveway and Charlie placed his cell phone on the hood of his car on speaker so we could both hear. It rang three times before it was picked up. A pleasant sounding woman answered. She spoke English but had an accent.

"Thank you for calling Vivanta by Taj. How may I direct your call?" Charlie pointed at me. I had been prepared for a cell phone or house phone personally belonging to my aunt. By the look on his face, he had shared my assumption.

"Hi," I spoke to the air in front of us, "I'm trying to get ahold of my aunt. Her name is Catherine Thorne." I quickly added, "My mother gave me this number to reach her."

"I'll check to see if we have her registered." I figured this was a hotel but wasn't certain. My instincts said not to ask, if it was it was a miracle they were even looking into it and I didn't want to say anything that would deny us access or at the very least, cause a delay. I didn't realize I was holding my breath until I had to breathe. Charlie looked equally anxious. "I can connect you to her room. Have a nice day." Music played as we waited for an answer. It sounded like something you'd hear at a spa or for meditation; plenty of flutes and string instruments. Just as my body began relaxing we heard our aunt's voice.

"Hi, this is Cathy." My brother and I almost fell on top of each other.

"Aunt Cat," I started yelling, "Are you okay? This is Calli."

"It's Charlie, where are you?"

"I'm not available right now," her voice continued, "I'm currently on an evaluation assignment in Peru. I will return all calls upon my arrival in two weeks. Thanks and Namaste." There was a beep to leave a message. Charlie did it. I was too deep in thought. A sharp click then the call ended.

We exchanged glances as we returned to the car; his face mirrored my frustration. He put his phone away and we drove inside the gate and parked behind my Toyota. Nana's pickup was still missing from its spot in the car port.

"What the hell is wrong with our family?" Charlie shook his head and stormed inside. He didn't slam the door but he closed it firmly. I didn't follow him. He had a right to be angry, we both did.

Growing up, Charlie and I hadn't really fit in much with the rest of the kids. I had it a little bit easier, due to my athletic prowess but still felt some of the same cold isolation. We were like aliens with no memory of our home planet. Not feeling we belonged where we were but not knowing where else we could. Your family was supposed to offer comfort, was supposed to act as a safe haven where you could feel accepted and welcomed. So why did we feel like ours was jerking us around?

Pissed off I went for a long walk around the yard then took the back stairs to my room. I didn't see him the rest of the day and told him 'goodnight' through his closed door.

The next morning, I quickly showered, dressed and headed down for coffee. Charlie was just pouring a cup which he slid over to me.

"Thanks," I grabbed some creamer out of the fridge and he passed me the sugar.

"You look rested," he sounded resentful

"Nana's magic tea," I smiled and nodded to a canister next to the coffee maker. He picked it up and opened it, taking a deep breath.

"Nana's drugs are minty," he grinned. "Make me some later," he gave me his puppy dog face.

"Sure, tonight before bed and after my appointment."

"What appointment?"

"Well after everything going on I thought about what you said and I agree, I think it's time to talk to someone. Well a professional someone."

"Dr. Phil?"

"No, Dr. Erin Yes."

"Is she related to Dr. No?" He grinned. "Make sure to take your laser pen and handbag that doubles as a bullet proof vest."

"I'm not worried about that aspect of her name, just the first part; Doctor"

"Who referred her?" He stirred more sugar into his cup.

"No one, I saw her ad on TV yesterday. I think. Maybe I heard it on the radio." Though I couldn't remember the actual source of the information I distinctly recalled the conversation on the phone late yesterday afternoon when I made the appointment.

"That sounds comforting." Charlie's zings were extra sharp this morning but I knew it wasn't personal so I let them go.

"It actually is. I feel like I should start listening to my gut and stop overthinking everything so much and taking action."

"Well as long as you 'carefully evaluated' and selected the right brain doctor." Charlie was acrimonious, "At least my guy's building had a glass elevator and a cool water feature in the lobby. What does yours have?"

"I don't know yet but I'm thinking a Charlie wouldn't be a bad idea. Want me to book a double appointment?"

"No, no, I need my crazy to fuel my intelligent research. Let's just work on the women of the family okay?"

"Better not let Mom hear you say that! Maybe I should call her."

"Oh speaking of, the answering machine is flashing I don't know how to work it. I think it's from the 80's. Might be secret agent Nana requesting clearance to return to the nest or hive or whatever."

"Wow, I can see why your research is so important, too much free time is turning you into a freelance comedian and not a very good one." I motioned him over, and pointed to the play button. "Push this." I refreshed my coffee as an all too familiar voice sounded in the room.

"Calli, we need to talk. Can you meet me at Regent Square at noon? It's important. There are some things…"

"Turn it off!" I waved at Charlie.

"It's David," Charlie stared at me stunned.

"I know who it is; turn the damn thing off now!" Charlie looked wounded as he found the stop button. I headed for the stairs.

"Calli, wait."

"What?" I said without turning around.

"We should go."

"I'm beginning to think you're the crazy one. I don't want to be anywhere near him." My eyes started misting just at the sound of his voice; I couldn't imagine what state I would be left in if he was physically near me. My mind flashed to the scene in 'The Wizard of Oz' when Dorothy threw the water on the wicked witch causing her body to melt into a dark puddle. Yeah, that would be me.

"It could be good information for your therapy. Maybe he can give you some closure." Charlie was crossing a line. I turned and faced him.

"I appreciate you caring Charlie but no, I'm not going. I don't care what he has to say." My tone said more than my words and like a pup who's been swatted with a newspaper; he quit chewing, though he wasn't keen on it.

"Alright, I'll leave you alone. I need to pick up some things from Mom and Dad's anyway." His shoulders sagged in defeat.

"Are you sure you want to stay," I asked, afraid of the answer.

"Of course, I'm not going to leave you."

"I'm sorry I snapped."

"It's okay you're going through a lot." I waited for another joke but he was silent for once. I offered one to him.

"Well I am balancing a lot; newlywed, possible burglary accomplice and unemployed photographer." He didn't laugh but he smiled faintly. "Damn, I really need to go find my camera one of these days. Keep an eye out for it if you go back by the bank."

"We both know I'll be going nowhere near that tree or the water but if I see it in the safe confines of the house or deck, I'll grab it for you. Good luck with your appointment today. You need anything from the Mom's?"

"Not that I can think of."

"Okay, see you later." He forced a smile as I ran upstairs to the hall bathroom. Stress topped with guilt, topped with more stress was making it hard to keep food down. I prayed Nana had a cure for this too.

The good Dr. Yes was situated in a strip mall on the outskirts of town. Out of the five buildings only three were occupied; Al's Deli Mart and Liquor and Quick Finish Cleaners were the other two. Many of the shopping centers had suffered when the giant mall was built 20 years earlier. They still rented out but it was more of a revolving clientele that never stayed more than one season.

It wasn't exactly the idyllic spot for therapy but I decided to reserve my judgment for after the meeting. After all, I was paying for quality care, not a fancy location. The inside provided no more promise of professionalism. It wasn't that it wasn't decorated very well, it wasn't decorated at all. The reception area contained a couple boxes, no seats, no desk and no receptionist. My intuition tingled slightly and I started to turn back towards the door.

"Hello, you must be Calliope," Dr. Yes emerged. She was a large and short woman with hunched shoulders. Her hair was jet black and oily and was in a sloppy bun and her cheap tweed suit tensed with every movement as though it would burst at the seams.

The worst aspect was her face which also appeared slicked with oil and was stretched so tight her grin resembled that of the cat that just swallowed the canary. Her mouth was closed but I imagined her teeth would be sharp as daggers. I turned back towards the door but she had deftly maneuvered me into her sparsely furnished office and onto a leather couch.

"I think I have the wrong place." My interest in leaving wasn't reaching my feet.

"Of course you have the right place Calliope, you made the appointment yourself." Her voice was rough and grating.

"I don't go by Calliope; everyone calls me Calli." Why was I still here and making conversation?

"Not everyone calls you that I'm sure." She eyed me intently.

"My grandmother doesn't but she's the one who named me." I sat up and planted my feet firmly on the floor needing some balance.

"I bet she did," she said and offered another closed grin. "This works better if you're lying down. Allow me." She grabbed my legs and flipped them up on the couch in one swift motion. My stomach swayed for moments after.

"I'm not feeling too comfortable; I don't think this is what I had in mind." I tried to keep my panic out of my voice but it was near impossible.

"And what exactly did you have in mind Calliope?" She had her back to me at a desk.

"Something less physical and creepy..." my head was getting woozy and I tried to sit up. "What is burning?" She turned to face me a long stick in her hand; I assumed it was incense. Was this some sort of alternative therapy?

"That is a little concoction of mine of Aloeswood and Musk Seed; it helps you get into a dream state. That way when I ask you questions you can't lie to me, at least you'll not want to."

"That sounds awfully threatening. I don't think you're allowed to do that." In my mind I was standing and marching out but my body refused to follow.

"Hah," she barked in my face. "I do what I want and you'll do what I want. We're going to take a little trip to grandmas and see what you got there. That is where it's located, right?" Her eyes gleamed and her face was drenched in perspiration making her face appear even more waxy and plastic. This time she did smile teeth and all and I swear they were sharper than I had imagined. I began to suspect the incense was some sort of hallucinogenic.

"I don't know what you're talking about, I thought I was supposed to talk about David and my broken engagement and how it's making me crazy and I'm having weird dreams about getting married." My vision started to blur and I tried to stand. "Are you sure you're licensed?" My stomach turned as the smoke invaded my nose and mouth.

"Married? To who?" I couldn't read her expression; concern, surprise or fear. "Hades," I mumbled as I swayed in my seat. She hurried over to the couch intending to grab my left hand but instead ended up with what was left of my lunch on her shoes. She jumped back quickly.

"Disgusting, you are a disgusting mortal! I'm infuriated! I'm going to enjoy hurting you!" Suddenly we were both thrown to the floor as the ground began to shake. I screamed and crawled towards the door; unable to recall anything about earthquake safety but acknowledging the open outdoors would be far safer than a tiny office with a lunatic.

I risked a glance behind. Through the smoke I was barely able to make her out. She was bent forwards, her clothes tearing. Gradually she stretched out taller and taller, as though she had been folded up inside that hideous outfit. I was convinced it was a hallucinogenic when her face split, actually split revealing some vulture like head and then enormous feathery wings sprouted from her shoulders.

I continued crawling through to the front office. A lot faster now thanks to the added motivation. As the air became clearer so did my mind. I quickly located my purse and wobbled out the door. The doctor was screaming in the office like a banshee. As soon as I managed to my car I locked the doors and drove like a bat out of hell.

I made it about a mile down the road before I was forced to pull over on the side. I yanked open my door and heaved. I found some napkins in the glove compartment and my bottle of water and cleaned up best I could. I decided to call Charlie before I went further as I was too shaky to drive straight.

"Hello," Relief flooded my face as I heard my brother's voice.

"Charlie, oh my God, are you okay? How are Mom and Dad?"

"I'm fine...we're fine. Are you okay?"

"Yeah, the earthquake shook me up but..."

"Earthquake? Where are you? Argentina?"

"Outside that crazy quack of a doctor's office. You were right, I should have gone with yours. She tried to drug me and wanted me to take her to the house."

"Are you safe?"

"Yes, I'm not there anymore. I'm west of town on that back road near the sugar factory."

"Need me to come get you?"

"No, I can drive now." My voice did sound steadier. As the effect of the drugs was fading I felt more confident in my ability.

"Go home, I'll meet you there."

"Ok."

"I mean it, drive straight there. Don't stop anywhere else."

"What's going on Charlie?" His concern was expected but I sensed there was more.

"I don't know about that but there's more stuff we need to talk about when you get there." His voice was strained. I said goodbye and slowly pulled back onto the road, my eyes darting to the rear view mirror all the way back to Nana's.

Charlie beat me there and he had a visitor; David. I pulled up the drive and parked next to them.

"Hello Calli," David's voice was serious as he climbed out of the car. "Thank you for loaning me your jacket Charlie." He tossed it on the seat and strode over to me; his hands and face were sunburned. I bristled at his presence and glowered.

"Charlie, what is he doing here?" I climbed out of my car and slammed the door so there was no question about my mood.

"I went to talk to him for you." He stayed a safe distance away.

"You did what?"

"Calli, you can be mad all you want later but for now just listen. He knows about some of the things going on."

"Can we get out of the open, maybe inside the house?" David made a move for my hand and I pulled it away.

"You're not welcome here." I doused the statement with as much venom as possible.

"Listen, if you just let me explain," His words were cut off by the blip blip of a siren as the Sheriff's car pulled up the drive. It wasn't unusual to see them driving around the area, not only was this their territory, as the police were limited to city limits but a couple officers lived out here as well. What was unusual was to see one in your driveway with their lights on.

"I need the three of you to put your hands up where I can see them and don't' move." We did as he asked. He motioned for Charlie to join David and me near my car. "We received a report of screaming and possible shots fired from this address." The color drained out of my face.

"How long ago," I struggled to keep frozen.

"About 10 minutes ago," he said after consulting his watch. I risked a glance to the right at the car port; Nana's pickup was parked.

"Oh my God, Nana," Charlie looked over at the carport and shook his head.

"Officer, my name is Charlie Bennett and this is my sister Calli Bennett. We're staying here with my grandmother Thalia Thorne."

"Who's your friend," he asked suspiciously. I noticed he didn't have his gun in his hand but the holster was unhooked if he needed it in a hurry. He was conveying our information over a walkie talkie clipped to his shirt.

"David Bradley," David spoke for himself.

"Were you invited here," he asked Charlie and I. Luckily he answered before I could.

"I brought him here with me."

"Officer, we just pulled up moments before you so if anyone might be hurt or in trouble it will be our grandma." I pleaded for him to hurry.

"Any vehicles here other than yours?" We glanced around but no strange cars or trucks were present. We shook our heads 'no'. "I need you to stand right here," He indicated a spot about five feet from the front of his car. I suspected he had a camera, most of the law enforcement vehicles did now a days, even the county. "You can put your hands down but keep them in front and out of your pockets." We each sighed in relief but remained tense. He slowly made his way up to the front door, staying low out of sight of the front windows.

The curtains were drawn, which was unusual, as Nana preferred them open during the day, but not alarming.

"What do you think," Charlie spoke to me while keeping his eyes on the sheriff. I shrugged.

"I don't know; I mean it could be nothing. Sounds carry so the screams and the gun shots could have been on another property or properties. The person who called in may be wrong but..."

"Why hasn't Nana came out to investigate our noise?" Charlie filled in. I nodded fighting back tears. I couldn't imagine any reason for someone to hurt Nana or her to hurt them.

I looked up at Charlie who was gnawing on his lip and about smacked myself in the head. No, there were several reasons and they were lying under my bed. I shook my head 'no' before he could say anything out loud in front of our mixed company. This was family business.

The sheriff slowly pushed the open front door and peered inside. The tension was too much and I ran up beside him. He jumped and cursed under his breath, glaring at me. I ignored him, straining to see past him.

From outside the house looked normal but inside it resembled the aftermath of a hurricane. The coat rack was overturn in the foyer, scattered coats and scarves, the formal living room furniture was completely flipped, flowers strewn everywhere.

"I'm gonna ask you again to wait outside," the sheriff whispered. I turned and noticed that David and Charlie were right behind me.

"Can't we help," David asked. The sheriff shook his head.

"I called for backup as soon as I saw the mess." He motioned for us to move back, which we did until we were off the front steps. Charlie grasped my hand.

"It will be okay, nothing can happen to her." He tried to smile at me reassuringly but failed miserably. As soon as the sheriff had cleared the foyer and living room, turning out of sight into the hall that led to the kitchen and family room, I let loose of Charlie's hand and ran upstairs to Nana's room, David followed close behind.

The second floor appeared to be untouched. Nana's bed was still made. I heard some muffled conversation below. David went to the head of the stairs and motioned to them that it was clear.

"Charlie is with the sheriff. They want me to keep you up here while they look around." I started to lose it and he pulled me in for a hug. "Shhh it's going to be okay babe." I allowed it for a moment, needing the physical contact and comfort to ground me but once I was calm I slid out of his grip and left the room.

"Calli, listen," he began to talk but I cut him off with a sharp look.

"I don't believe now is the appropriate time, do you?" He hung his head and then motioned to continue downstairs. Charlie and the sheriff were already outside, I cried out when I saw the damage done to the den; books shredded and the sliding glass door was in a million pieces on the floor but worse of all was every family photo was fractured. Then I saw the blood pooled at the doorway and out to the deck.

"Could be an animal," Charlie offered. I nodded numbly praying he was right. The crimson trail twisted through the maze, past the garden, down to the bank and into the water.

"I found something," the sheriff motioned us over to the fence that separated the backyard from the riverbank. "Recognize this?" There were strips of torn flannel; Nana's favorite gardening shirt. The world around me went black as I fainted. I awoke in darkness and screamed. Light suddenly illuminated the hallway and spilled into my room through the partially open door. Charlie was at my side in seconds.

"Nana," I asked weakly. He shook his head.

"I'm sorry Calli, it doesn't look good." He sat on the foot of my bed. His eyes were red and raw. "Not only can they not find Nana but I told them about that doctor and they went to question her. I guess they figured it was some sort of burglary scam that went awry. David went to see if he could find anything out."

"Burglary? My doctor?" I tried to sit up but the room started to spin.

"Careful, you fainted pretty hard out there. Do you want to go to the hospital?"

"No, I think I'll feel better if I stay here, thank you." Charlie patted my leg. "In case she comes back." His eyes averted mine. "You didn't tell them about what we found did you?" He shook his head 'no'.

"Not yet, I mean I will if it comes down to it but since we don't even know if it's real or not or really anything right now then better to keep it to ourselves I think and let them focus on the leads they have." I nodded in agreement. He sat up, kissed me on my cheek and headed for the door.

"Charlie, wait. Earlier today you said that David knew what was going on? What did you mean? Was it about Nana and how weird she was acting?"

"It doesn't matter right now Calli," he made to leave the room. "We'll talk in the morning."

"Charlie, I want to know…no, I need to know, please. I can handle it. Was it Alzheimer's? Did he recognize signs or something?"

"Actually, he didn't really offer much on Nana's state of health or mind, rather," he paused and scrunched up his face, "more like he thought she was involved with criminal types."

"What? What do you mean? Are you saying that woman I thought was a doctor and Nana?" I sat up in bed, ignoring the stars that played out before my eyes.

"No, we don't think that she was," he sighed exhausted, "You need to rest and I think you should hear it from David, rather than from me second hand. Actually there are some extremely important things you need to know. Not tonight but tomorrow if you're up to it."

"Okay, I'll listen but I want to know everything, don't hold anything back." Charlie nodded and turned for the hallway.

"Oh and Calli,"

"Yes?"

"You might just want to keep that ring handy?" My eyes immediately darted to my bandaged finger. As if reading my mind, he added, "The diamond engagement ring." The house became dark again but I didn't need light to see that my right hand was bare, in fact the last time I remembered wearing David's ring was the day Charlie and I sat by the river; the day David had broken off the engagement but insisted I keep the ring in the letter. Where had it got to? I sighed and shifted on the pillows, my mind abuzz with too much information.

Sleep didn't come until the tears did. Hades didn't call for me that night; my mind obviously preoccupied with more important things. Perhaps that spell had been broken, as well.

French stories for newbies

newbies

Funny, easy and French

By Monique Brue

Made in the USA
San Bernardino, CA
07 April 2019

Eight

Q & A

"Charlie said you wanted to talk to me?" David smiled sheepishly from the doorway of the den. My aversion to the man who had broken my heart was overridden by my curiosity and I had asked Charlie to invite him back over. In the days since the sheriff's visit, the room had been mostly put back in order; the sliding glass door was taped up until it could be replaced and all the photos were missing their glassy sheen as we just removed the broken glass and left them in their frames.

Being Charlie's room I had insisted he take mine and I moved into my grandmother's. I steeled myself and motioned for David to sit next to me on the couch; not wanting to have to face him. He sat a respectable distance away which I appreciated as his familiarity was too tempting to fall back into considering the chaos going on.

"Yes, he told me you had information that was helpful." I forced my voice to remain even and calm.

"I think I do." His voice was relaxed, a little too relaxed. I felt my anger stirring but held it down. I needed answers, not a fight.

"Do you know what was wrong with my grandmother? Why she was acting so odd?" Charlie hadn't elaborated on anything he offered the other night. He just kept directing me to David. I didn't know if it was an intentional move to try and get me to talk to him or sincere ignorance. Either way, here we were and if I wanted answers, here I'd have to stay.

"No, I don't. I'm sorry. However, I do think because of whatever condition that was plaguing her she was able to be sucked in with a corrupt organization."

"My grandmother wasn't a criminal," I turned to face him, eyes flashing. He held his hands up defensively.

"I'm not saying that she was, in fact, I'm saying the opposite, that they had her believing she was doing something good."

"And how do you know all this?" I found it suspicious that the person furthest from contact with her allegedly had all the answers. However, it didn't make sense for him to be trying to worm his way back in my life when he was the one who had left it either.

"Well, this is the harder part for me. This actually involves you and me."

"What do you mean?" The strain was evident in my voice. I had a feeling I was going to be hearing something that would cause the floor to drop out from beneath my feet. I was right.

"I was assigned to you, as your boyfriend, to investigate your grandmother." There it went and I was suddenly emotionally suspended above empty air. I clung to the couch cushions and started hyperventilating. He reached out to touch me and I swatted his hand away.

"Okay that's enough for me." I stood up intent on running back to my room.

"Calli, you have to let me explain," his voice pitched and tears were streaming down his face. "I loved you, I still do. I defied orders proposing to you. I should have whisked you away somewhere and eloped. By the time they found out it wouldn't have mattered." He stood in my way, trying to wrap his arms around my waist.

"Get out!" I shoved him hard though he barely budged an inch. "She never liked you and now she's gone, possibly forever and you have the nerve to use her in some ridiculous concoction. What purpose do you have here? We are done, you or they made sure of it and I'm all the better for it."

"You don't mean that Calli," he pulled me in his arms. I struggled and managed to kick his shins but he wouldn't let go. "Shhh, listen to me and I promise if you still want me to go I will." I relaxed only because the effort was futile and exhausting. He held tight so I couldn't run away. "Okay, I work for an organization..."

"What organization?" My voice muffled in his shoulder.

"I can't tell you which one but I can tell you we are the good guys." He didn't feel my eyes roll. "I was assigned to this group of rebels."

"What rebels?"

"Mediterranean rebels from Greece. Anyways, they led me to your grandmother and we did research on your family and that's when they decided to have me infiltrate your family by becoming your boyfriend." I tensed in his arms and tried to pull away. "But...but I fell in love with you and asked you to marry me, which was not part of the plan but I truly do love you. That's why I asked you to keep the ring, because once I got things sorted out with this mission I planned to make good on that promise.

"I know it's hard to believe and even harder to believe that you would forgive me, let alone marry me once I accomplished that but it's the truth. Only now, things have gotten more complicated and obviously more out in the open."

"Where's my grandmother, is she," I was unable to finish the sentence. There wasn't enough blood to speak the worst but it was plenty more than was necessary to raise concern. The fact the trail led to the water also wasn't definitive; I had mentioned the boat to the Sheriff but they had dredged the water and found nothing, which was a hollow hope at best. For the fact remained; Nana had to be somewhere and there weren't many places nearby to hide. This was open farmland.

"I honestly don't know. I can only speculate that either the group figured out we were onto them and wanted to prevent her revealing them or they have competition or it really was a simple burglary." I was reminded of the treasure Charlie and I found; had we set Nana up?

Bile started to rise up at the thought I might have contributed to her disappearance. I smacked myself mentally before I started shaking. We didn't know if there were 'boat people' who smuggled stolen artifacts under the tree, we didn't know they were authentic until Aunt Cat could evaluate them and there was this whole David mess with criminals that could or could not be associated with her disappearance and may or may not be involved with the stash. My head started to spin and I closed my eyes to steady myself.

"I'm sorry baby," he kissed the top of my head. I relaxed and he released his hold on me then I pushed him away with all my force. He staggered but didn't fall.

"So you guys were watching her because she was somehow involved with some foreign regime in a country she's never been to and you are the good guys but weren't capable of protecting her? Do I have it all straight David?" My icy stare made him shiver.

"You're right, I fucked up. She should have been safe but we underestimated her cunningness, for an old woman she was very clever. She lost nearly every tail we put on her; she just disappeared."

"Yes she was clever and good. I'm sorry but I'm exhausted so if you don't mind you need to leave." I left him in the den and headed to my room; head buzzing with unanswered questions, swirling with intense emotions. My David situation was more complicated than ever and we weren't any closer to finding out about Nana.

The next two weeks were like a nightmare I couldn't wake from. After the investigators verified the blood was indeed Nana's they became convinced it was a homicide. I couldn't cope, I became a zombie and I refused to leave the house. David came around as often as he was allowed, first by Charlie, who had taken a break from school, and then eventually by me. It was harder and harder to keep him away but I didn't let allow him more than role of casual acquaintance, though he tried daily to get closer.

I didn't know what to think of him or us. I had spent, no wasted so much time grieving and pining over the loss of this man but compared to the loss of my grandmother it meant nothing. I really didn't give a damn anymore and I told him so. My mother moved in for a while to help get things in order for the funeral. There was a casket to order, I guess for show and she collected important documents and Nana's more personal belongings. She appeared to be looking for something specific but she never asked Charlie or me to help find it or even hint at what it was exactly.

Like a robot, she went through the necessary motions, like performing any other mundane chore. She must have been in shock because I never saw her cry, which made me cry even more. I was afraid to dream and afraid not to; the former won out and I was taking Nana's sleep mixture every night. The funeral came and went; a blur of faces and names I couldn't keep track of. It was a small simple service at a plain hall.

Aunt Cat expressed her condolences through a card and bouquet of tiger lilies. I was torn between wishing she could have attended and being glad that she hadn't; I wanted to punch her. I was angry at her absence over the years, at her lack of availability for me and Charlie to reach her now when we needed her and for keeping her kindness and comfort to herself.

My two favorite emotions of late were sadness and anger. Charlie was having difficulty spending much time around me but he did; God bless him. I suspected it was to keep my mother off my back. I knew she was dying to get me back home and under close supervision. I slept in Nana's bed but kept her side open. There had been nothing in the coffin; no body not even ashes. I yearned for closure but it evaded me so I couldn't really say 'goodbye'.

The stress caused me to eat constantly, my clothes were becoming uncomfortably tight but what did I care? I was grateful the nausea was gone, perhaps it was because I no longer worried about what might happen to her. She was gone, everyone had said so; the sheriffs, my parents and even Charlie. I said this with fake sincerity. I didn't feel it in my gut, there was no calm certainty, only questions that buzzed around like mosquitos offering nothing more than confusion and pain but without any alternative I had to convince myself that she was really...dead. That one word like a nail pounded into a hollow wooden cabinet. No. Yes. Maybe. I was desperate to let go while still clutching a frail whisper of hope. If I hadn't been mad before I was on that path.

David and Charlie had whispered conversations about me in the hallway outside my room. Charlie was now an advocate for me moving into Mom and Dad's and David thought I should stay. His theory was taking me away from the farmhouse would be like taking Pops and Nana away from me again. I appreciated that, I had never felt more at home than I did now though I didn't even know if it was my choice anymore.

I hadn't asked about the will and no one had mentioned it. When I couldn't take any more of their hushed ruminations I asked them to run an errand in town for me. I took a long hot shower and then dressed in some warm sweats, a t-shirt and zip up jacket. The kitchen phone rang.

"Hello," I knew who was calling without the aid of caller id. "Calli," Charlie's voice was frantic, "why is the gate locked?"

"Look, you guys have been great, I appreciate you looking out for me but I want to be alone for a little while. I'm not going to do anything rash, I just want some time to try and process all of this. It's too hard with the two of you hovering over me all the time."

"Calli…" I hung up the phone, poured a glass of wine, grabbed a blanket and headed out back. I felt bad for pushing my brother away but I was suffocating emotionally. I walked to the back of the yard near her garden, the sound of the ringing telephone fading with each step. I laid the blanket next to the stone mermaid statue and just sat, breathing in the fresh air. I needed to feel closer to her and this was the spot.

I sipped on the wine, remembering varied conversations and events connected to the different plantings; some memories were fuzzy, like the kangaroo paws but others were strong, like the laurel tree that was planted the year my grandfather died. I finished the glass and stretched out on my back on the blanket, counting the stars that began to make their appearance as the sky darkened. My last thoughts were pondering which plant I would dedicate to her; possibly sunflowers. Yes, sunny, happy sunflowers.

"Come to me NOW!" His voice reverberated my entire being. I didn't remember the steps but I was already walking through the metal door. Again there were two tunnels.

"I don't know which tunnel to take," I cried out, panicked and afraid of what to expect. He must have sensed my fear for his voice softened.

"I'm sorry my lovely, I have just been so worried about you and need to see that you are alright. My mind had conjured up the most horrible reasons for your absence at my side." I felt the sincerity of his words and relaxed a little but still two tunnels stood before me. "Just think of where you want to go and you will find the way."

My heart, body and soul yearned to go to him but I felt a resistance deep inside. Was there somewhere else, or rather someone else I needed to see? Yes, it was time to use these dream trips for that closure I desperately needed.

"I need to see my grandmother one last time," I whispered. I felt the ground shake, not harsh and angry but more of a shudder, like weeping. The tunnel on the left slowly became brighter and I could see that it travelled upward. "I'm sorry," I apologized to the air and ran forward.

This was the shortest tunnel I had travelled and the sweetest smelling; jasmine. The scent immediately reminded me of Nana and her garden. I came out in the middle of a moonlit forest and gasped; the trees were illuminated by millions of tiny lights that moved to soft music, like humming. The stars, what I could see through gaps in the lush canopy above, twinkled brighter and were much larger than any I'd seen on a California night. I smiled as the lights began coming toward me, swirling and spinning.

"Stop right there," a harsh masculine voice sounded from the dark behind me. "Do you have any weapons? If so, throw them down now, you're surrounded." I laughed and turned towards my wannabe captor. They remained hidden from view by the dark shadows of the trees.

"Is that so? Well I'd hardly be afraid of lightning bugs," I called out sarcastically. The lights scattered as an arrow whizzed past my face and embedded in the tree behind me with a loud twang. "What the hell? What kind of dream is this now?" I yelled to the air as though there were some unseen creator and not my own subconscious responsible.

"Dream, I'm afraid not. You are in very real and very serious danger unless you prove otherwise. That arrow missed on purpose, I will not miss again."

"What am I stumbling onto this time? A secret meeting? Enemy territory? What am I now, a spy?" Rough hands suddenly reached out pulling my arms behind me and pushing me forward. "Ow! Let go of me!"The ground shook beneath our feet almost knocking me to the ground. He cursed in alarm but still didn't release me.

"Slinking through the dark, using words like that, you're lucky I don't do you here and now. You can tell your story to the captain, spy." He spat the last word out like it was poison.

"Fine but I'm walking myself, you let my arms go," my demand was ignored and I screamed in frustration as he wrapped a blanket around me and tied my wrists in front of me. He wore a dark robe, the hood hanging over his face. All I could see was his strong bearded chin, mouth and nose. He turned and yanked on the longer remaining strap causing me to fall forward like I was some kind of pack mule. I almost tripped, as I was wearing flip flops rather than hiking boots but he never relented and he never slowed until we finally reached a curtain of greenery.

He whistled and it opened revealing an illuminated campsite. By this time my feet were cut, bleeding and I was missing a shoe. Apparently the quality of my dreams equaled the quality of my mood at the time. I began to seriously question my choice of tunnels.

The faces of the camp that greeted me were hard, full of hate and dirty. Most were wearing simple tunics but a few wore armor. They all looked dangerous. Of course, marrying Hades wasn't enough for my daredevil mind anymore. He took me over to a wooden post and handcuffed me; arms above my head. I hoped that the bondage and the group of men wasn't part of my burgeoning sexual appetite, I shuddered violently. I looked down at my feet and noticed scarlet splotches in the soft dirt and had a feeling that wasn't my worst fear after all.

"She's over here; I caught her spying just outside the south side of camp." My captor had removed his hood. He looked scarier in the light and I silently begged him to put it back on. I hoped the person he spoke to wasn't worse.

"How did she get past the defenses," a strong woman's voice sounded somewhere behind me and coming closer.

"I don't know Captain, magic perhaps," he eyed me with raw suspicion as though daring my powers to reveal themselves.

"Our defenses are very strong and very sensitive, we must be careful with her if she was able to get so close before we knew it." I strained to see over my shoulder but was restricted by the chains.

"Well, I'm sure we'll get the information out of her one way or another." His grubby, bearded face was suddenly inches before mine, his breath hot and sour. His grin was twisted in both form and intent. He would enjoy making me talk. A small cloaked figure came around him and he stepped back to give them view of me.

"Release her immediately, that's my granddaughter!"

The woman pulled back her cloak and I almost fainted. Even though this had been my intent, it was still overwhelmingly emotional seeing her in the flesh...well in the dream flesh. She looked good no, she looked better than ever; vibrant and strong and confident. I felt my warm tears slide down my cheeks, amazed once more at the clarity and details of these dreams. She brushed them away gently with her hand.

"Bring me the keys," she said harshly to the closest man. "What are you doing here Calli?" She deftly worked the key and unlocked the shackles. I rubbed my sore wrists.

"I know it's a dream now because you called me Calli, instead of..." her hand clamped down on my mouth.

"Names have power, there is so much you don't know and I don't have the time now to teach you. You must go back home."

"But..." I started to question her as she grabbed my arm and led me back towards the forest. "Wait, if this is my dream then why are you making me leave?" I dug my heels in and forced her to stop.

"Calli, do as I say," her tone was stern but her eyes were soft and pleading.

"Nope, my dream so I'm going to do what I want. Maybe I'll just start dancing...yes, I think I feel like dancing." I proceeded to bob and spin until I resembled a gorilla attempting ballet. She shook her head in disapproval.

"Calli Marie, you listen..."

"Nope, now I think I want to sing...yes definitely singing. The hilllllllssss are alive, with the sound of muuuuuuuuusssssiiiiiic!" My grandmother slapped me hard on the cheek. The sound echoed off of the trees and intermingled with the 'oohs' and 'ahhs' of our burly witnesses. It hurt like hell. "Whoa, what was that for?"

I forced myself not to cry. I was suddenly missing my dysfunctional romantic dreams. She gently walked me into a nearby tent, sat me on a cushion and proceeded to create a pack to put on my cheek; it smelled awful but felt good.

"This is not a dream child. This is very real and very dangerous." She sounded tired.

"Not a dream but Nana, you're dead. We had your funeral."

"Oh good, the diversion worked. I wasn't sure your mother could pull it off."

"Mom?" Visions of my mother smashing our family treasures, overturning furniture and spraying the family room with Nana's blood did not sit well. I became nauseated once more. "But...Mom?"

"Listen Calli, we don't have much time so best to hurry and ask the questions you want answered before you go back home."

"I don't want to go back home, yet." I sounded like a spoiled child but didn't care. It was bad enough having people boss you around when you were awake.

"You have to; your mother expects it."

"Well I expected my mother to be honest with me. Why did you fake your death?"

"I have things to do here and it's going to require a lot of time, people, most notably you and Charlie would have noticed my absence." She noticed my feet and brought over a bowl of water and gently cleaned the wounds after removing my sole flip flop. "I have something you can wear. Any other questions," she went to a corner of the tent and returned with a pair of leather sandals.

"Where is here?"

"Here is Ancient Greece." My mind raced to the most probable conclusions. I had concocted a scenario where my grandmother was alive and on our dream trip only it involved the soldiers that David had mentioned. Yes, my attempt at closure was being thwarted by my own mind wanting to believe her alive and well. Though I understood this I couldn't stop myself from asking questions.

"What? How did you get here?"

"Too long of a story," her voice was curt. Of course, I hadn't thought that far yet.

"What is this place? Who are these people?" Nana gently placed my feet in the sandals and laced them up.

"This is a camp; the people here make up an army."

"Whose army?"

"Their own army. They don't belong to any ruler. Some are from Thebes, Athens, Corinth and others. I'm their captain."

"You're the captain," I asked not hiding my surprise. She looked offended.

"I'm perfectly capable in the position," she scolded me, "More than capable in many respects." I nodded quickly. "Any more questions?" She eyed me sternly like she very much did not want any more.

"I'm finished for now," I said, wondering if I would push it so far that the illusion would shatter and leave me in a worse state.

"Good, I have one for you; how did you get here? Did someone bring you?" Her voice sounded calm but her eyes appeared worried.

"I don't know, I fell asleep and I'm here." Sounded like a dream to me, though I couldn't remember any that I actually had to argue the point. This must be one of those lucid dreams I had read about where you're dreaming but know you're dreaming and therefore can dictate what happens. However, I decided I should just follow along with her, arguing about it just got me slapped. She walked to the door of the tent.

"Erwin, I need…" Nana's request was cut off by the appearance of a beautiful woman with long red hair and eyes that looked like fire. She wore a floor length tunic of emerald green. "Cassandra what brings you here?"

"Thalia," she inclined her head at my grandmother, "Welcome child," she beamed at me. We were soon joined by a boy, about twelve. He couldn't seem to keep his eyes off of her. My grandmother maneuvered him out of the tent. All the while he twisted to view Cassandra. "Erwin, I need you to get a message to my father. Tell him 'the wind has carried the seed off path'. That is all." She gave him a swat and he bowed and then scampered off.

"The child continues on a course you didn't predict," Cassandra eyed my grandmother knowingly.

"It will be fine; her mother will see to it from here." She waved her hand dismissively.

"I do not speak of her apparent love and ability to travel." Her voice was melodic yet tinged with danger. I shifted uncomfortably.

"Accidents happen, I'm sure it's easily explained." I'm not listening to you is what she was really saying. Cassandra took a seat and gave her a firm look.

"You know of which I speak, of what I spoke of before and you did not believe. Will you be so foolish now?"

"Because that is impossible," Nana's voice lacked conviction.

"Vain woman you are to believe you can outwit the fates. You would do well to believe me Thalia, or do I need to remind you of the tragic events of Troy?"

"Alright, that is enough! Would you two quit talking about me like I'm not here?" My face was flushed with anger. I was losing control of this dream fast.

"We need to get you home," Nana pulled me to standing. I stared at Cassandra.

"Please tell me what you are talking about, I know I'm going crazy but I need the truth."

"You know the truth; why don't you share it with your grandmother?" She asked instead. Nana eyed me suspiciously. I shot daggers at Cassandra.

"What is she talking about Calli? What did you do?" Her eyes were wide and it appeared she was running several scenarios through her mind, none of them pleasant.

"Nothing," I stared at my feet. I wondered if I could will the dream to fast forward to somewhere more enjoyable. Perhaps some island in the Caribbean sipping fruity drinks spiked with lots of alcohol.

"Wait, those strange dreams you were having, did you 'go' somewhere? Did you come here?" Nope, I was stuck here for now. This was beginning to feel like "Inception", having a dream talking about dreams, with my dead grandmother! Maybe it was time I moved out of Nana's and into a mental institution.

"Yes," I decided to play along, "I once came to a place much like this only with a lake, it was beautiful but most times I was at a castle." I blushed and glanced down at my left hand. I hadn't replaced the bandage since Nana had gone missing. She grabbed my hand and started to faint. I caught her and eased her onto a cushion.

"Nana, are you okay? What's wrong? What did I say?"

"The ring of Minos," she shook her head from side to side. "Then he broke the oath but how?"

"I spoke the truth," Cassandra stood with a serious look on her face, "and you know there is more."

"That is enough for now," my grandmother waved her away.

"She will learn soon enough, with or without your telling," she turned toward the tent entrance, pausing before exiting. "The question remains; which way of learning will be better for her ultimately?"

My grandmother waited for her to leave then wrapped a hood close around me and quickly led me outside. There was no one to be seen though I got the sense there were guards above us in the trees on lookout. She took me back to the tunnel and kissed my cheek.

"Goodbye dear, I'll see you soon I promise. Give my love to Charlie...oh wait, better not. Don't mention any of this to anyone, especially your mother."

"Nana, what did you mean by 'he broke the oath? What do you know of this ring?"

"Not now, another time. We're preparing for war and you'll only get in the way. Go home and stay safe."

"I'm staying here, I can help and I still need some answers."

"Goodbye Calli."

"I'm not a child, you can't order me about," I yelled at her.

"Watch your tone with me, I'm still your grandmother even if I'm presumed dead, trust me I'm very much alive and kicking."

"I know," I rubbed the tender spot on my cheek and glared. "I'm just asking for some more answers before you rush me off. I got this ring from Hades," I felt the ground rumble; "if you don't want to tell me what's going on, I'm sure I can persuade him to."

"Do not involve him anymore than you already have!" Her tone was suggestive.

"What do you mean by that? You are so damned mysterious that every question I ask just leads me to more questions. And why are you angry with me, I didn't do anything wrong!" I was falling back into the charade but couldn't seem to help myself.

"You obviously did," she glanced at my crotch and I flushed from anger not embarrassment. "I'm well versed in marriage practices here. Now hurry and go home where you belong. Your mother will take over."

"Take over? I'm not a chore, I'm a person, and I'm your granddaughter! You know, I think I will talk to him," I leaned down towards the ground and yelled, "Hades, get your ass up here now, I have questions and you damn well better have answers!"

The ground started shaking almost knocking me off my feet. The earth churned and crumbled revealing a deep chasm that stretched half the length of a football field; the mixture of heat with the smell of sulfur was overwhelming and all too familiar. A black chariot sprang forth; it was pulled by dark horses with red ember eyes, their mouths frothy and wicked tails swishing angrily. Hades leaned down and grabbed me placing me gently at his side.

"I think I'll take my wife home now," he said icily to my grandmother; fire shown bright in her eyes.

"I can't let you try and take her again," She warned while fidgeting with something behind her back.

"Again?" I looked from one to another awaiting an

answer. Everything was a blur as we suddenly travelled

beneath the ground. The last thing I saw was my

grandmother wearing a look of shock, fear and regret.

Nine

Love and Marriage

"What was that all about," I demanded as we exited the chariot within the stables of his castle. Hades looked as though he was struggling with something enormous but said nothing. Silently, he unharnessed the horses and after pawing the ground for a moment they sauntered to their stalls where they crammed their heads into feedbags. He left the chariot where it was and turned toward a short hallway, ringing a bell on his way.

"Show her to her room," he instructed the little winged beasts that answered his call. I stood there unsure of where to go but sure of one thing; I wasn't following anyone else tonight. I chose instead to wander my own course while I sorted things out in my mind.

Hades' home was opulent and grand which I found odd as it seemed there were no other residents or visitors to speak of. It was also a confusing labyrinth that surprised me at every turn. I would take stairs up only to find myself on a lower floor, doors led nowhere or everywhere and I began to think the castle itself was toying with me. Every so often one of the creatures would tug me one direction or another but I shrugged them off and went where I wanted; if I was truly Hades' wife then this was my home too and I had the run of it like it or not.

Exhaustion pleaded with me to find my bed but the day's events still tossed around my mind like clothes in a dryer and every time I tried to grasp a thought, it slipped through my hands. My frustration added to my exhaustion only complicated the process further and eventually I found myself walking merely for some purpose. I was like a ship that kept sailing because it didn't want to dock. My wanderings eventually led me to the grand entryway.

The front door loomed larger than I remembered; ten feet tall, solid marble with door pulls that looked eerily like they were crafted from the bones of a very large and odd creature. Immediately to the left was a formal seating area with a large leather couch, well I guessed it was leather, who knew what things were made of here! In addition to the couch were two matching stone chairs, chiseled finely and adorned with silver cushions. To the right was an open door, which begged investigating. I wasn't disappointed.

It was a large room, very much a library with the towering walls of books, but the more I observed, the more it resembled a 'war room', at least what I had seen in movies. It had several maps on the long walls, one window, a large stone desk and an enormous table that took up the entire center of the room. I inspected the desk first.

It was smooth quartz with silver spiral legs and tall enough that I was almost on my tip toes to see what was on top. There was a partial glass of wine in a heavy gold goblet, a sealed envelope addressed to no one, some letters written in what I assumed to be Greek and a picture frame; the subject was a young girl of about sixteen with wild dark hair, wearing an emerald green tunic and wielding a bow. There was a naturalness about the photo, not posed and unexpected. It was almost intimate in a way, as though she was unaware of her image being captured. I found myself entranced and only set the photo down when I was distracted by a noise across the room.

I was alone in the room and soon discovered the sounds were coming from the large table. Its legs were formed from some sort of tusk and the base was petrified tree and the top was translucent glass and the sounds were murmurings like listening to a conversation in a restaurant several tables over mixed with the clanging of silverware. The closer I got the more I realized that the table wasn't really a table but rather some sort of three dimensional map of the world; though not the world I was familiar with.

I followed the sound to the body of land that I believed to be Greece. When my hand accidentally brushed the spot, it was as though zooming in on a satellite image; clouds, then mountains, then a shepherd herding sheep. I touched the table top and slid my hand to the right and the image changed. Suddenly I was watching some huge wriggling mass of arms and legs. Another tap and it became clear that it was some sort of battle. I zoomed in more and saw the grimacing face of a man in armor as he shoved the blade of his sword into an opposing soldier. Unlike movies, the movement was not smooth but rather jagged and very gory.

"No," I screamed. The wounded man turned towards me and gasped for breath only to choke on his own blood. More bodies continued to hurl themselves at one another and I hit the table top several times in an effort to clear the atrocities from my sight. The imported sea breeze tossed the curtains of the open window and I ran to it hoping to stave off the bile threatening to overcome me.

As long as I kept my eyes closed I could imagine I was above ground and inhaling clean open air. Of course the illusion was ruined once the nausea passed and I ventured a look around. Thankfully much of the underworld was ink black, so I couldn't detect the oppressing walls and ceiling. The only glow came from the fire lake and the occasional torch on the wall of the west wing which was clearly visible from this part of the castle. My eyes were suddenly drawn to a new and different light several feet up on my left.

A dark figure was illuminated by a green flame that grew brighter revealing a balcony; it was Hades. His face was pained and creased with worry. My heart ached in response but I didn't call out. I couldn't remember details but felt a mild irritation mixed with confusion for him.

My overwhelming exhaustion all but forced me to my knees but I made it out of the room and into the seating area. The last thing I remembered, as a wave of dizziness took me, was falling onto the leather couch as I whispered his name.

Stars. So…many…stars. Just as my eyes focused, they shifted position. I rolled over slowly on my side and got my bearings; I was in Hades bed chamber or rather 'our' bed chamber. I felt him behind me, shifting to wrap his arms around me and murmuring my name in my hair.

"What happened?" I whispered weakly.

"You fainted," he whispered back as though I was so fragile one loud word from him would break me. He gripped me tighter and sighed. "I'm sorry I think you've had too much excitement. I would very much like," his voice caught in his throat, "I would prefer if you would stay here and rest where it's safe, if you please." I sighed contentedly and snuggled closer to him.

"Why would I ever want to leave? Where would I go?" Though somewhat rested, the thought of leaving the bed, let alone our home was exhausting. I tried to think of something, anything that needed to be done but could recall nothing. He hummed my lullaby and I fell into a deep slumber floating away on a cloud of bliss.

"My sleeping beauty, come, let's have dinner shall we?" He roused me gently and helped me to my feet and down the steps. I struggled, feeling the weight of heavy sleep. "I have something more appropriate for you to wear." Draped on the chaise lounge was a beautiful ebony tunic with diamond accents across the bodice and hem that shimmered like fire was contained within them. He helped me dress, the light caress of his fingers causing my heart to race and a long happy sigh to escape from my lips.

I evaluated myself in the full length mirror and attempted to smooth my hair. "I like it this way, "he said through a smile, "let's go eat." I yawned and stretched and reluctantly followed him. The dining room was situated on the floor beneath our chambers on the east side of the castle with large ornate windows that revealed a view of an illuminated meadow in the far off distance. There were blue skies, clouds and birds above, vibrant grass and flowers below, as well as stately dwellings. It was a bright contrast to the dark gloom of the Underworld and I found myself unwilling to turn away.

"The Elysian Fields", he informed me. It made me a little homesick and something tickled at the back of my brain but didn't reveal itself. "Darling, your seat," He waited, chair in hand, at the spot directly right to the head of the table. I tore myself away from the window and allowed him to push my chair in. The table was beautiful, quartz, the preferred stone down here, though you couldn't tell with all of the food loaded on top. There were so many different types of meats, breads, pastries, vegetables, soups and wines. It was like an all-you-can-eat-buffet. Until I had seen the food, I hadn't realized I was hungry but I couldn't remember when I had my last meal. "Tell the plate what you want," he instructed. I gave him an odd look and giggled.

"That's okay; I think I can handle wielding a spoon." I made to get up but he placed his hand firmly on my arm.

"You are my queen now and must learn the appropriate customs." He released my arm and waved a hand over his plate, immediately a large turkey leg, mashed potatoes and asparagus appeared.

"You didn't say anything." I looked sideways. He smiled warmly.

"I said you had to tell the plate what you wanted, not that you had to speak out loud. Try it." I glanced at my plate and watched it fill before my eyes; the same selection as his. I tried not to overthink that somehow he could read my mind and instead, took to investigating my food. I probed the mashed potatoes with my fork.

"Hmmm, feels solid enough," I mused. My stomach gurgled loudly and I blushed

"Tastes divine, try a bite," his eyes were suddenly very intense for a simple dinner. A glass of wine appeared and I raised it eagerly to my lips. A sudden knocking on the dining room door caused me to pause. With an annoyed look on his face, Hades motioned the unseen visitor to enter, it was Hermes.

"Whatever it is can wait for after dinner." Hermes edged closer to me then turned his back so he had full view of Hades and I had none.

"They want to meet immediately." His voice was all business; unlike the first time I had met him.

"Impossible, she is unwell and needs my full attention." Hades' was dismissive.

"They insist."

"As soon as I see to her comfort I will come."

"You are to bring her." Hermes was firm and unrelenting and I found it odd that he could speak to Hades like that. I was pretty sure he worked for him not the other way around.

"Nonsense, I will do no such thing," Thunder rumbled in the distance, loud enough to make the glasses shake. "Fine, after she eats, her health is weak." More thunder that sounded even closer. "Alright," he slammed his fists on the table. Hermes turned, bowed then left the room. Hades stood and took my hand, helping me out of my seat

"What's going on," I asked timidly. He shook his head. His face was creased with worry.

"I fear for the worst," he whispered and pulled me in for a tight hug. I pulled away and searched his face for more.

"I'm afraid," I whispered weakly. A single tear slid down my cheek. He brushed it away lightly and forced a smile.

"Don't be, it is not for you that I fear." We headed toward the door and my stomach growled like a tiger.

"Maybe just a roll for the trip," I said as I turned back towards the table. I saw his eyes light up for a moment then darken.

"Better not my dear," His voice echoed a familiar pain that I could not seem to place. "I'll see to it that you are fed when we get there." I nodded and followed him out of the room.

Soon we were loaded into the chariot and flying off to some unknown destination. The sights were breathtakingly beautiful but my companion was sullen. I tried to lift his spirits but eventually gave up and enjoyed them myself. My experiences in this land so far had been limited to our night time trip to the meadow and the countless visits to the castle underground. I knew there was so much more to this world but had failed to envision even a fraction of its true wonder; the majestic mountains, thriving cities, the ships riding the high seas.

We flew higher and higher into the air until the ground below looked like a colorful quilt. I was immediately reminded of an exhilarating hot air balloon ride I had taken in my youth; the quiet peace of the altitude, humans looking like ants below, feeling on level with the birds and clouds. Though, soon the similarities ended.

The air became heavy and fragrant and the clouds became so dense I couldn't see an inch in front of my nose. I groped around in a panic until I found his hand and clasped it tightly. Before long we came to a stop on what felt like level ground. He swung me down carefully from the chariot and I tested my weight hesitantly on the cloudy bank below my feet.

"You may walk if you prefer," he said with a slight smile that seemed to take all his effort. "Or I can carry you if you allow me." I smiled and jumped into his arms. He cradled me, kissing my forehead, then my nose then my lips. "You are so precious to me."

"As you are to me," I tried to smile but could not; feeling the heavy weight of expectation. "Where are we going?"

"To see my brother," his voice seethed with animosity.

"And then?" Judging by his face this seemed to be the question that mattered most. Something very important and possibly life changing was about to be decided.

"We shall see," his voice choked and he pulled me in closer. "Just remember that I love you. I always have and always will."

"Of course," my voice muffled by his shoulder, "Of course. I love you too."

"Remember that," he held me so I could read his face. I nodded numbly.

"Here we are," he said despondently. I turned and gasped. Before us was a glimmering city of magnificent proportions. We had arrived in Olympus. I would have expected Olympus to have more fanfare, perhaps the streets teaming with various fantasy creatures, exotic sights and sounds; like Carnival in Brazil or Mardi Gras in New Orleans.

It was disappointing and I felt a little like Dorothy landing in Oz a week too soon. Though the streets were marble and the buildings were towering and bedazzled with gold, silver and jewels I kept expecting tumbleweeds to blow across our path. The place appeared to be deserted.

"Where is everyone?" I searched the entranceways and windows for signs of life but saw none. He gently set me to my feet and clasped my hand in his, motioning with his free hand.

"This is what you'd call, the back entrance if you will. The main entrance is where the festivities take place and there are the greeters; the satyrs, nymphs and occasional muse. I probably should have brought you that way, showed off my new beautiful wife but I didn't want to overwhelm you."

"Aww that's so sweet," I beamed up at him. I thought I saw him blush. "You're always thinking about me."

"There are usually people milling around here but they are probably at the palace for court."

"Court? Is there a trial going on?"

"Not a trial per se but things are to be discussed and then decided."

"Is that why we are here, because you have to help decide something?"

"Not exactly," he stopped short and kneeled before me. "Tell me, do you remember anything about this world?"

"I remember the meadow and your castle and some woods and a camp." Something at the back of my brain buzzed quietly, trying to get my attention. "Why?"

"You don't remember anything before that, before we married?" I strained but nothing came to mind. The buzzing still tickled but revealed nothing. I shook my head 'no'.

"Why do you ask? Do you think I've been here before?" The feeling behind the statement felt real but the sound of the words sounded ridiculous. How could I? I wouldn't have forgotten a place as magnificent as this.

"I know you have." He spoke to the ground. I laughed nervously.

"That's impossible," I spoke the lie in earnest. He stood and took my hand and began leading me back down the road. I suddenly became nervous and stopped and tugged him towards the opposite direction.

"What are you doing agapimeni?" He stood firm.

"Let's go home. I want to leave." Suddenly I didn't want to understand. Knowledge I felt would devastate me. Knowing was the tiger and me its frightened prey. A tender smile crossed his face, it was tinged with pain.

"We can't, we have to go to the palace, my brother demands it, as well as your grandmother." At the mention of Nana, I dropped his hand. The buzzing in my brain became an explosion of thoughts and memories. It was like a wave washing over me; everything was jumbled and out of sequence but it was there. I fell to my knees and clapped my hands over my ears. I saw him speaking but couldn't hear. I didn't dare release my hands until the pressure in my brain had ceased significantly.

"Are you alright," he asked again but this time there was sound. I backed away slowly and shook my head as tears began to slide down my face.

"I remember." Those two words seemed to drive a stake through his heart. He winced and hung his head. "I...remember...you." I forced the words out like they were toxic.

"Listen, I think if you take some time to sort your thoughts..."

"This place is real, not a dream. I have been here before. I used to come here a lot until...until my family said you had to stay away from me. You tried to take me. It was a long time ago; I was a kid." He recoiled from the sight of my revulsion. "That photo on your desk was of me."

"Just let me explain please." He looked unnaturally human. Like a character from a monster film.

"You're not denying it, that's essentially an admission of guilt."

"There is a lot to discuss, please I love you."

"You love me? I don't think you know what love is. Possession is not love. I remember the story of Persephone and how you took her and made her," realization dawned on me, "she couldn't leave for months at a time because she ate food while in the Underworld; pomegranate seeds, right? That is why you insisted on dinner isn't it? So I would be your prisoner, too."

"I admit that I would have liked the extra assurance but you needed sustenance. You are not well." He reached for me and I backed away.

"I admit, is enough, thank you." I turned and walked towards our original direction, unsure of where I was going or what I would find. I was fueled by betrayal, anger but mostly overwhelming sadness. I had been happy for a brief while; blissfully ignorant. A hole in my soul, that I had been unaware of until it had been filled, was violently emptied once more. My emotional bandage was ripped off and suddenly I was overwhelmed as all of my suppressed feelings of David came back nearly knocking me off my feet.

Hades moved to my side and I pushed him away, not bothering to hide my revulsion. He kept his distance but shadowed me until I came to an intersection. I looked back at him and he motioned to the left. I had no choice but to trust his directions, though I was wary and stayed in the middle of the path. The road began to climb slightly and soon I was able to make out a large palace in the distance. It was so far and I had become so weak from lack of food or water, emotional exhaustion and physical exertion but I dared not ask him for help.

I heard him whistle and I was soon greeted by a satyr pulling a cushioned cart. I didn't argue, just climbed inside and curled up on my side. I felt beat up, emptied and wrung out. I was roused from a deep sleep what seemed like only seconds later. Hades helped me to standing but had the good sense to keep his distance after. For an immortal ruler he looked small and weak. My heart ached and I fought the urge to comfort him.

Oh how I longed for the days of sweet disillusion when I thought all of this was a mere dream. We walked up steep marble steps, I clutched the railing the entire way. He stayed a couple feet behind me, as though he was readied to catch me if I fell. I wondered if it was another deception of his or a sincere approach. Could he be both the nightmare of my youth and the man of my dreams? Did it matter? As I stopped to catch my breath I pondered this. However, my emotions were a big ball of yarn that became more and more tangled the more I tried to make sense of things so I pushed it aside for the time being. Anger was a more comfortable hat to wear anyhow, especially with the painful stitch in my side.

"Are you okay?" He was suddenly beside me, worry on his face. I shook him off and continued up the last two stairs.

"Don't." I crossed the pavilion to the entrance. Two large doors made of gold swung open and I hurried inside. The room beyond seemed to go on forever, both in length and height. It was crowded with creatures, gods, goddesses but only one human; my grandmother. I pushed through the throng and threw my arms around her.

"Nana, oh my goodness I can't believe everything that's been going on. Can we go home now please? I just want to wake up in my own bed and forget everything." I was surprised how my voice sounded like that of a panicked child. She looked at me kindly and shook her head.

"I'm sorry Calli; we have to deal with this first. Then you may be able to go home but sadly I cannot." A wave of dizziness threatened to knock me over and I felt her grip my elbows tightly as she maneuvered me into a nearby chair.

"Can we get her somewhere comfortable and fed and watered while we sort this out?" Hades' voice sounded loudly beside me. I gripped the chair tightly, anticipating someone to remove me then clutched my grandmother's arm.

"Decide what? Why do I need to be here? Why are you here? Why can't you leave?"

"Child we are deciding your fate. We will be determining whether you will be remaining in The Underworld as Hades' wife or returning to your own land as a free person." The male voice boomed and reverberated throughout the room.

"Oh really and who are you to decide what happens to me?" I asked angrily.

"My name is Zeus and I would appreciate some respect little one." My Nana pointed across the room, I left my seat for a better look but stayed close. Several giants were seated on brilliant thrones that formed a half circle. One throne, positioned in the middle, was grander and more opulent than the rest. It's occupant, a handsome tan blond man waved to me and smiled. He was dressed in a gold tunic though he'd look just as at home in a pair of surfer trunks.

Unlike the graphics I'd been accustomed to he looked no older than 20; hardly a wizened ruler. As though reading my mind he aged 50 years complete with full white beard and flowing hair. In a blink he was youthful again. I staggered a little but remained standing.

"He's also your great great grandfather," Nana added matter-of-factly. My brain attempted to process this new twist to the family tree.

"Zeus is my great grandfather," I babbled, my eyes wide and searching.

"Great great grandfather," Nana corrected. I stared through her.

"You're not really dead and I'm really married to Hades and we're having a big meeting to decide what to do about it. Does that about cover it?" Nana nodded, as well as Zeus. I turned to the gods and goddesses seated about him. "And you are all the other," I started to say people but thought better of it, "gods, like "Poseidon," I guessed of the man seated to Zeus's left, wielding a trident. He smiled and winked, "and goddesses Hera," The beautiful woman with flowing red hair to his right gave me a stiff nod and no smile. "Athena?" A tall golden woman gestured. Nana turned me towards her and gently grasped my chin.

"Sweetie, we have a lot to discuss, you can meet everyone after, okay?" I nodded numbly and sat down.

"What is your case Thalia, they are married," Zeus took control of the proceedings.

"I contest the validity of it," My Nana; the lawyer.

"She consented and wears the ring and it was consummated." Zeus spoke of my personal affairs as casually as though reading minutes from a stockholders meeting. My cheeks flushed furiously from both anger and embarrassment.

"He broke the truce; he was to leave her alone." Nana's voice was firm but respectful.

"Brother, what say you?" Zeus motioned to Hades. I didn't turn in my chair to look. I was too busy staring at the floor wishing it would open up and swallow me whole.

"Can we please move this to private chambers? Must she suffer the indignities of such a public setting?" Hades request tugged at my heart strings and again I willed my anger to crowd it out. We wouldn't be here if not for his selfishness. I felt another wave of dizziness and shut my eyes tight. "Thank you," his voice sounding slightly muffled.

I opened my eyes and saw I was in an antechamber to a larger office. It was oddly modern looking, like a lawyer's office I had visited once with David. It was weird not hearing the sounds of people typing, making phone calls and other work related activity. It gave the area a false presence, like a hologram. I was seated on a sofa, which was very real and solid, within hearing but not in view of the next room where I assumed Hades, Nana and Zeus had convened.

"Okay brother, what is your response?" Zeus voice was clear as though travelling through the wall.

"She came to me first," Hades announced to the room. "I didn't coerce, deceive or physically remove her. She visited me several times as a matter of fact."

"Liar!" That was definitely Nana's voice. "She had no means of travel."

"Thalia, I'm sorry that you are upset but we are married whether you like it or not. She is my wife and will be returning home with me. I love her and she loves me."

"Do I get to say anything about what I want or what happens to me?" I gripped the doorframe tightly afraid of falling and losing my dignity. I wasn't sure if it was the air or the circumstances making me so dizzy. Zeus and Nana shook their heads. Hades remained still and quiet.

"That's not how it works here," Nana explained, "that is why you have to be very careful about what you do and say. Contracts can be made with a whisper." Her eyes were kind but I sensed disappointment. It pissed me off.

"I had a dream…" The three of them turned back to one another, ignoring me. "I want an annulment!" I screamed at the top of my lungs. Suddenly I was on the other side of a closed door. "Fine, I'm leaving!" I stormed out of the room and down the hall. As I wandered looking for the exit I pondered how to get back home. I looked around and once assured the coast was clear, clicked my heels three times while reciting quietly 'there's no place like home'. Slowly I opened my eyes and groaned. I guess I wasn't Dorothy after all.

"You look parched; may I get you a drink?" The woman's voice startled me. She had braided hair the color of golden wheat and wore a beautiful green tunic. She motioned for me to follow her down a side hall until we reached an archway which led outside to a beautiful garden. A table with delicate little sandwiches and a pitcher of amber liquid beckoned me forward. "Have something to eat, as well."

"It won't trap me here, will it?" I asked hesitating with the morsel of food mere inches from my mouth. It was torture. She smiled and shook her head.

"No young one, it will not."

I eagerly bit into the sandwich and it disappeared, my hunger a bigger force than I thought. I waited for her approval before claiming another and then another. Soon the plate was empty but I was still ravenous. She offered me a plate of fruit and soon that was gone too. It wasn't long before I was satisfied but still thirsty. I gulped down three goblets of water she filled from a live spring. She then poured some of the amber liquid into the goblet and set it before me.

"Try this, you will like it. It's called ambrosia and it's the favored drink of us here in Olympus." She poured some into another glass and drained it in one gulp. I smiled and thanked her and raised the cup to my lips. The smell was divine and intoxicating. "Excuse me, I will return. I'm going to fetch my daughter. I think you two should meet." I thanked her again as she disappeared, leaving me in a rested and blissful state. I was almost considering returning to the meeting and then remembered the goblet of ambrosia and raised it once more to my lips.

"Don't drink that it's poison," the man's voice caused me to drop the goblet. It crashed noisily onto the table.

"David, what the hell are you doing here?" My ex fiancé was standing in the middle of a garden in Olympus. Was I dreaming after all? He was wearing a blue tunic that hung just above his knees and brown leather sandals that ended right below. "It is you?" I had better use more caution I warned myself.

"Of course it is," he shrugged. I put my hand up to stop his progress, my look loaded. "Um, something that only we would know," he started getting the hint, "Oh, I know, for your 25th birthday I took you to a bed and breakfast in Carmel. No one, including you knew about it and it was unforgettable," He smiled conveying more of the memory without words. I almost blushed. "We good," He asked before continuing. I nodded. "Who gave you that?" He scanned the area quickly as he made his way over.

"Some woman dressed in green with a cornucopia bracelet." My fuzzy brain began to clear a little. "Was that?"

"Demeter? Yes," he kneeled next to me and examined my eyes. "You are sure you didn't drink any?" I nodded quickly.

"Are you sure it's poison? She drank some too." I didn't want to find fault with the beautiful woman, she fed me and well I didn't want to think anyone would want to kill me. I was funny that way.

"Ambrosia is the drink of the gods, they can handle it because they are immortal, but to us mortals it's instant death."

"No! But why would she want to kill me?" Anger tried to rise but it was cancelled out by my overwhelming fear and hurt. I couldn't help it, as irrational as it seemed, the fact people didn't like me, and especially enough to do me harm or in this case do me in, wounded me. Not the thing to focus on, I know but such were the way of emotions, right?

"Look who her daughter is? You are the other woman, no?" He eyed me knowingly. I faltered for a moment. The tangle of yarn was getting tanglier by the second.

"How do you know?" Was there an Olympic version of E!? Was an otherworldly Ryan Seacrest interviewing heroes and recounting tales of the infidelities of the gods? 'Up next; Dionysus talks rehab!'

"A centaur told me in the square. I was here looking for my mother." His voice was somber.

"Your mother?" I gaped as David pulled me to standing.

"We don't have time for this; we need to get you out of here." He hurried me past a stone water fountain, down some stone steps and along a path bordered with hedges. I glanced behind me repeatedly wondering if it mattered. Maybe she could just mutter words and strike me down or think me dead, regardless of the distance. I stopped to catch my breath. He looked uneasy and pulled me into a shadowed clump of olive trees. I sat on a gnarled root begging my heart to slow.

He sat next to me and put his arm around me pulling me close. I could smell his aftershave, which was very much an artifact from the mortal world. I imagined we were both unwilling tourists fleeing for our lives back to our homeland. We were united in a single likeminded quest and I relaxed until my common sense intruded.

"How are you here? Why are you looking for your mother in Olympus?"

"I came after you, you left the door open." He meant this literally. I didn't doubt his honesty. I remembered the door and all the trips I had made through it. Of course if I hadn't been dreaming then it would be very real and very functioning.

"Where's Charlie? Did he come with you?" I glanced around almost expecting to see him.

"We took different approaches to get in after you locked us out. Don't worry, he's not here he's back at your grandmother's." I breathed a sigh of relief. As much as I wanted to see my brother I didn't want to pull anyone else into this mess. "Look, I know you have a lot of questions but we need to focus on getting you out of here."

"What about your mother?" I worried about the task I was pulling him from. He read my concern.

"I can find her later," he assured me, "Calli, she's not a prisoner or anything." He smiled so I would follow him.

"How will we leave? Can we climb down?" I tried to remember any 'facts' about Olympus.

"We'll fly. There is a stable of Pegasus just a little further ahead."

"Won't Zeus be angry I left?" Caution jabbed at me again like a persistent nag.

"Did you not notice how insignificant they view us mortals? Trust me; if Zeus wants you he'll summon you and you'll immediately be brought to him. Right now, there is a conspiracy afoot so let's go."

"What conspiracy?"

"Wrong place, wrong time."

"Why doesn't my grandmother like you?" He stopped and regarded me thoughtfully. Then he shrugged and pulled me onward.

"I don't know. You're the great granddaughter of Clio and Apollo; maybe she doesn't think I'm good enough. Maybe she heard a prophecy." He said 'prophecy' like he was saying 'gossip'.

"When I met her at her camp there was a woman with crazy hair and eyes."

"Cassandra," He asked I nodded. "Look, there are prophecies and they are very popular with the people here. They like to think that they are immutable and fixed and anyways they are usually very vague. You know like fortune cookies. If the prophecy said you will meet a tall dark stranger for instance, it could mean a man, woman or even a zaggart."

"What's a zaggart?" My mouth had a hard time forming the word.

"Something very tall and very strange. My point is, when it's vague you can twist it whichever way you want it to make sense with the person or situations you're dealing with. The prophecies aren't even as straightforward as that example. They are long and worded so that three different people can hear the same thing and come up with vastly different conclusions."

"So my grandmother might have heard a prophecy and thinks you're a bad guy?"

"Maybe or perhaps she intended you to be married to another." He nodded at my hand. I shook my head violently.

"No, not him," I said instead of Hades, afraid he might hear and pop up suddenly, "that's why we are here, she's contesting it."

"I didn't mean him," he smiled kindly, "no one in their right mind would wish that on anyone."

"He didn't seem that bad," I said quietly, the yarn ever more tangled. "At least while I thought it was a dream."

"It was a rouse. He cares about no one. You're lucky to be free of him before he showed you his true colors. He's a nightmare." He let me absorb that and I didn't even bother to think of a rebuttal. How could I? I was in Olympus, possibly facing deportation to the Underworld because he tricked me into marrying him. None of those things could be misconstrued as noble, could they?

"Why do you think he wants me so bad? I'm not anyone special." I didn't mean this in a manner that reflected on low self-esteem, rather I was looking at it objectively.

"I wish I knew. Again, maybe there's a prophecy. The reason doesn't really matter does it?"

"I don't know, I think I should go tell Nana and Zeus what just happened with you know who."

"Sure, tell Persephone's daddy that her mother tried to do in her husband's mistress turned wife." He waved his arms laughing.

"What? Oh that's right, everyone is related. Why is it considered normal here but very backwoods where I come from?"

"Calli, you exhaust me. Look I just saved your life. Can you just please trust me?"

"I don't know," I sighed loudly, "I feel like I keep making the wrong choices; caught in some horrible karmic loop."

"Well here's your chance to make the right one."

"Do you promise once we're away from here you will explain everything to me?"

"I promise full disclosure."

Riding a Pegasus was not the thrilling adventure I thought it would be; rather it was a fear inducing aerial version of a bucking bronco. It did not like me on its back and did everything it could to try and pitch me. I had ridden horses before and had assumed it would be similar; not taking into account the two large wings that protruded from its shoulder blades.

In order to accommodate this, the saddle, which was thinner and more flexible than a horse's, was positioned so that the rider's stirrups were further back by the hind legs which didn't move much during flight.

Obviously this would throw off your balance so the solution had the rider's upper body lying flat towards the neck. We had gone far enough that both the earth below and Olympus above were equal parts blurry and undistinguishable. Not far enough for me.

My nausea was threatening again as my steed reminded me once more of his dissatisfaction. I eyed David envious with how well his was behaving. He constantly flew circles around me waiting for me to catch up.

"You have to relax," he said in a tone that was drenched in a little bit too much condescension for my taste. I glared at him. Seriously, he was going to reprimand me for not riding a Pegasus correctly? I could barely think the statement, let alone say it out loud it was that ludicrous. "It senses your fear."

"It senses correctly," I snapped at him. He flinched as though I'd slapped him and I regretted it immediately. He was only trying to help. "I'm sorry, I'm scared, confused and several thousand feet up in the air." He smiled to let me know he accepted my somewhat apology.

"I understand," he smiled again, wider this time, "release your grip on his neck and firmly but gently, wrap your hands in his mane." I nodded but it took an eternity before I finally relaxed first my right hand and then my left. I shut my eyes tight, prepared for the impending fall. When it didn't happen I risked a peek and found we were flying even with David, my Pegasus's wings beating in a calm and steady rhythm. I laughed amazed at the change. I leaned forward and kissed my steeds neck, thanking it over and over.

"I knew you'd get the hang of it," David grinned. His smile faltered and grew further away as suddenly my ride changed course and headed back. I panicked, tugging left and right but it would not turn for me. David was quickly beside us, though I noticed with great difficulty; my steed was moving in a fevered pace that his was barely able to match. He reached out for my hand. "He can't maintain for long, you're going to have to jump Calli!"

Several problems arose in my mind simultaneously, each shoving for my attention; the deadly height, the moving target, the fact that they weren't used to carrying two passengers and the overwhelming fear I was getting into more and more trouble. I sighed and shook my head 'no'. The look on his face was unreadable, was it shock, betrayal, fear? It didn't matter as soon his face and the rest of him were gone. I watched my arrival back to the stables through salty tears.

"I'm sorry Calli," my grandmother's voice sounded from nearby as strong hands lifted me firmly and led me away.

I heard the door opened and squeezed my eyes shut even though I was facing away. My bed, no longer our bed by my decree, (though I didn't know how long I could get away with it), had been my sanctuary ever since Hades had brought me back. I heard the sound of a tray being set on the table by the window, listened to the steps that moved across the floor and held my breath in anticipation as I felt the bed shift and a gentle hand stroked my hair. Then came the sigh, steps and then the closing of the door.

This had been the routine, three times a day for how many days I couldn't recall but I knew it had to be something like four or maybe five. It was hard to track time in a place where sunrise and sunset were nonexistent. I slowly slid off the bed and over to the table. It really didn't matter whether I ate or not. I knew this because I had tested the theory for the first couple days.

It was better to be complacent in this regard as it gave him less reason to bother me. I knew though, in the back of my mind, the sooner I made peace with my situation the easier it would become. As usual I wondered and worried about David. If only I could see or at least speak to my grandmother I could implore her to find out. Maybe knowing his whereabouts or at least that he was safe would help ease my transition here. Then again it could put him in more danger. Either way it mattered not, the only person (and I used the term loosely) that I was allowed any contact with was my husband.

Apparently Zeus had thought a honeymoon was in order to help gel the union. Only once that was achieved I'd be allowed visitation rights. I realized that my disposition and isolation was keeping me away from my grandmother longer but I could not embrace quiet complacency. I ate until I wasn't hungry and pushed the plate away with content. Seconds later a knock sounded at the door. I didn't respond and eventually it opened and he entered. He smiled as he noticed the empty plate.

"I'm glad to see you are eating, agapimeni, it brings me joy." He leaned down to kiss my cheek and I turned away. He tried to put his arms around me and I pushed him off. Every move I rebuffed or deflected. In a final gesture he was on his knees before me. "Please, can we not talk about this?" I risked a glance at him, at his fake concern and glared in return. "I love you," was what he was saying before I kicked him in the jaw. Now he had crossed the line, though now I guess I had, too.

"Leave me alone, I will die before I allow you to have any part of me," I screamed at his back as he shuffled out of the room. I stood at the window breathing heavy from both my actions and the anger that had instigated it. I knew I had probably screwed up my chances of seeing my grandmother and I suddenly had a new target for my anger; myself.

I paced for the rest of the afternoon. Dinner was brought in by one of his creatures and I began to think I wouldn't be seeing him anytime soon. I was wrong.

He was carrying a long plush robe, a bath sheet and some slippers; bath time. I nodded towards the chaise at the end of the bed for him to leave the items. He remained standing and I knew then that he intended to be 'involved' in the process. Slowly I was losing battles previously won. I glanced at my bed wondering when that too would be invaded. I sighed and followed him into the master bathroom.

The master bath was as opulent as any room in the castle but he had gone to great lengths to ensure my comfort. A small toilet room and a wash basin were immediately to the right of the room, on the smallest wall. The left side of the room was dedicated to a large pool, many times larger than a bathtub and much deeper. It had steps leading up to the wall and then down into the water. It had no faucet handles but rather tasseled pulls that hung down from the ceiling above. These supplied the hot and cold water that fell as rain from a spot near the middle, closest to the mirrored wall.

The tiles were painted with sceneries that were richly detailed and silk hangings offered privacy if desired. Those were usually closed by me. This wasn't the first time he had insisted on intruding. The room was usually infused with a soft purple glow, relaxing and peaceful. I noted right away that while the lighting was still soft, it was much brighter and more of a white light. I looked for a control of some kind, intent on changing it but saw none. The look on his face was controlled and even.

I went over to my changing screen, which was conveniently near the steps furthest away from him. As soon as I neared, it flattened against the wall. The loud smack of wood against tile reverberated throughout the room. I stifled a gasp, not wanting to give him the satisfaction. So he was forcing me to undress in front of him? Show me who was boss? Fine. I gritted my teeth and started to unclasp the metal bindings of my tunic on each shoulder, keeping my back towards him. The material fell to the floor in a heap around my feet.

I didn't feel cool, he kept my rooms warm, until I met his gaze in the mirror before me. When did that get there? I covered my breasts with one hand while my other hand flew to my crotch. He continued to stare at me wordlessly, his face hard and unfeeling. I awkwardly made my way up the steps and down into the water. Once I was submerged I swam over to the side closest him and grabbed the edge of the silk curtain.

I heard him clear his throat and looked up at him. He shook his head 'no'. Angered I pulled on the curtain, intent on blocking him from my view and more importantly me from his. With a wave of his hand all four curtains fell to the floor with a low swoosh.

I couldn't stop the tears then and just gave in, clutching the wall before me, my head tucked into my elbow. I heard him enter the water behind me. His hands found my shoulders and I allowed him to turn me towards him, prepared to fall into his arms and receive the comfort he'd been longing to give me that I had been refusing since we came home. I had spent my very last ounce of will power; I gave up; he could have me.

He pulled me to standing and held me at arm's length. I looked up into his eyes, confusion playing across my face, they were like ice. A chill ran down my spine as he stepped back further. He motioned toward the shelf over the bath that contained a sponge, some bath salts and body scrub. He wanted to watch me clean myself. I grabbed the sponge, applied some cleanser and quickly started scrubbing as much body as I could; my arms, breasts and stomach.

A firm hand grasped mine, the one holding the sponge and he dictated its movement; slowly up from my stomach up to first my right breast, circling my nipple then repeating with my left breast. The pressure was painful, not overtly so but definitely unpleasant and such an extreme contrast to his normally gently nature. I feared I had awoken a sleeping monster with my angry poking.

We dipped the sponge in the water, applied more cleanser and began on my legs. I dropped the sponge as it headed upwards between my thighs. I was done helping. Anymore he would have to do it himself. He gave me a knowing but emotionless look, reached into the water and retrieved the sponge. He took my arm and guided me under the shower spot and wrapped the ropes around each wrist. I yanked my left and was suddenly scalded. I yelped and pulled on my right; cold water doused my inflamed skin.

He propped me against the wall, wrists even so the water that fell on me was warm. He kneeled down beside me then proceeded to clean me, starting where I left off. There was no thrill from his touch there. I felt invaded and used my hate to extinguish any desires that attempted to flare up. He wasn't as rough as he had been while using my hand but he wasn't gentle either.

He moved me away from the wall, the spray of water hitting me square in the face. I was only able to turn my head to one side or another, not reducing its effect on me by much. I struggled with my wrists but the pressure only increased. He stood before me and scrubbed my shoulders, neck and my breasts again. He leaned over and bit one nipple hard. I gasped out in pain. He lowered himself further and repeated the gesture, my knees struck on either side of his face but he didn't move until he had bit and sucked to his liking.

He took the sponge and reached behind me, scrubbing each butt cheek, the small of my back and back up to my shoulders. I was pinned against him and felt his arousal pressed firmly on my stomach. In a blur of movement, he was suddenly behind me and inside me. The force of his thrusting threw me against the wall. I threw out my arms to balance myself then adjusted them to keep the water temperature even. I don't remember when I stopped crying.

He finished, cleansed me once more then my arms were released. He half carried me down the steps where I waited to be wrapped in the bath sheet. He carefully dried my body and hair then helped me slip on the robe and slippers.

"This is what you asked for," he whispered as he left me in my bed and shut the door. I was too exhausted to cry and fell into a deep slumber; my only safe place for now.

We spoke of the different facets and functions of the Underworld, supplemented with tours and boat rides. In addition to the Styx, there were four other rivers though my favorite was Plegethon, a river of fire. In a land of cold death, it made me feel most alive. I lit up watching the flames dance and twirl. He also introduced me to the three judges at the gate, Radamanthus, Aeacus and of course Minos, who eyed his ring on my finger with such fierce animosity that I begged not return.

Cerberus, my big puppy, was an unexpected treat. Though he had to lie completely flat on the ground, and I had to be aided by a ladder just to scratch his heads. We talked endlessly about music and literature and art and of other aristocratic things, he had an eternity of experience and exposure but we never ever broached the topic of what happened in the bath.

We had exchanged a silent agreement in that neither of us mentioned it. It was an unthinkable and therefore unexplainable blight that dirtied any attempts at 'honesty' with me so I cast it out like a stone into a deep chasm, flinging it far away in the hopes that it would stay gone. This made my 'role' easier to maintain. I hadn't given up hope of getting back to Nana and then home, possibly with David though that situation had become very strange and complicated but until I had a great plan it served me best to be complacent.

He had come back into our bed; I had known he would eventually. We were husband and wife, in ALL respects, something he had made very very clear. However, he didn't force himself on me because I didn't force him to. My willing acceptance, at least on the surface, gave him no need.

The first time was maybe seven days after the incident, a time during which he left me completely alone. He had snuck in sometime during the night, or what amounted to night anyways, while I slept. His hands were chaste, only holding me gently around the waist but his other appendage was not so innocent. When I ascertained that he had no intentions of 'forcing the issue' I decided this was an opportunity for me to gain some favor points.

I rolled over, facing him and smiled. It was forced but convincing. The look on his face, before it changed to pleasant surprise had been sullen and almost guilt ridden. Had he regretted his hateful actions? I found I wished too much for that for it to be true and pushed those feelings aside. When he tried to speak I covered his lips with mine, tongue thrusting forcefully inside his warm mouth. He relaxed and when he did so I maneuvered myself on top of him.

I released him from my kiss and he began to speak again, it sounded like the start of an apology. I wasn't having that. I shoved my fingers in his mouth and eased my way down. He was dressed in a sleeping gown and I had to remove my fingers to ease it up. Luckily he was naked underneath. I placed him in my mouth and rendered him speechless. When I was done, but before he was, he flipped me on my back. I prepared to be ravished and my body almost welcomed it, this being strictly sex, only physical. He surprised me by taking his time.

He slowly removed my nightgown, completely, though not necessary. Contrary to the harsh examination I had endured from him in the bath, his gaze lingered with appreciation. Again I was probably giving him more credit for feelings and not enough for deception but I was grateful none the less. Being objectified in such a harsh manner had left me feeling empty, hollow. He was at least treating me like a person. I relaxed a little. He sensed my apprehension and leaned over me on one elbow while he stroked my hair and face with his other hand. Soft kisses rained over my face and then my neck.

My eyes closed and my back arched in automatic response. My body cared not the cause or origin of these impulses. I chided it mentally for its looseness, where was the dignity? I lost my train of thought as his lips moved lower, grazing my shoulders and working towards the valley between my breasts, which he cupped with each hand, his thumbs rubbing in a circular motion over my nipples. I let out a small gasp, as my traitor body took the reins from my complicating mind. The message was simple; submit.

I finally relaxed my body and in doing so felt new sensations creeping through my body. This submission was different; it wasn't coerced or subjugated. I realized I wasn't giving in to him as much as giving in to myself. It wasn't the mind blowing sex from our blissfully ignorant dream days but I allowed myself to enjoy his attention without reprimand. His member throbbed on my leg as he repositioned himself above me, parting my legs bringing my knees up. I awaited the thrusting and plunging but instead felt the tickle of his beard as it moved up my thighs.

His tongue was warm, firm and flirty; darting around the hard nub that would send me over the edge. I would get swept up in a wave, about to crash then he would turn his attention to the inside of a thigh or the back of a knee. When I was finally breathing steadier, he worked his tongue into a spiral, darting in and out until I was panting heavily and grabbing the sheets with such force I thought they'd tear. Then it would subside. He kept this up maybe a dozen times before I begged him to finish.

He timed the last one perfectly, just when he knew I was at orgasm, he sat up and pulled me onto him. The in and out sliding motion enhanced the experience and I actually cried out. He slowed but didn't stop. He used his thumb to get me there a second time and then twisted without pulling out until he was beneath and I was riding him. This time we came together, afterwards lying in a heap where we had finished, our feet pointing towards the head of the bed. I heard his whispered words but didn't comprehend them as I fell asleep. This was the night I learned how to gain my freedom.

Many women would find it laughable, my inflated confidence at coming to such an obvious conclusion about a man; give him sex and he will be happy. However, Hades wasn't a man, at least not in the technical aspects. None the less, he reacted the same; with overwhelming generosity and sweetness. Every day he presented me with a new dress, hair adornment, jewelry or other purchase. One day it was an elaborate golden harp that played itself, the next, a rose garden with a swing. I laughed a lot that day. I was noticing that his resolve was crumbling at a faster rate when he saw me visibly happy.

It was in these moments, before we'd depart for dinner or sometimes before bed, that I would see him slip out a glass orb, hold it near his lips and then place it back inside his robes. I was afraid of undoing any progress I had made; my questions might make him upset. I had learned after a couple failed attempts in the beginning of my campaign, when I was too desperate to see my grandmother in his opinion. I hadn't asked anything of him since. This seemed to be the right approach; still my curiosity was getting the better of me.

"What is that," the words fell out of my mouth before I could stop them. He halted, orb almost back in its resting spot, clenched tightly in his hand. We had just spent dinner 'outside' in the garden, the plants and flowers illuminated by fairy lights. Not real ones of course, just a simulation, the end result looked as though the stars had fallen from heaven like snow.

It was a magical evening, filled with music wine and dancing and I found I didn't have to work so hard at 'enjoying' myself. I was beginning to wonder if the line was becoming blurred. Perhaps that explained my lack of forethought. I stared at a nearby rose bush, counting the petals on one bloom, silently cursing myself for my failure. I heard him sigh then he sat on the nearby bench and pulled me onto his lap. I forced myself to look into his face, he wasn't angry, he appeared to be sad.

"Agapimeni, this," he held up the translucent pearly orb, "is a memory globe. It contains recordings all of my memories." My evaluation of it was skeptical; it was no larger than a medium apple. "Well not all my memories," he added as though guessing my thoughts, "but they are all my memories of you." Several emotions flooded me at once making it difficult to sort them out.

"May I see them?" I asked confidently. He offered me neither the desired look nor response.

"I'm sorry, I would very much like to share them with you but I don't think you are ready to handle what it contains. Remember I said some of your memories might be jumbled." I nodded, fully understanding the meaning of it all; here were authentic recordings of events, that concerned me and he didn't want me to see.

"But those," I indicated the orb, "are not jumbled." He nodded his head in agreement and then the orb was gone, most likely stashed back inside his robes. "You want me to see those," I waited for him to incline his head in agreement, "but not yet." He nodded again. "I'm not ready," I finished.

"As much as I wish you were; I can't take that risk." Of course you can't! The conversation was over. He helped me to standing, pulled me in close, breathing me in and then kissed me with a passion that was filled with painful longing. It felt like a goodbye kiss but when he finished he took my hand in his and led me back into the castle.

I was shaken from the kiss but my resolve was firm; I was going to get that orb and the evidence it contained back to Olympus and win my freedom. I had no clue my opportunity was closer than I could imagine.

I was sitting in the library reading, surprisingly enough a Jane Austen novel; Sense and Sensibility. I had just reached the part when Marianne receives the letter from Mr.

Willoughby explaining his engagement to another woman when Hades walked in smiling.

"I'm sorry to intrude," he bowed low and kissed my hand. I placed a marker on the page and set the book on a nearby table.

"Of course not, don't be silly," I smiled. It was easier to do since I learned he held evidence of his betrayals. I allowed him to help me off of the chaise and we walked out into the garden. Although it was beautiful, it always pained me to see it, missing the sunshine and all. He must have sensed my mood for he squeezed my hand gently and led me to one of the stone benches. Its legs were carved with the images of gargoyles but I thought it was magnificent, not scary.

He knelt before me, reminiscent of the night of our wedding; the time before the knowing was how I referred to it in my head. I twisted the ring unconsciously while I stared into his face for clues.

"Today I am taking you somewhere special for lunch," he smiled at me, "how would you like that?" I nodded in response, what else was there to say? He must have not received the reception he had hoped for. He grinned wider and pointed above him. It took me a moment but I soon caught his meaning.

"Above ground? We're going up there?" I squealed and jumped, nearly knocking him over. I threw my arms around him and pulled him to the grass, kissing him all the way. "Thank you," I whispered.

He hadn't noticed anything was missing when he helped me up and led me to the stables. Soon I would be, too. We arrived at our spot in a strange way; we just popped out of the earth. One minute we were headed straight for the ceiling and the next, we were treading sunshine and blue skies.

He parked the chariot near the olive trees and after helping me out, removed a basket. Instead of going towards the pond, he lifted me and carried me up the hill. I glanced as we went but couldn't make out the tunnel we had taken previously to come here. Was there was a chance I could get home; a chance I hadn't even considered until now? I would be safe there I just knew it. I turned my focus to the landscape ahead and gasped. Here was the ocean and it was spectacular.

We made our way to a wide ledge that was close to the water but far enough where the spray wouldn't wet us. He laid out a blanket, then retrieved far more food and wine than could have fit reasonably in the basket and placed them around us. I lingered longer over eating than normal, relishing the fresh outdoors, the smell and sound of the ocean and the songs of the birds. I lie on my back, taking it all in and smiled. He came to sit next to me, fumbled in his pocket then stood up again turning in circles.

"I must have dropped it," he muttered.

"What's wrong darling," I purred up at him, "come lie with me." My voice was intentionally seductive. He started to follow then stopped and admonished himself.

"I will, but I must find it first." I sat up to follow him and he urged me to stay. "I will be right back, I'm sure it's somewhere on the path." I smiled and nodded.

I waited until he had turned out of sight and hurried in the opposite direction. I knew from my careful exploration during lunch that there were three ways out of here; back the way we came, into the ocean or down the rocks to the path parallel to the water. My first instinct had been to jump, but again, were there dangerous creatures in the water and if those weren't an issue, if I didn't clear the surf I'd be bashed against the rocks.

The third option was my only viable one but the most difficult. It's hard to be quick and careful and I slipped a couple times before I had managed a third of the way towards the water. Luckily, a well-worn path cut into the ground though it was still slow going and I had to use roots and tree branches and jutting stones to maintain my balance. I was sure he would see me but the ground curved around further away.

I considered tossing my tunic into the water to misdirect him but that could backfire and I didn't want to be caught naked. I prayed that I could make it back to the tunnel before he found me. I felt for sure this time there would be real hell to pay.

Ten

Dirty Little Liars

Hades noticed I was gone. I know big surprise! It wasn't that I thought he wouldn't but I had hoped it would have taken him longer. He had taken to the sky in the chariot to better search for me and came close to spotting me once and I pressed myself tight against the mountain wall praying the entire time. Luckily there was a depression, not quite a cave but deep enough to hide comfortably.

I decided it was probably a good idea to stay put for a while in case he doubled back. I was wet and cold, the surf being much closer, but I was determined. The sun began to set and I reluctantly moved out again, not quite believing he was gone from the area but sure I didn't want to be stumbling on the wet rocks in the dark or worse, hiding in the cave. What if the tide rose and flooded me out?

Once around the sharpest bend of the hill the path became less steep so by nightfall I had managed my way back towards the meadow. I slunk low, careful to stay to the shadows. I wasn't sure if he was capable of magical tracking that would render my stealth ridiculous and unnecessary but I had to try I reasoned.

I searched the rock wall desperately for the tunnel but to no avail. Panic started to swell until I realized I was further back than I had originally thought. Several yards further I pushed against the wall and fell, tumbling a little way in the dark. I stood up and dusted myself off. The torches weren't lit like they always were but then again I had always been with Hades or used my key.

Instinctively, I reached up to my neck though I knew the necklace was back at the castle. I understood the repercussions immediately; I would not be able to return. I laughed at that thought; would I ever want to return? I realized that I did. I wanted to see Nana but more than that, I had fallen in love with this world. I would have to work that out later. I took a deep breath and fumbled forward into the darkness towards HOME.

Time is a funny thing, or at least our attachment to it. I found myself wishing I had my cell phone or a watch, anything that would tell me how long I had been traveling. I don't know what it would accomplish, not practically anyways. I would be done once I reached my destination; no sooner, no later. Of course it seemed like it was taking an awful long time, a lot longer than before. Of course, with no light I was taking it slow and cautious I reminded myself again.

The only comfort in time would be if it told me what I wanted; that I had mistook hours for 30 minutes and therefore was so close I could smell it. Come to think of it, I did smell something. Whether or not it reminded me of home was the question. I smelled barbecue. When I finally made it out of the tunnel it was like coming up out of the water for air. Not literally of course, I could breathe adequately in there but I was beyond relieved once I sighted open sky.

I had known something was wrong as soon as I exited the tunnel. Instead of the stone cellar of Nana's I was standing at the base of a hill. For a moment I worried I had come full circle; the tunnel did twist and turn slightly. However, though I had only the light of the moon, I could tell this hill was grassy, smaller and not located within the mountain walls. Also missing were the grove of olive trees and the salty air of the ocean. I pondered my situation while I sat on a nearby stone. If I reentered the tunnel would it take me back to the picnic spot or somewhere else?

I wasn't sure how these traveling tubes worked exactly. Twice on my way to visit Hades there had been two tunnels; one to the Underworld and the other to where ever else I had wanted to go. I wanted to go home and didn't end up there but I couldn't remember how the tunnels worked backwards only forward. I hadn't taken the tunnel to get to the picnic spot, at least not recently. Another thought crossed my mind, were these tunnels only for me or public use? If it was the latter, then who knew where I was or where it would lead me next.

I had no choice but to try and find my grandmother. She of course would be able to send me home or Zeus after I showed him the evidence contained in the… My face fell as I searched my empty robes repeatedly for the memory globe. I sighed loudly and sagged on the stone. I was stuck in a bad situation; if I tried to leave, if I was capable of leaving, without proving I was coerced, then they might return me to Hades and he might punish me. I shuddered at the memory of the bath. Had I turned him that way or had his true nature finally come out?

"Calli," a familiar voice called over to me. I was too deep in thought and gnawing on my fingernails to take much notice. "What are you doing?"

"Trying to figure out what to do next," I mumbled through my fingers. Nana had already shown her hands were tied when she handed me over to HIM, I reverted to my original calling of him, as though the name whispered in my head might lead him straight to me.

The gods, including my great grandfather Apollo would be even more bound and less likely to help. Not that they seemed to care. I noticed none of them had clamored over to get a closer look at their descendant. What I needed was someone who was capable but not so connected. I was going to have a hell of a time trying to spot that.

"Are you hungry," the voice asked, oblivious to my ruminations. Another interruption? Here I was trying to align puzzle pieces that would determine life and death! Okay maybe not that drastic but if I was sent back to the Underworld I would very much wish to die.

"No David," I snapped. "I'm busy can you please just give me a mom..." My smile grew a mile as I leapt up nearly knocking him over with my hug. He laughed and twirled me around then set me gently on the ground, his hands still around my waist.

"I thought I'd never see you again," he frowned, "are you okay? Did he hurt you?" I sidestepped the latter question.

"I'm good," I nodded, "better now. Oh and yes, I am actually hungry, thank you." He laughed and took me by the hand, my right, fingers laced together. It felt good. He led me to a campfire beneath an Aleppo pine tree. Nothing was on the spit that bridged across the hot coals, by the looks of things David had already eaten. However, he motioned to a fallen log and handed me a clay plate of some type of cooked meat (I didn't want to know) some berries and a flask of water.

In between bites I filled him in on my journey. He nodded and occasionally asked questions to clarify but didn't add anything himself. I noticed he was very interested in the memory globe and disappointed when I mentioned I lost it.

"You don't need it," he told me after I had finished eating. We were lying on a bedroll next to the fire. I didn't mind his close proximity, I actually appreciated it. I felt myself falling into a relaxed stupor.

"Need what," I asked blankly. He chuckled.

"You don't need the globe; in fact, you don't have to go through Zeus or any of the others at all." I sat up suddenly, my sleepiness suddenly dissipated. "You can initiate a separation from him. That is if you still want it."

"Well he's been trying to kidnap me for years so yeah I think I still want it. Why would he want me? I'm just an ordinary mortal."

"He didn't tell you?"

"No," I looked down at my ring somberly. He had told me many things but never the most important. "Do you know?" David's gaze shifted from me and he was up on his haunches poking at the fire. "David, do you know?"

"I don't feel it's my place." He said without looking at me.

"Then whose place is it? Hades? I don't see him telling me the truth." David motioned at me to be quiet.

"If you want him to find you then keep saying his name. Has anyone told you?"

"Names have power? I think I might have heard that once or twice. What power does mine have? I noticed my Nana keeps calling me Calli here."

"I don't know, but let's not find out. Most likely he'd at least be able to find you. Like reverse tracking."

"Why is he so interested in me?" My resolve was clear in my tone. I was not going to let this go.

"Do you remember me telling you about the prophecies?" I nodded, not wanting to interrupt while he was being forthcoming. "There is one about you," he motioned me silent when I made to speak, "I don't know what it is, I've never heard it. Anyways, I believe that he wanted to possess you so he could control the prophecy. Use you as a pawn or a weapon."

"Why? He's lord of the Underworld. What more could he want?"

"Olympus, his brother's throne, maybe he wants to use you to take over your world."

"You're sure it's about me?" Maybe it was a case of mistaken identity, in which case I would be absolved. I entertained myself with visions of supernatural detectives. A chubby satyr with a checkered hat and a pipe in his mouth would present the evidence proving it was actually a nymph from Crete who had a secret crush on well, you know who. They would run into each other's arms and he would sweep her up and away and I would live happily ever after. Maybe that scenario was seriously flawed but it still gave me hope.

"Everyone thinks so," he answered, popping my bubble. I thought about what was probably happening, what had happened after I disappeared. Ha...HE had to have gone to Zeus and my grandmother with the news (complaint) of me (his property) running away. My grandmother must be in a right state.

"David, I have to let her know where I am." He looked puzzled. "My grandmother, I have to let her know, she's probably freaking out."

"Look, while you're still bound to him it's not safe for anyone to know." I began to protest and he held up his hand. "But we can send a message to her letting her know you're okay." He reached into his pocket and withdrew a small leather satchel, poured some crystals into his palm and then threw them into the fire. It flared up, changing to blue then green then normal once more. "It's done."

"That easy?" I asked not quite convinced. He spread his arms wide.

"That easy."

"Thanks," I mumbled, suddenly feeling ridiculously simple minded. He moved closer to me.

"What are you thinking," His voice was soft and comforting. I sat on the bedroll and snorted.

"How stupid I am for falling for a guy, thinking he loved me and not realizing it was all a ploy, a game to get what he wanted." Tears formed at the corners of my eyes. David sat next to me, his face pinched with concern.

"I'm so sorry babe," he gripped my hand tightly. "I never meant to hurt you." Realization hit me like a sledgehammer; oh yeah, I had fallen twice! Stupid, stupid me.

1

"Seems to be a habit of mine," my voice wickedly sharp. His cheeks redden as he noted his mistake.

"Yeah, well."

"Unless you have anything to add from the other day, save it. I'm in no mood for a repeat." He nodded solemnly.

"So about your problem, the one with," he nodded towards my ring hand. "We have to initiate a separation, a divorce."

"How do we do that?" I shivered from the cold, though thankfully my tunic was finally dry. He reached behind me and unrolled a wool blanket then wrapped it tightly around me, his hands lingering longer than necessary. I focused on the fire.

"I know a witch." He said with a hint of excitement.

"Of course, probably aren't any divorce attorneys hanging around here," I wasn't thrilled with the prospect of meeting a witch though it sounded like this was my only course of action. "So where is she or he?"

"Borghild? She is from Hunland."

"Are we going there?" I wondered how far we'd have to travel. I hated being out where I could be identified and captured. Was there a reward? How much was I worth? I mentally slapped myself for my sideways train of thought.

"Iceland? No, we don't need to, she's coming to us. We'll meet up with her two nights from now outside of Thebes."

"David, when can I go home?" The words came out without me consciously thinking of them.

"You mean to California?" He asked cautiously.

"Yes, that is where I live."

"I don't know how to tell you this but I don't think you can." His words sounded false, they had to be.

"What do you mean? I can't stay here." Anger flared up without a target, though my words were aimed at him.

"Why not?"

"Why not? I have a psycho husband looking for me, for one thing," my voice was pitched.

"Once the divorce is initiated he can't touch you," I raised my eyebrows, "I swear he can't."

"My life is back there."

"What life?"

"Mine, the one I was starting before and again after you."

"Why not start here, again?" He stared at his feet, "with me."

"I don't know if I can do that? I don't trust you anymore."

"You left Olympus with me and we're all alone out here, that's trust Calli."

"Different kind David, I'm speaking about my heart. Look, maybe I'll feel differently once all this is sorted out but you have to give me time. I've been through a lot in a short amount of time. I mean, what the hell are you doing here? I didn't know you knew about this place. You said your mother was in Olympus, who is she?"

"Chaos."

"That's for damn sure."

"No Calli, my mother is Eris, the goddess of chaos. My father was a mortal, a fisherman from Crete."

"How did you get to my world," I wasn't sure I could claim it as mine just needed the label to help me understand.

"She banished me."

"Why?"

"That's family business." Was all he'd say about that.

"How long were you in my world?"

"Fifty years."

"Fifty, wow how old were you when you came over?"

"About 30 or so."

"You look like you're 35, how is that possible?"

"Look at your family, it's the genealogy; we age slower. Same with you and Charlie, though to a lesser degree."

"Charlie," I suddenly remembered my twin, "where does he think I am?" I wondered if the fire trick would work to get a message to him too.

"Calli, there's no easy way to say this. Charlie's dead."

"Excuse me, I'm exhausted. It sounded like you said Charlie's dead."

"We were ambushed outside your grandmother's. He was only protected inside the fence." David's voice suddenly sounded miles away.

"The hedera helix," I whispered faintly. That ugly vine that Nana insisted never be chopped down. Now I knew why but not knowing had cost me more than I could have ever imagined.

"Yes, I'm sorry there was nothing I could do to help him. I barely made it through to find you and make sure you were safe."

"I killed my brother." Doused in frozen realization I fell hard down a dark and deep hole. I was like Alice, with blood on her delicate little hands.

"No, you didn't. It was Lu Bu or rather his henchmen." He made to hold me and I pushed him away.

"I locked the gate...Charlie..." I broke and a flood of tears and emotions washed over me. Every memory, every detail of my beloved twin passed before my eyes. I recalled with clarity each moment from our time as children teaching him how to ride a bike to his math tutoring in high school and the last time we spoke, when I gave him his death sentence. As this last memory faded it was like a bright flame had been extinguished calling forth the cold which iced over my heart. A solitary emotion remained; revenge. "Where is this Lu Bu?" I didn't recognize the cruel voice that issued forth. It sounded of hardened steel and harder heart.

"He was last seen near Mount Penglai." David's voice caught, most likely taken by surprise at the evolution of my character; meek mouse to enraged lion.

"Where is that?" I stared at the ground.

"Why?"

"I'm going to kill him." If ever there were a time this statement would be laughable, it was not now. These weren't mere words but a promise made, a contract signed in blood and unbreakable. I would travel to the ends of the earth and this world too if necessary, I was certain.

"Calli, I understand you are upset but I think you need to rest and think things through."

"Upset?" I laughed and finally met his eyes, he shrank from my gaze. "He killed my brother; upset doesn't quite cover it."

"Look, we just need..." He was silenced by my wilting glare.

"Enough! I've had enough. I'm tired of everyone telling me what to do and lying to me and pulling me into their shit. We aren't involved with whatever drama is going on here. At least he wasn't. Sweet clueless Charlie was just there for me, to help me and it got him killed. That's it, I've been pushed past my limit of what I can take and still try to be nice and sane. Now I'm killing Lu Bu and his men and anyone else who gets in my way. You want to regain my trust, then help me or so help me stay out of my way." I stood and he followed.

"Okay. Look, this is overwhelming and I know you want revenge and I'm going to help you, I promise. I was involved as much as you. First, though we need to perform the separation ceremony, and then we need to get to your grandmother's camp."

"We don't have time for all that. We need to hurry while we know where he is."

"Listen Calli, you've been here for what five minutes? Let me offer you some advice from someone who has the military skill and experience of this world. First off, as long as you're connected to Hades you are bound to his will. He's not going to let you go running around killing people like some Greek vigilante. As far as Lu Bu, he's not secretive about his whereabouts; you can map his progress by the destructive wake he leaves behind. Not to mention you should probably get word to your grandmother, also."

"You knew," I turned on him quickly, "all this time you knew and you let me go along thinking everything was fine. That the only problems were mine and mine alone. How could you lie to me like that? You talk about building trust and you can't even be honest about one of the few people I truly love in this whole crazy existence." The tears came again, great waves of ugly loud sobbing that had me in his arms being rocked while he whispered softly and kissed my hair.

"Baby, listen to me. It's not your fault, no one told you about the protection spell so how could you have known? I'm sorry I didn't tell you about Charlie before but I was trying to help you escape from Hades and that would have slowed you down," he felt me clench, "and it wouldn't have changed the fact. I waited until there was a better time for you, for you Calli, to hear the truth. While I do regret what happened to Charlie, I don't regret keeping that news from you. Do you understand?" I nodded numbly in response.

"I need some time alone, to process." My voice was barely a whisper but he motioned for me to follow him to a nearby trunk with a clear view of the night sky. The beauty was wasted on me, the wide expanse of stars was just cold and empty space. I eventually took to inspecting the trees, shrubs and other foliage around me. After about an hour I stumbled back to the camp. "Alright but after that will you help me?" My voice was small and pleading.

"Yes," he rummaged in his backpack and pulled out a blank sheet of parchment and lay it on a flat stone.

"I need to know where your grandmother's camp is located." I looked at him quizzically. "We might need your grandmother's help."

"In the woods," David grabbed my hand and placed a quill in it and motioned towards the paper.

"I can't write directions or draw you a map?"

"Yes you can, just empty your mind and relax then think of only the camp and the people there."

"This is ridiculous, nothing is coming to me and anyways I only ended up there from a tunnel at my grandmother's house."

"You can do it; you're the great granddaughter of the muse Clio and the god Apollo. You're special." I frowned at him and shrugged. It was a ridiculous notion thinking that I could conjure up a map to a place I didn't even know how I arrived there but I couldn't move forward without at least trying. I closed my eyes and tried to relax but images of Charlie laughing and smiling assaulted me. I felt David's arms on my shoulders.

"It's okay Calli, let the thoughts flow, even thoughts not about the camp. Eventually they will come to you. Think about your grandmother, people you met there, details about the tents, were there horses, whatever will help your mind recall." I took a deep breath and let myself go limp; my body, my mind and my emotions. It was a miracle I remained standing as I suddenly felt like a leaf trembling on the breeze.

I focused on my Nana's face, the fringe on the hood she wrapped me up in, Cassandra's wild eyes and hair... Suddenly I felt as though a cord was running through my arm and my hand started flying across the paper. Once the movement subsided there was a map. David quickly rolled it and placed it inside a leather satchel. I was too exhausted to be impressed. As I child I had loved all things magic, as an adult, I was finding I could do without it just fine. All it had brought me was trouble.

"Perfect. You should probably get some rest."

"I don't know if I can. I'm so overwhelmed with thoughts and emotions, mostly Charlie. It's like a thousand TV stations blaring simultaneously." I sank on my bedroll and hugged my knees. I felt like all my nerves were being shocked at once. He came and sat behind me, wrapping his legs around and hugged me tight. His embrace seemed to quiet some of the noise in my head. His strong hands began working on my shoulders and neck and I slumped a little against him. "Wow, that's helping a lot." I whispered gratefully.

"I have magic hands remember." His voice wasn't suggestive but the memories they conjured were. My body tingled and my back arched slightly. "Calli, I know I've got a lot to make up for but I promise I will not rest until I've made things right and I will not let anyone else hurt you ever again." He kissed my cheek and then continued moving his hands down my back and then closer to my breasts, sliding down my sides to my hips and back up again. When I didn't protest he went a little further. "I'll only continue if you want me to, I don't want to push myself on you after all you've been through." His breath felt hot and wet on my ear. I maneuvered until I was facing him on my knees.

"After everything I've been through I can't imagine anything better right now." My need for comfort was great and laying her in misery wasn't doing anyone, least of all me, any good. He reached up and wrapped his fingers in my hair and firmly pulled me in for a kiss. Within seconds I was naked on my back with him on top. I had forgotten how lean and strong he was. His touch wasn't rough but it wasn't soft and gentle either.

Like floating along a river, my body relaxed and gratefully he did all the work. It was equal parts sensual and consoling; like a sexy hug. I drifted off afterwards, still wrapped in his arms, my mind quiet at last.

"Good morning sunshine," David's mouth was close enough to plant a kiss on my cheek, which he did. He seemed to be waiting for my reaction before he did more. I smiled and he kissed my lips softly though I was pleased when he told me we needed to pack up camp and get moving. As much as I appreciated the activities of the night before, I wasn't ready to move forward in a full on relationship with David.

As far as I was concerned he had a lot of ground to cover, more questions to answer and a whole lot of promises to fulfill. Perhaps once I had divorced, exacted my revenge and was assured he was being completely honest with me I could entertain ideas but not a moment sooner. After a quick breakfast we were packed and headed down the road.

"I want to learn how to fight," I surprised him as we struggled up a rocky hill. "I want you to teach me."

"Now," David smirked as he firmly grasped my hand to help me navigate a particularly steep spot. I shook my head vigorously.

"Well not this exact moment but when we make it to level ground."

"Okay," his smile stayed but his voice was serious. "I think you should train."

My training was postponed. Every time I suggested an ideal spot, David told me to wait and be patient. Around midday my patience was thinning as we came across a small camp. David pulled me into the shade of a clump of trees and motioned for me to be quiet.

"Why are we hiding?" I asked David but when I turned he was gone. Near the tent a sharp noise sounded sending a flurry of doves into the air. A large man emerged and quickly headed the direction of the birds. I almost shrieked when David returned and grabbed my arm.

"Mercenary, looking for you." He handed me a rolled sheet of parchment. I reluctantly unrolled it only to see a crude but adequate representation of me. The script was in Greek so David had to translate for me.

"Charon is offering 6,000 minae for your return."

"Hades is sending people after me?" David cringed at my slip but nothing happened.

"Of course he is, why am I surprised? He's probably pissed that something he wanted got away."

"He wants you really bad, 6,000 minae is almost 600 pounds of silver!"

"Wow, maybe I should turn myself in. That'd buy a lot of shoes."

"Maybe I should turn you in," David joked and got a punch in the arm. "Ow, kidding, kidding. You're not supposed to train on me."

"I can joke about it, you can't. Wait, what do you mean I'm not training with you? Who am I supposed to train with?" David pulled me out of our hiding spot and yelled out something Greek. I struggled but his grasp remained firm. "What the hell are you doing?" I shrieked as the large man returned. He looked mean but smiled as David continued speaking.

"No David, don't do this."

"You said you wanted training, fight him." He shoved me towards the man who looked eager but confused. He asked David a question, which he answered as he threw a sword at my feet. "I'm not going to fight him," I yelled at David as I moved to run away. The large man blocked me. "David help me!"

"I am helping. You said you wanted to learn how to fight, here it is; on the job training." The man and I circled the fire pit slowly. Luckily there were flames, otherwise he would have already lunged across and grabbed me.

"I don't want to do this. Isn't there another way?" My heart was pounding so loudly in my ears I could barely hear him.

"What other way is there Calli?"

"I don't know but not this!"

"But you want to avenge Charlie, you want to kill Lu Bu."

"Yes!" It was getting hard to concentrate on both the mercenary and David.

"Well this is the best way. If you fight me, you know it's not real. You have to learn to fight under extreme duress. I hardly feel this even qualifies; he's only one man."

"David, please don't make me do this."

"I told him that you are a beast and he will have to fight hard if he wants to bring you in."

"Tell him I'm the wrong person, get me out of here."

"I can't, he wouldn't believe me and I won't because you need this." I tripped on a rock and almost lost my balance. The mercenary made a move to grab me but I side stepped and ran to the nearest tree. "Oh Calli, I should probably warn you, you're wanted dead or alive." He handed me the sword just as the mercenary came up behind me.

The sword was awkward and heavy and I managed to slice my shin before landing a blow on my assailant. I scanned the area for a better weapon while holding him at bay with the pointed end. We had been dancing along this way for what seemed like forever. If I didn't figure something out fast,

I'd fall over from exhaustion. It didn't help that David was cheering him on in Greek. The mercenaries' looks began to range from the horrified to the determined. This was not how I expected my training to go; I imagined standing atop steep stairs triumphant, maybe pounding on some slabs of meat.

"Quit talking to him," I snapped at David.

"The reward money wasn't enough motivation; I had to convince him he was doing a public service. I told him you're an empousai on a murderous spree killing any men you meet." I managed to extend my middle finger while maintaining hold of the sword. An impressive feat I thought. I noticed a hard wooden staff near the tent and maneuvered my way over.

"And how is it that you fared my wrath? I mean, I do want to kill you." David laughed, diverting the man's attention long enough for me to grab the staff. I held both weapons awkwardly not wanting to give my sword to my adversary.

"I told him I drank a spell that makes me appear like a weak helpless woman in your eyes." I managed to toss the sword in a thorny thicket. David swore under his breath and it was my turn to laugh.

"What makes you think you'd have to use a spell." The mercenary lunged, seeing me with what he assumed was a less threatening weapon. I sidestepped and rapped him hard on the back, he stumbled towards the tent and I kicked him hard. The tent didn't break under his weight but it sagged enough to make it difficult to return to standing. Before I could run he flipped over and threw himself towards me. I grabbed his shirt and used his momentum to hurl him into the closest tree. I wasn't sure if the loud crack was from his head or the trunk. I waited a moment, staff at the ready but he didn't move.

"That's our only sword," David complained as I sat on a nearby log. My breath was ragged and I felt as though my heart would pound right through my chest. "Good job though."

I couldn't muster enough energy to get angry. A small part of me had to admit he was right. Fighting someone who wanted to kill you was a lot different than fighting someone who would rather kiss you.

"Can I borrow this please," he aked helping me to standing then using the log propped up the thorny bush and retrieved the sword. He placed it in my quivering hands and led me over to the tree. The man was snoring. "Finish it Calli."

"What?" I looked at him with dismay, disappointment and a small ounce of hope. Surely he was joking. He didn't really want me to kill someone.

"You need to finish him," he stated as clear as possible.

"No, I won't." I backed up and he blocked me with his body.

"To get to Lu Bu you will have to fight and you will have to kill. You were lucky today; one guy, caught by surprise. You will be facing hundreds of men, of warriors all intent on killing anyone taking on Lu Bu." I shook my head no.

"I'll find another way. I'll sneak in." He laughed and unrolled the wanted poster and shoved it in my face.

"Let's not forget your darling husband wants you dead as well. Kill this brute, this man who was willing to kill you for money." I twisted to face him, tears welling up in my eyes. I wasn't a killer, who knew if I could even kill Lu Bu. Deep down

I knew my revenge plan was just to cover up my grief so I could cope but I wouldn't let it overwhelm me.

I kicked David hard sending him to the ground and threw his sword beside him.

"Fuck you David," I cried then ran. I pushed myself hard and fast, driven more by rage and sadness than fear. Actually try as I might, I couldn't summon that emotion. It was relieving, like a weight was being lifted from my shoulders. I by no means felt invincible but I no longer felt the restraint. I thought of Charlie and sped forward. The tears made it hard to navigate and I felt the ground suddenly get soft and wet and then I was under water.

My nose stung as it was assaulted with fluid and I choked; struggling for the surface, my robes weighing me down. The prospect of death itself didn't scare me in itself but I wasn't ready to go. An alien form headed towards me, reluctant yet curious. It was humanoid with large eyes, scaly skin and sharp teeth that it revealed a little too close for my comfort. So this was one of the dangers in the water? It lunged closer and tugged on my robes pulling me neither up nor down but towards some dark and murky destination.

Several more passed by in my peripheral. I desperately searched my databanks of mythology to come up with a solution but it was in vain. I had no idea what this creature was or what to do. For all I knew it could be a servant of Hades, bringing me back to him the old fashioned way, as a corpse. There was a disturbance in the water and then David was there. With a flash of his knife I was soon out of my robes and heading towards the surface.

He quickly pulled me up to shore and laid me on the soft grass. I expelled the fluid from my lungs with such fervor

I thought my ribs would crack. Exhaustion wrapped me in its embrace but it was lined with grateful. No matter how many times I had come close to death I would never take it for granted.

"Are you alright?" He searched my body for signs of damage. I nodded my head weakly.

"You saved me." The surprise in my voice seemed to wound him.

"Of course I saved you, I love you," his voice was rough. I tried to respond but soon his mouth was on mine and his hands were moving all over my wet and naked body.

After our erotic encounter David wrung out my robes, they had washed up on the shore near us, and helped me fasten it together enough for decency's sake. I was emotionally and physically wrung out and begged to rest where we were but he insisted that we had best be on our way so our friend didn't catch up with us to avenge his wicked headache.

When we made camp for the night I was wishing I'd worn my Nikes, as the leather sandals were wearing blisters on the bottoms of my feet. David was looking over the map as I made known my discomfort. He motioned for me to sit at the makeshift table consisting of wedges of lumber and rocks. It was unusual seeing David in this new habitat with skills I'd never guessed he possessed. Hell I never knew he liked camping. I had to say I was a little more than impressed.

"Unbuckle these," he touched my feet gently. I heard him rummaging through a pack while I removed my shoes. Luckily they were short, with just a single buckle around the ankle. I couldn't imagine wearing the taller style. I had never considered myself pampered before now. He returned shortly with some strips of linen and a flask. He took one of the clay plates, laid the strip of cloth across and doused it with the thick liquid from the flask. "Olive oil," he informed me as he thoroughly soaked the material. "Wrap your feet and leave on for a while."

I started on my left while he soaked some more cloth. The map caught my eye or rather a particular word on the map.

"Delphi," I motioned with a dip of my head. "Is that, the Delphi?" He started working on my other foot, his lips tight.

"I know what you are going to ask," he started firmly.

"Is it true?"

"Is what true?" He finished wrapping and tied off the ends, gently propping my legs on the bedroll so my feet wouldn't touch the ground.

"Do they really have an oracle that can give me some answers?" I wondered how it worked; was it a 'one and done' type deal or could you ask as many as you wanted. He sensed my excitement and laid a hand on my arm.

"Yes, they do but we can't risk it."

"It is right there," I pointed at the map. "We're heading south to Thebes, why not veer slightly west, hit Delphi, get some information and then continue east?" I couldn't tell by the map how many extra days we'd have to travel but it didn't look far. Of course nothing looked far on maps when you were used to the luxuries of cars, trains and planes. He shook his head 'no'. "My great grandfather is Apollo, surely I could get a message to my grandmother through him."

"Wow, I see I'm going to have to educate you even more than I suspected. Your grandmother really never discussed this world with you, not even as a bedtime story?" I shrugged. "Calli, the gods are as far away as you could possibly imagine. They don't care about humans or demigods or muses or even great granddaughters." I started to protest. "Give me a break, did you meet any of your 'family' while up in Olympus? I doubt it, because when I found you, you were alone with a goddess hell bent on revenge. Where was he then? Where were any of them? Save yourself some heartache and learn this lesson fast. Olympus has no love for those on Earth. It's like a TV show just waiting to be canceled once they're bored."

"Maybe so, but I still want to go," I tried to hide the hurt in my voice. Was it so shameful to want your family to love you?

"We might miss Borghild if we do," he faltered as he said this, noting my apprehension. "You are scared of the witch." It was a statement, not a question. I nodded. "You were hoping to find an alternate way to handle the situation?" I nodded again. "I promised you I wouldn't let anything hurt you." He said this last bit weakly as though my lack of faith wound him like a sharp dagger. I didn't know how to react. I chose honesty.

"David," I struggled to find the right words, as confusion clouded my mind. I couldn't afford to lose his aid and if I was really truthful with myself, I just plain didn't want to lose him. "Yes, I'm scared. Can you blame me? I never, well I don't remember dealing with a place like this, with creatures like these. I'm trying to trust you; I know in a lot of ways I should. I want to trust you and..." I stopped short before I started pledging feelings. That wouldn't be fair to him if I changed my mind. "It would comfort me to know I knew all my options first. Is that okay?" I tilted his chin up to look in his eyes. They looked like the ocean on a cloudy day. He smiled at me and kissed my hand.

"Of course," he pointed to the map, "We're here, the junction is here," he motioned a couple inches below, "if you still want to go then I'll figure out a way to get Borghild to wait longer, just in case that's our only option and I'll take you." I smiled up at him as relief passed through me. I noted he was strained. He gripped the back of my neck firmly and eyed me hungrily. "I have a few questions, myself." His kiss was intense but brief. I thought maybe he would follow it up with more but he released me and stood. "It's getting late, I'm going to finish setting up and maybe hunt us up some dinner. I'll bring you a basin for your feet." I nodded my head heavy with thought.

Dinner was pheasant, which was surprisingly tasty, some olives and fresh water. We didn't talk; something seemed to be playing on his mind so I let him be. Afterwards I laid on my back watching the stars until their patterns became familiar to me. That memory was so painful I was forced to turn on my side. David joined me, facing me.

"By the lake I told you I loved you. If I hadn't kissed you, what would have been your response?" His eyes searched my face for an answer. I was afraid to speak. I wasn't sure how I felt about him and knew what answer he wanted. He must have sensed my indecision for without waiting for an answer he rolled over. I prayed the devastation I saw in his eyes was a trick of the light. My heart was heavy enough with guilt.

I sighed and closed my eyes, hopeful that a good night sleep would help clear my mind. Little did I know I was in for one hell of a night. Dreams of fire and death plagued me and a laughing, unseen foe mocked me for being just a girl with a sword that was growing much too heavy in my unsteady hands. With each swing I was closer to the looming earth as I watched his shadow grow ever larger.

Depleted I swung one last time and then fell to the ground. An unfamiliar voice; much like that of a serpent being granted the ability of speech, sounded near my right ear.

"It's your destiny to suffer and to inflict it on others. Stop denying it and join me. You will be my queen of destruction and millions will bow down to you starting with those arrogant gods and goddesses in Olympus. Join me or die with the others after you watch all those you love perish at my hands." A shadow hand reached down and grasped my shoulder causing intense heat and pain!

I bolted upright, a scream lodged in my throat. It took a moment to get my bearings; I was under a large tree, near a river and David was nearby cooking breakfast on our camp fire. He ran over quickly and assessed me.

"Are you okay? You look terrified."

"It was just a nightmare."

"Do you want to talk about it?"

"Not in the least but I would like to wash up before breakfast." He eyed me warily but handed me a rough cloth and pointed towards the river. The cool water was a refreshing contrast to the dream and I took my time scrubbing first my face and hands then feet, legs and arms. My tunic was surprisingly undamaged considering my recent journey but not practical. I would need to get different clothes.

"Need a hand?" David's voice startled me out of my trance. He took my hand and helped me to standing then took the cloth. He drenched it with water then lifted the back of my dress. Lightly he wiped starting with my ankles and working his way up. The combination of his proximity, the breeze on my wet bare skin and the ever more daring places he moved the cloth was enough to make my head spin.

My body, against my will, relaxed allowing him access to my inner thighs. He only went so far, then wet the cloth and moved up and along my buttocks, then my lower back.

"David..." My protest came out as a whisper. My mind was more clouded than ever meaning I was even further away from resolving my feelings for him. His hand moved higher on my back then he swept my hair to one side to get my shoulder. I cried out in intense pain as the cloth made contact.

"Who did this to you?" He asked in alarm.

"What is it?" I craned my neck to see but could barely make out some pink flesh. I touched it gingerly and winced. He led me to the camp and handed me a polished metal mug. The reflection was warped but when I held it to my shoulder I could make out the shape of a hand...with claws.

"In my nightmare, he touched me."

"Who?" His face was intense with worry.

"I don't know but he was evil."

"Your husband, he's trying to scare you. We need to hurry and do the separation." I nodded numbly, defeated, wondering when my crazy dreams became an even worse reality.

We ate in silence then packed and began walking towards Thebes. With an optimistic heart I prayed this was the right choice and the rest of the journey would be better. It couldn't possibly get worse.

"Calli wake up," David nudged me gently. I smiled up at him but received no warmth in return. His eyes looked glazed and distant. I couldn't blame him. I was no closer to answering his question than I was before. I glanced around the makeshift tent, allowing my eyes to adjust to the dimness.

It was barely after noon when we had stopped to make camp so I could rest. I exhausted so quickly anymore. I hoped it was some sort of inter-dimensional jet lag that would soon pass.

"Borghild, she's ready," he called out to the darkness. A figure came into view. She had shock white hair that was tangled and dirty and she wore a thin crude tunic that was draped awkwardly over her bony figure. She smiled or rather leered at me revealing blackened teeth and she smelled earthy, like she slept in the ground. I could almost imagine worms and other insects crawling all through her hair and along her body.

I shuddered and looked at David for help. I was beginning to second guess this supernatural divorce proceeding. He turned and left the tent.

"David," I called out in a panic. She shoved a crude wooden spoon in my mouth filled with liquid that tasted metallic and somewhat familiar. I coughed and sputtered and she quickly refilled it and forced more into my mouth. "What is that?" I demanded.

"Blood," her accent was thick.

"Blood?!"

"Yes, from a fairy."

"Why?" I asked revolted, bile rising in my throat."

"It will help. We need to remove the ring."

"How is that supposed to remove the ring?"

"It's not, this is." She pulled out a large cleaver; it was rusty but wickedly sharp.

"Make a fist." I struggled but suddenly found myself feeling very sleepy. She moved my left hand onto a nearby table or log and extended my ring finger. I screamed but didn't hear it, as my vision went black but the sound of the knife hitting the table was loud and unmistakable.

Unconsciousness claimed me and I was only too eager to follow. I swam through thick deep water until I broke the surface and gasped for air. I was lying on the makeshift cot, drenched in sweat, my left hand wrapped in gauze. I began to wail as the severity of the situation became apparent.

"Oh good she's awake," David's voice sounded from the foot of the bed. I could barely make out his shape through my tears. I was suddenly aware of severe discomfort causing me to shrink back on the bed and glare at him.

"Why am I sore down there and why did you chop off my finger?" I bit my lip, amazed at the absurdity I was uttering. How could this be happening? With David, of all people? My heart would have broken to bits if it hadn't been beating erratically out of fear.

"So many questions Calli, let's see. Oh, yes I didn't chop off your finger, Borghild did. So without fanfare you are now officially divorced. You are welcome." I continued to glare, while slyly scoping my escape options; I saw none. "What no gratitude? Okay so next question. Again it was Borghild, she had to examine you."

"Why," I didn't bother to hide my revulsion.

"To verify the pregnancy. I'd say congratulations but you don't look like celebrating."

"Wait, you and me?" I was suffocating under a pile of confusion and he kept adding layers.

"Silly girl, no. Thankfully the father is in a position of great benefit to us. The big guy, Calli, he's the father.

"I'm pregnant with Ha...with his baby," I forced out slowly. David wagged a finger at me.

"No worries, I know you're unprepared to be a single mother so I will be taking it off your hands." I was still trying to wrap my head around being pregnant that his words were almost lost on me.

"The little bastard put up a fight; I shouldn't have been so gentle." Borghild came out of the corner holding a large and long metal probe. My stomach turned but I felt a smile tug when I noticed her right arm was blackened. "Like that do you?" She moved across the room her arm raised to strike, David knocked her to the ground so fast I never saw him move.

"I think you've had enough fun for one night. You can go." His demeanor was calm and all business. She wiped the blood from her mouth and leered at me.

"You won't have it for long anyways according to the prophecy."

"What prophecy?" My voice was frail.

"Child of the sun will bear a child who will spend eternity in darkness." She laughed hysterically as she grabbed a leather sack and headed out the tent. "Oh thanks for the dress, I pried off all the pretty jewels to spend at the market. As you could see I need new tools." I didn't need to look to know I was wearing her nasty tunic. I could smell it. That bitch was added to my list of people to kill; I might even get her first.

"Why are you doing this to me?" I overplayed the crying, hoping to lure him into a false sense of security. I didn't know where I was or where to go or even who to trust but I knew I had to get away. I'd rather die trying to escape then linger in this nightmare any longer.

"Well without boring you with needless details, I was cursed by my mother and expelled to your world. I wandered around for many years until I happened upon your mother, her sister and your grandmother. I wanted to learn how they traveled back and forth, I tried to befriend Thalia but she was suspicious, so I waited thirty years until I could get close to you. Only she must have figured out who I was or at least suspected where I came from and cut off contact with you. Oh yeah and I killed your grandfather, how could I forget that part? When was that, a decade ago?"

He waited for a response but I gave him none. I had to keep my head clear and my emotions in check.

"Nothing? I figured that would make you just a wee bit mad. Anyways, this is your traditional revenge plot, I am working with a powerful leader who is going to conquer this entire world and make those arrogant giants his slaves. You were my ticket back my dear, though I was worried you wouldn't figure out the key after your grandmother went missing. That crafty old bitch had me believing she left you stranded but I hoped, oh how I hoped and you came. Then another surprise; you and Hades betrothed. What a setback!" He laughed hysterically.

"Why did it matter that we were married?"

"You are aware of your history, right? Persephone and her mother?" He sighed loudly exasperated. "We never had fall and winter until he stole her daughter, while she was with

Hades our army had a bridge to cross over from the north but by marrying you, Persephone was allowed to go home to her mother so now all that ice will be melting."

"So why bother with me, more revenge?"

"Please, I don't have time for such folly. My dear you haven't figured it out yet? I was going to ransom you in exchange for passage through the Underworld but now I have an unexpected bonus, you and your baby!"

"My baby? You monster!"

"Monster? You haven't begun to see monsters Calliope. Just you wait, you're going to see things that will make all this seem like a child's fairy tale. Besides, it will be better off with daddy anyways. Did you see the number it did on poor Borghild? Damn! Now that's a monster! And anyways you have an important role in all of this. You my dear are going to be a new bride." I quickly scanned the tent for an unexpected gap or weak spot. "We're going to have to do some repair on that hand first but don't worry, we won't skimp; you'll probably get a solid gold finger, much better than that old flesh one."

"You think I'm going to marry you? You're crazy!" He sat on the foot of the cot and ran his fingers up my leg. It took every ounce of self-control not to kick him in the face.

"Oh not me, it is a shame to let such a hot piece of ass go but once he claimed you I had to back off." I craned my neck towards my burnt shoulder and he grinned.

"Finally, you are figuring some stuff out yourself! See, I knew you weren't that stupid."

"Who?" I tried to repress the images from the nightmare as they struggled to overwhelm my mind.

"Oh no, I want you to be surprised!" I waited for him to turn his back to dive under the largest gap of the tent. "We can't have you running around in your condition." I felt a sudden intense pressure on my head and everything went black...then there were stars.

The stars reminded me of Hades and the doomed child within my womb. I awoke to stars; real stars and fresh air. I was on my back in a moving cart pulled by a horse or pony. I could hear voices towards the front, meaning David wasn't alone.

My head felt like it was splitting open and I almost gave up on another escape attempt but the thought of being subjected to more torture was too much incentive. Not to mention I was a mother now and had to protect my baby, whatever it was or however long, at all costs.

My maternal instincts surprised me, considering I had no idea what was growing inside me or the extent of Hades evil. I just knew deep down that this child, my child, had no one else. Perhaps taking charge and care of someone else helped me feel less out of control myself. At the very least it gave me purpose.

The portion of the cart where I lay was flat with no sides. I dared a peek to my left and right being careful not to move too much or too fast. We were on a path with the river to the left and thick woods to the right. If I rolled quickly I could be on my way before they even realized I was gone. I would fight if I must but in the state I was in I hoped that would be unnecessary. So which escape should I choose?

I weighed the pros and cons of each while working loose cords off my wrists. The woods were thick and would offer cover for hiding, especially in the dark but I would be unable to see where I was going which meant possibility for twisting an ankle or breaking my leg or getting eaten.

The pro for a water escape would be less chance of injury but again, creatures in the water. Not to mention if I passed out I would surely drown. I began to worry that neither option would work when I realized they wouldn't but there was a third option I hadn't pondered before.

The wagon had been gradually moving up hill, eventually it would travel down again meaning the road behind would be obscured. Surely, they wouldn't expect me to go backwards. In the time spent searching the woods and water I could make it far enough to find a more ideal hiding place or help if help was to be found in this area.

For a brief moment I contemplated calling out to Hades. The baby moved in my belly as though to give its consent to that plan. Even if I escaped I had no idea where I was going and after David's deception it was possible that he didn't have a bounty on my head. Then again I could be jumping out of the frying pan and into the fire.

Hades had proven to be a liar and a kidnapper so the only person I knew for sure I could trust was Nana. The wagon began to descend downhill and I waited for their conversation to become loud enough to cover my movement then I carefully maneuvered my body and rolled off the back.

I landed with a rough thud on my side, hopefully doing as little or no damage to the baby. I started to roll after the wagon until I turned into a seated position and dug my hills into the ground. A triumphant laugh sounded in my head and I smiled with satisfaction. I quietly stood once they were a little further down the hill and turned...into two guards.

"I thought she was out cold," the gruff man on the left questioned the equally gruff man on the right. They both wore swords but neither reached for them.

"Well she obviously woke up." Gruff man on right made a move towards me and I kicked him. "Whoa missy, let's go back to the cart."

At the mention of the cart I risked a look behind me. David and the other man had stopped and were making their way up the hill though they were dark figures with no discernible features in the dim twilight. When I turned back the two guards moved together towards me.

I grabbed their arms and used their weight to throw them off balance enough to run past them. Okay so slight change in plan; four was more than two but less than six or twenty or whatever number that would make me feel lucky. I could do this, I had gravity on my side. I ran down the opposite side of the hill quite easily and then I couldn't stop, which would have been a good thing if I weren't hurtling towards the river; somehow I had veered off course. I turned sharply and slipped, injuring the very same ankle from the incident at my grandmother's house.

I managed to stay on my feet but barely and they were all four advancing on me now. I couldn't run and I dared not go into the water. I picked up a large tree branch and prepared to fight. The men looked startled and I laughed to myself imagining what I must look like; crazed woman wearing a dirty tunic, missing a finger and wielding an oak branch like it was a sword.

"She's a feisty one," Gruff man on my right commented.

"Don't hurt her," Gruff man on left warned him. He watched the other man advance on me. I twirled the branch and brought it down on his left arm and then up on his right. He fell backwards and cursed.

"You're worried about me hurting her?" He scowled. The other man shrugged in response. I used the opportunity to limp towards the woods.

"Your turn." He hung back while his partner grabbed me from behind. I slammed my head into his face and he screamed. I felt warm liquid in my hair and smelled the faint copper smell of blood. He dropped me and I staggered, the blow a big mistake considering my previous head trauma. The two men from the cart caught me as I fell and I was able to see their faces in the moonlight.

"You're not David," I said to them both. They looked on in disbelief as they carried me to the cart.

"Let's hurry and get her to her grandmother before she kills one of us." The bleeding guard sat up front while his partner took his place behind with the other cart guy, massaging his wrists as they followed a safe distance behind.

"You're taking me to my grandmother," I asked tears in my eyes and hoping beyond hope that I heard right.

"Yes, our orders are to deliver you to Captain Thorne." He said disdainfully as though he felt the errand was beneath him. I broke down and sobbed, finally able to stop and mourn all that had happened and been revealed. He seemed to soften a little and his companion seemed ill at ease. I turned to the bleeding man on the front seat.

"I'm sorry I hurt you, I didn't know who you were. I'm...I'm pregnant and he tricked me away and they cut off my finger and assaulted me and I tried to escape and he knocked me out and when I woke up I was here." I turned to the men behind the cart, "I'm so very sorry. Thank you for rescuing me." The cart stopped abruptly and I was soon swept up in one embrace after another.

"You poor child."

"That evil bastard."

"No older than my own daughter."

"Don't worry we won't let anything happen to you." Once they were assured I was okay and seated comfortably the cart resumed its progress.

"Are you thirsty or hungry?" The injured man on the seat smiled at me, dried blood smeared across his face. "My name is Thelius, this is Agapenor and the two men behind ye are Borus and you've met Mecisteus." He chuckled indicating the man I hit with the branch.

"There's some food in a sack next to you and a flask of water." I found the sack and pulled out a loaf of bread and broke off a chunk.

"Thank you, my name is Calli." They nodded in response. "Do you need some?" I offered the loaf to each but they declined. There was also some cheese and some large green olives. I ignored decorum and ate greedily. This was becoming a habit. I would have to take better care of myself now that I knew I was pregnant.

"Who is this man that abducted you?" Borus asked quietly. I followed his lead and kept my voice low.

"His name is David. I met him in another place; we were engaged to be married."

"Is he the father?" Mecistius asked. I shook my head and questioned whether I should divulge the father's identity just yet.

"That's none of our business," Thelius growled from the front. Mecistius put his hands up defensively.

"Just asking a question, not meaning to pry."

"It's okay," I assured him and he gave me a slight smile. "No, he's not the father. Where is he? Is he still alive?"

"We went where we were directed and found you bound and alone," Agapenor offered, "what else can you tell us about him?"

"He said he's the son of Eris."

"Magnes, the dirty bastard," Borus grunted, "But he was exiled."

"Perhaps we should save any more talk until we get to camp," Thelius advised.

"How close are we," I asked nervously. I suddenly felt vulnerable out in the open.

"Don't worry Calli," Borus assured me, "We are close. Can you see the fairy lights, just over there?" He pointed to a spot on the horizon and I squinted but couldn't see anything.

"It's okay, you'll see them soon enough, it just takes practice."

Before long we left the road and stopped at the edge of a thick cluster of trees. I expected to be taken off the cart as it was impossible to travel any further but Thelius whistled. There was a rumbling sound and the trees parted long enough for us to clear and then resumed their positions once we were on the other side.

"Clever, eh," he grinned. I nodded in a daze.

Once in the glen we were surrounded by faint lights of every color imaginable. A shimmering blue fairy flew close and landed on the leather sack beside me. Incredibly tiny, she could have fit comfortably on my hand, her wings were iridescent like a dragonfly's and her features were human like but more pronounced and pointed. She was clothed in a garment that appeared comprised of flower petals. The blue light she emanated vibrated with energy and I wondered if I touched it if I would feel a shock. She peered at me with intense curiosity.

"Hello there," I smiled weakly. She ventured closer to me and sniffed, inhaling deeply. Suddenly she squealed loudly causing everyone to stop and stare. The look on her face was pure terror and she flew away quickly. I had the distinct impression that she knew what I had ingested and was sharing that gruesome news with her fellow fairies. The men didn't question but they hurried me into the camp.

Eleven

All Fired Up

"May I enter?" A woman's voice sounded from the entrance of my tent. I recognized it as belonging to Ophira; a woman younger than myself, though she seemed years older in mannerism. She was tall and lithe and looked like she belonged in a castle rather than a battalion encampment tending to me. I pulled my fresh and clean night gown over my slightly bulging belly and shifted to sitting.

"Come on in," I smiled as she entered; she and I had hit it off, making her the closest thing to a girlfriend I had in years. Of course, she was also one of the few people here who spoke English as well as ancient Greek so there was that.

Apparently she had been a ward of my grandmothers for years. In addition to English she was teaching her about our world, I guess that was in case she ever had to travel with her. She sat at the edge of my bed; her eyes kept darting to my stomach.

"Is my grandmother back?"

"No, not yet," her eyes met mine, "but word is she'll be here by morning if not sooner." Her eyes fell back on my stomach. "She knows you are here and mostly unharmed."

I had arrived at camp only two hours earlier so the trauma of my physical assessment was still fresh, though I think it troubled her more than it had me. My finger or lack thereof rather, didn't hurt and the site was already smooth and pink as though it had been removed years, not hours earlier. Most likely this was due to the fairy blood.

A small part of me was grateful for it but a larger part argued that it wouldn't have been necessary if they hadn't cut off my damn finger in the first place! Not to mention I would probably be hunted by the fairies.

This was the point where I began beating myself up for trusting David, hell for coming here in the first place. I had taken this guilt trip several times since my rescue and I was getting dizzy. You'd think I'd find better use for my time, now that I had the luxury of just lying here thinking without the threat of capture or death.

"Thanks," I chewed on my lower lip, a bad habit that revealed my mental duress. Ophira sat up to leave. "Wait," I stopped her, "where I come from there is a device that can see inside you so you can see the baby." She eyed me quizzically and sat back on the bed.

"What is its purpose?"

"Well you can tell if the baby is okay, that they're healthy and how old and sometimes you can tell if it's a boy or a girl."

"Wow." She grinned enjoying one of her new words.

"The reason I bring it up is I'm wondering if you have something like that here." She scrunched up her face in thought. "Maybe Cassandra."

"No, I think I've had my fill of prophecies, besides I don't believe in them." Ophira gasped, her hand flew over her heart.

"Calli, how can you say that? Everyone is bound by the prophecies."

"Not me." My face was set with grim determination. "Well, you must have great powers to be able to thwart the fates."

"Mind over matter; I make my own decisions and create my own destiny." My voice sounded harsh and foreign to my own ears. I attempted to soften it, "Thank you for everything Ophira."

"No problem, as you say," she laughed. "Tomorrow if you like and are feeling up to it we can tour the camp and I can introduce you to everyone."

"I would like that very much. Goodnight."

"Goodnight Calli." She leaned towards my belly, "Goodnight morakee." I glanced at her questioningly. "Little baby," she smiled and swept out of the tent. I leaned over and extinguished the candle on the bedside table. The bed, though quite firm, was the most comfortable thing I'd slept on since Nana's and I was finally safe and well fed and warm. The combination ensured I drifted off to sleep quickly but not before kissing my hand and rubbing my belly.

"Goodnight little one," I whispered. I felt a slight kick in response and sighed contentedly.

"Calli," Ophira's voice pierced the silence and I winced. My physical safety had been ensured with my rescue and subsequent care but mentally and emotionally, that was a different story. All night I had been assaulted by a nightmare collage, pieced together with real scenarios and exaggerated fears. At one point I had almost fallen out of bed and was forced to sit with my head between my knees until the nausea passed.

"Good morning Ophira, can I have a little longer please?" I rolled over on my side and pulled my pillow over my head. I smiled to myself thinking how I used to respond to my mother this way when I was a teenager when she wanted me to get up early on a Saturday morning for one chore or another.

A flash of guilt hit me as I thought of my parents and the grief they were going through alone, without me. What if they thought I was dead too? Did Nana have a way to communicate with them? I sat up suddenly, my eyes blurring with tears.

"Um, your grandmother is back and asking to see you in her tent. I can tell her you aren't well enough." I wiped my eyes with the back of my hand and shook my head.

"No, just let me change and we can go." Nana, or rather Captain Thorne occupied a tent that was larger than the rest. Inside it was divided into two rooms; a bed chamber and a command center. The command center was empty so we entered the bedroom. Nana was sitting on the edge of her cot pulling off tall leather boots. Her face aged about ten years when she saw me.

"Oh Calli," she pulled me into a tight hug and then led me to the bed. She examined me from head to toe, crying out when she saw my left hand. She saved my belly for last, lightly moving her hand along, frowning. "I think we should send you home," she dabbed at the tears forming in the corner of her eyes. I smirked and she looked at me with surprise.

"You think," I asked her sarcastically. She shook her head. "Nana, I'm okay. I mean I'm not okay, I've been through hell and back but I'll be okay."

"You've always been a tough cookie."

"Yeah well I learned from the best," I nudged her and elicited a slight smile, though it faded fast. "I am ready to go home and see Mom and Dad and bury Charlie." My voice caught and I broke down crying.

"Charlie? Whatever do you mean child?"

"Oh my God, that's right you don't know; he's dead Nana."

"No, Charlie is not dead."

"Yes he is," I insisted. My voice rose in irritation. It was hard enough to process the information myself and here I was having to convince her. It was like ripping off your bandages to convince someone you really did have wounds.

"David said he was killed at the farmhouse; he was outside the fence. It's all my fault; I sent him away and locked the gate."

"I assure you Calli that Charlie is safe and sound."

"How would you know?"

"Because I talked to him just last night," her voice was firm.

"Charlie's here?" I jumped off the bed practically flying from the elation of the news. She grabbed my arm and gently pulled me back.

"Charlie isn't here," my face fell and she quickly added, "not here at camp anyways but he is on this side. He's working with Daedalus on some innovative weapons combining our two worlds; bright boy that Charlie."

"That lying bastard," I growled. Try as I could I was unable to sustain my anger for very long, the knowledge that my brother was alright, hell that he was still alive caused me to grin. "Everything's okay!" My grandmother raised her eyebrows. "Well we still have things to sort out but I'm feeling optimistic." She slipped on some sandals and changed into a gray tunic. "Thinking I lost Charlie made everything else seem less important, insignificant really."

"When did you talk to David and why on Earth would he tell   you   that?"

"How much do you know?" I settled in on the bed prepared for a long conversation.

"I know that you tried to escape Olympus on a Pegasus and then successfully escaped your husband and ended up in trouble." She nodded to my hand. "I wish you had stayed put, if it weren't for an anonymous tip then we would never have found you."

"David was at Olympus; I was leaving with him. He followed me through the door in the cellar." She didn't look surprised just disappointed. "But he's been here before. His mom is Eris. He said she banished him and he's been trying to get back for fifty years." This last bit of info caused her to perk up.

"He's a demigod, I can't believe I never noticed." She shivered uncomfortably.

"How can you tell?" I asked as I inspected myself for any signs of magic.

"There's an essence, kind of a visible aura around children of the gods. He obviously suppressed it somehow. I definitely would have noticed." "He said you must have suspected and that's why you kept your distance while we were together."

"I noted other undesirable qualities; his selfishness, greed and desire for power."

"You never said a word to me, why?"

"It wasn't my place. It's something you had to decide on your own and they were merely my observations, suspicions." I chewed on that for a moment and realized she was right. If anyone had said anything differently I might have held on tighter. Still, a part of me was resentful for not being told her true feelings. I wondered if my mother had shared her insights. If she did she never showed it, though I couldn't imagine her being as good an actress as Nana.

"Well your suspicions were right on target though understated; he's responsible for my missing finger. He brought a witch and performed a separation. I guess on the bright side I'm not married anymore." This news didn't please her like I assumed it would. "He also claims he's working with some evil emperor from China I think and they are planning on overtaking your world like Napoleon. They want to challenge the gods."

"We did notice some activity in the south, which is why we recruited men from that ridiculous battle."

"Which battle?"

"Between supporters of Hera and supporters of Aphrodite, a violent bit of business all to decide who is favored more."

"Like the Helen of Troy incident?"

"Yes and countless others. The Gods can be quite short sighted and childish at times. I was on an expedition based on a tip about a plant, we noticed the activity and started responding. If he thinks he can take Olympus with that little army he's delusional."

"The south, no he told me he was planning an attack from the north but I messed up his plans."

"He was probably lying, trying to get you to misdirect us."

"No. The separation was done for his new plan. He planned on ransoming us to gain access through the Underworld. He said with Persephone free from her marriage, there would be no passage across the north on the ice."

"Because there would be no more fall and winter," she realized. "I guess that makes sense. We can check that out. Either way, they're stalled for now."

"I hate to bring up a delicate subject but how did grandpa die? Was it really cancer?" Nana sat next to me on the bed, her eyes suddenly misty.

"No, he was murdered," she looked away and dabbed at her tears. "Well attempted," she corrected. I didn't say anything, just raised my eyebrows. "Your grandfather is alive but not in human form, my father helped me change him into a laurel tree."

"Our laurel tree; the one with the bench?"

"Yes."

"So you were talking to Pops out in the garden," my heart grew lighter at the thought of him being alive. "So why did you change him into a tree? Can you change him back?"

"We were ambushed at the house, by monsters, but I don't know why. He drew them away from me and he was stabbed by a dagger dipped in venom. It was killing him slowly; the only hope was to turn him into a tree until I could find a cure. I was schooling you not for a quiz show but so you could come and help me."

"It was David," her eyes flashed, "he confessed but I hoped he was lying just trying to hurt me. He was trying to use your portal to get home." Something suddenly occurred to me. "Why didn't he use it then? Why did he go through the whole relationship act with me?"

"The portal requires two things to travel; firstly, you must be of blood of the one who created it or traveling with that person. Second, you must have a key. How did you get it?" She asked pointedly.

"From David, it was in the envelope he left me. How did he get it?" I knew the answer as soon as the words left my lips.

"Your grandfather was wearing it, the day he died. He never would travel but insisted when I wasn't that he wore it for my safety." Her voice sounded far away.

"I'm sorry," was all I could think to say.

"What else can you tell me?"

"I can't think of anything else. If I do I will let you know right away."

"Yes, please do. We don't have much time before you go home."

"I'm really sorry Nana," I stared at my feet. She hugged me tight and kissed the top of my head.

"Listen, I want you to go with Ophira for a little while, get some breakfast and hang out. I need to meet with the men and go over some maps. Afterward we'll figure out what to do with you." I stood up suddenly.

"Map. Nana, David knows where the camp is, he made me draw a map. I don't know how I did it but he knows. They didn't find him when they rescued me, he could be on his way now!" I struggled to keep the panic from sending me fleeing but it was my grandmother who succeeded in calming me down. She wrapped me tightly in her arms and rocked and shushed me until my breathing began to slow and my heart didn't race so fast.

"It's okay, we prepared for that. Of course he'd have had you draft a map. We have very strong protection spells and we're invisible and impossible to plot. Even if he were standing outside he couldn't see nor gain entry, just keep wandering in circles."

"You're sure there is no way he can get in?"

"It would take some huge magic for him to do so. Don't worry. Go eat and come back in an hour. We have a lot more to talk about."

The camp was enormous, more like a small town, with various tents and buildings for everything from weapons repair to stables to lodging and food and drinks. The latter is where Ophira led me. It was an open space with rough wooden tables and benches. The cooking was done using a metal oven and a massive grill over a fire. There were a few other people, mostly women, seated near us.

"The soldiers are either training or on missions," she offered as we took a seat at a table furthest away from the others. Soon after two young girls brought over plates of porridge, bread, grapes, myrtle berries, olives, figs and jugs of water and wine.

"Thank you," I said to them, they smiled in response, then to Ophira once they were gone, "Isn't it dangerous for them to be here?" She bit into a fig and shook her head.

"No, it is safer here. What's dangerous is leaving, we never know how many men will return until the party comes back." I tried not to think of my grandmother and her recent mission.

Several women at a table a couple rows over were whispering and darting glances at us, or rather me.

"What's up with them?" Ophira shot them a dirty look.

"Stamata," she called over to them. "Don't you worry about them; they are just old gossips. They are obviously bored with all the fighting and killing."

"They were talking about me?" I couldn't imagine anyone knowing who or what I was but their attention was more than evident.

"Just a stupid, did I use that word right, prophecy" I nodded to her and smiled, her English was very good. She loved learning slang from my world but I had to be careful, as earlier while on the way to breakfast, a fight almost broke out when she misused the word 'sucks'.

"It's okay, I already heard about my baby." Ophira's eyebrows raised and she sighed loudly.

"Oh I'm sorry," she paused for a moment, "but it's okay because you don't believe in any of them."

"That's right," I took a swig of water and almost choked, "wait, did you say them, as in more than one?" She nodded reluctantly as though torn about the action. "Tell me please."

"It is better if you eat and don't worry?"

"Ophira, this could be important information."

"No, eat," she commanded.

"Look, it could mean the difference in how I'm treated and how seriously I'm taken, do you understand that?" She appeared confused.

"Okay, it's like if that girl over there told you not to eat those grapes because they were poisoned but someone else told you they heard the girl had a habit of lying." Comprehension played on her face. "I don't want anyone to eat the poison."

"Gotcha," she smiled and winked. "Okay, if you think you can handle it. I know two, well three now, one says you will help win a great war but die and the other says you will rule over an army of death. I'm not sure which is first. Then the one about your child." I silenced her with a wave of my hand.

"It's okay, I've already heard that one. Damn, usually my horoscope says stuff like 'beware of loans from friends' or 'you will take a trip today!' You're sure they're about me?"

"Well yes, it refers to 'Apollo's seed travelled from afar' so everyone, including your grandmother believes it speaks of you."

"Apollo is my grandmother's father?"

"Yes, I've seen him twice," her face lit up like a tween at a Justin Bieber concert.

"That explains a lot and raises so many questions." Ophira stood up and waved away a basket of food the girls had brought over while we were talking.

"Come, let us get back to Captain Thorne. Only she can tell you what you need to know." My grandmother snacked in between answering questions. First I asked about our family and whether everyone was involved or knew about this world. She told me that only her immediate family; meaning her two daughters and Charlie and I.

The reason I couldn't remember any visits here before was my mother had asked her to concoct a potion using water from the river Lethe and administer it to Charlie and I. I told her about my jumbled memories in Olympus. She quickly looked away biting her cheek.

"Well, here's the thing," she spoke slowly and carefully, "and your mother can never know. She was worried about you and the incident with him so she had me mix a potion to help you forget, which I did but water from the Lethe would have made it permanent so I used Lotus blossoms instead."

"I'm glad," I told her honestly, "not for the forgetting but you switching the ingredients. I want to remember." Her face scrunched up in thought.

"Word was sent to Hades concerning your torture and that you are with us and safe." She finally spoke. I was taken back. She said I was going home, I hoped that plan was still in place. Could I still be handed over to him?

"You won't be returning to him," she read the question on my face. "But we had to inform him."

"Why tell him anything?" I didn't bother to hide the annoyance in my voice, with her, with him and these damn prophecies.

"We couldn't have him making any rash decisions based on thinking you were still a captive. They sent him your finger with ransom demands." Her matter of fact tone irritated me. It was confusing watching her change from caring grandmother to crafty military leader. "Though we weren't told what they were we know thanks to you. He declined their request."

"And?" I edged closer.

"Well he of course knows of the pregnancy, they included that in their note. We didn't tell him."

"He didn't know? How could he not know or for that matter, how could he not come and rescue us?"

"Calli, you seem to be confusing the gods with God, they are not omnipotent, hell they aren't even wise or mature," a grumbling from the sky above, "Well it's true," she shouted to the air. "He probably didn't know or he would have but you worry me that you keep saying 'us'. Calli you need to distance yourself from that creature inside you."

"You mean my baby?" Though I myself had pondered what was growing inside me it pissed me off hearing someone else label it so grossly.

"It's not your baby. This isn't a mortal pregnancy, you are more of a carrier for his property and he will take his property back. So say your goodbyes now and be grateful. We will have someone remove it." She said this as casually as she would refer to yard work; don't worry, they'll remove all the weeds and bag up the leaves.

"You know that's the second time someone has threatened to take my baby from me and I won't hear it again." I couldn't believe I was having this conversation. What a misogynist world this was but dammit I was an American and I had rights.

"Calli," her voice strained.

"Discussion is closed."

"Fine, I won't say anything more to you on the subject for now. Is there anything else you needed to know?" I was quiet for a moment, suspicious of her flimsy surrender; Nana was a stubborn bulldog who never lost a fight. It seemed I would have to be on guard with her.

"The prophecies," I asked, more to keep her talking than anything else. She shut me down quickly.

"Ridiculous and should be ignored," she tilted my chin up and smiled tenderly, "I do love you more than anything. This is a different world and you don't belong here. You will go home soon as we deal with the 'situation'."

"Couldn't I stay?" I really had no desire to but I needed leverage. "I've trained since I've been here and could go with you on missions."

"Absolutely not! No, there is no room for discussion; you are separated from Hades you are free to return home. Your mother expects it. Now, is there anything else?"

"Yes, a demand rather; I will leave willingly but you will help me keep my baby." She took her time to respond, I could see the gears of her mind working quickly to come up with a solution where she got what she wanted. I had her tripped though, for she knew if she denied me I'd run and she wanted me home.

"Fine but you are taking Ophira with you." Worked for me.

"When are we leaving?" I asked Ophira as she loaded a sack. I tried to tell her the journey would be short, as in seconds and that Nana's house was furnished and I had access to money to buy anything she needed but she insisted. So I left her alone thinking maybe it was her way of processing the fact she was not only leaving home for the first time but the only world she'd ever known.

"First light, I'm told. Do you need me to wake you?" I nodded, while rubbing my belly. I was lying on my bed lost in my thoughts. "Did you ever see the baby?"

"No, that's the first thing I will do when we get back is go to the doctor. I don't care what anyone thinks, this baby is not evil and I will take really good care of him or her." She smiled and rubbed my tummy.

"And I will help."

"You can be Aunt Ophira," I smiled up at her and then frowned.

"What is wrong?"

"I forgot to ask my grandmother about my Aunt Cat. Weird, don't know how I could have forgotten but then again my mind has had to deal with a lot lately. She said she was in India. Is there an India here?"

"I don't know. You want to ask her now?"

"No, no need. I'll ask in the morning." We wished each other goodnight then I extinguished my candle. I snuggled in my blanket, said goodnight to my baby and prepared myself for an eventful morning. I'd like to say that for once I had a peaceful sleep but as usual bad dreams plagued me and this time they hit close to home. Then I awoke to a real life nightmare.

I heard a strange howling, like tortured metal but more organic then the crack of wood and then I felt the cool breeze. Before I could wipe the debris from my face and risk opening my eyes I felt incredible pressure around my arms and chest. I screamed as the pressure increased. Something sharp punctured my back and my eyes shot open.

First I noticed the stars that shown through the torn ceiling then a gigantic reptilian eye that was staring unblinking. My body began to shudder as the reality chilled me; dragon. I continued rising, the pain and movement in addition to the coppery scent of blood turned my stomach and made me dizzy. It reminded me of a ride at an amusement park when I was a teenager. Only that ride had a safety cage and wasn't trying to eat me.

It pulled me closer to its mouth, foul breath washing over me and stinging my bare skin. It inhaled deeply and roared loudly. I guess I wasn't on its diet. That brought little comfort as there were so many other ways to die; a fall from this height, I must be near 100 feet in the air, loss of blood, strangulation, bashed into a tree; the list could go on and on. Unfortunately, I could not. Out of the frying pan.

Did I really think that David and his witch would be my most terrifying fate? He had warned me about monsters. I had mindlessly involved myself in a tricky game as it were, only magnified by the Olympic players. Hades would get his property one way or another it seemed. I cursed them for their cold and uncaring view of mortals, we were like those little plastic army men, available for their cruel enjoyment then swept away at the first hint of boredom, disposed if broken.

Maybe Nana was right, maybe I was kidding myself. I had never thought about children, not even when David and I were making wedding plans. I guess a small part of me still thought I would make it out into the world to pursue my dreams. Hard to do with a baby strapped to your backpack. Yet as soon as I knew I was expecting, I immediately created this connection with 'my baby'. Had I been fooled again?

I couldn't blame the creature in my belly, which was becoming more like Alien 3 in my mind at this point, for selfpreservation. It wasn't like it had a choice who its parents were. I had two people to blame; Hades for being evil and myself for falling into his trap. It wasn't enough that I was in the clutches of a ferocious mythological creature, I mentally berated myself and when I didn't think that was sufficient punishment I spoke my accusations allowed.

I continued until too exhausted to think, let alone speak and welcomed the reprieve. Blood trailed from a gash in my head, stinging my eyes which were already blurred from smoke and heat. My dove white robes were stained crimson from additional wounds on my arms, legs and back; miraculously or perhaps not so much, my stomach was injury free.

My left arm was broken, a result of the monster crushing me in its claws as it yanked me from a restless slumber. The yells and screams from the camp below sounded like a dull roar as consciousness slipped away from me like water through a sieve. My last thought was of indifference; either option, whether life or death was no more appealing than the other. What did it matter? I was broken at last.

The dragon jostled me as it quickly ran towards the south gate then stopped abruptly then it quickly turned and ran the opposite direction only to stop once more. It was trapped. Desperate it beat its wings but one was torn and broken, my captor was grounded but surely this wouldn't prevent it from its mission.

"Calliope," I heard my grandmother's voice. It sounded miles away but was strong enough to keep me present. With my consciousness front and center I was suddenly all too aware of the pain. The lacerations were deep, there was muscle damage for sure, and I suspected internal bleeding. My lungs hurt, well one of them. The other felt useless, like it was full of holes or maybe the heat and gasses had baked it. I didn't think it mattered much, I knew beyond a shadow of a doubt that I was going to die. After all the close calls, the universe had finally succeeded.

I felt a slight kick. It was feeble and small yet sufficient enough to induce a wave of guilt and shame. Anger swelled up inside me; not for my diminished role but that of my child. I dug deep and summoned every ounce of energy I could and sent waves of loving energy to my belly. I would make sure that whatever it was it knew that it was cared for.

I felt a swift strong kick in response and smiled weakly. A wave of energy enveloped me as though she was hugging me. She? Yes, my daughter was sending me love back. I let go of the fear and anger not wanting to share those feelings and just imagined holding her in my arms, rocking her, singing to her, comforting her.

I wiped at the newly sprung tears and noticed writing was still on my wrist. "Thor," I laughed hysterically. Of all the people to think about as I was dying; a hunky hockey player from back home! There was a flash of light, everything went quiet and I floated just as I guessed it would be like. I wondered if I could still go to Heaven or if I would be forced to the Underworld because I died here. At least in the latter case I could haunt Hades for everything he did.

In either case it was all over; the war, my life and my rule over an army of death. I hadn't offered up myself for all this but I was glad for the sacrifice if it meant protecting so many. I just hoped my daughter would be okay. Surely, her father would take good care of her. Nana would see to it.

Zeus would have to intervene. A final solitary tear slid down
my cheek and I closed my eyes and welcomed death's kiss.

.

Twelve

Is That All?

"Get your tongue out of my mouth!" The heavy weight on my chest lifted. My eyes took their time adjusting so I heard the chaos around me before I saw it. There was yelling and screaming and the sound of trees and posts crashing and the unmistakable crackle and smell of fire.

When my vision focused I saw people were scrambling amongst debris and fire and Roth was leaning over me grinning like he was real proud of himself. We were on the hard ground outside the weapons tent. Or what used to be the weapons tent. It might have still been there somewhere underneath the huge lizard.

"You are not pleased," his eyebrows arched. I could only twist my head to the left and right, making it difficult to see everything.

"That you were making out with me during a dragon attack? No, not very and what are you doing here anyways? You're a hockey player for crying out loud."

"I was healing you and the foul creature is dead, I killed him for you after you called for me." He spread his arms wide, giving a full glimpse of what he looked like underneath all the padding and jersey. He was bare from the waist up, wearing some sort of leather pants, large belt, and metal gloves. His hair was untethered, cascading down his shoulders leading your eyes to his impressive chest. His pecs danced excitedly.

"Wait, what? I called you how?" My head was spinning from far more than the attack.

"You said my name, you said Thor."

"I thought your name was Roth," my voice was stiff.

"Yes, Joe Roth that is my mortal name, clever of me yes? I'm like Superman."

"Clark Kent?"

"Yes!" His grin was energetic and I half expected him to fly away. I wanted to sit up and found that miraculously I could put weight on my left arm.

"You healed me." I had tears in my eyes, from gratitude this time.

"Magic lips," he motioned and puckered. I had the feeling he desired to heal me some more. I shook my head.

"Thanks I appreciate that but where is my grandmother?" He shrugged and continued smiling and nodding to the crowd that had gathered. It was a mix of soldiers, tradesmen and women aids. Some were obviously hurt, others were in shock and most were in awe of Thor.

"Over here darling," my Nana's voice had never sounded sweeter. "Thor may we approach her please?" He must have approved because soon my grandmother was kneeling next to me.

"Another suitor Calli? I must say you share my mother's taste in strong men." Ophira appeared at my other side. Her eyes were glassy and her face slack, I began to worry that she had been injured until I saw the object in her sights.

"Ophira, this is Thor," I introduced them, he grinned, she swooned. My grandmother rolled her eyes.

"Why I chose a mortal." She whispered discretely. I managed to smile weakly in response. Mortals seemed to be the safer choice. "How are you feeling?" I performed a quick diagnostic of my body; bruised and exhausted but not broken anymore. 'You okay morakee?' I thought quietly. I was rewarded with a swift and strong kick in my belly.

"I'm okay, am I incredibly lucky, blessed or something else altogether?"

"You have Thor to thank, he killed the dragon and then," she choked up a bit, "brought you back."

"From where," I asked though I knew the answer.

"You died Calli," her voice cracked. Ophira gave me a knowing look but kept silent. "I don't know how that monster got past our defenses or how Thor came to be here but I'm grateful and you are definitely going home. Your mother was right."

"I wanted to talk to you about something," So much had happened since I had crossed over that I had temporarily forgotten events from home. "I do want to go back but I don't think it's as safe there as she thinks." I was recalling some of my 'accidents' prior to my vacation. She motioned for me to hush.

"Let's get you to my tent and clean you up and then we can get some sleep and go over everything in the morning." She sounded tired and old, words I had never before used to describe my grandmother. It took a lot of explaining to convince Thor that I was perfectly safe with him outside of our tent. I doubted anyone would be sending a second dragon. He pouted when my grandmother made it very clear he would not be sharing my bed.

Apparently he felt that was the obvious conclusion to the night's events, perhaps that was the usual routine where he came from. Now I knew what he meant when he had described his home as 'much further north'. Once cleaned up and tucked in I explained to Nana how we had met at the hockey game and his and the other player's strange behavior.

"Remember what I said about demigods? Your blood is diluted but you are still more than human and a muse, well that makes you even more special. When I made the potion for you and Charlie it shielded your essence as well. It must have diminished once you started traveling here. We'll figure out how to hide you again."

"A muse," I chuckled, "Funny the only thing I seem to inspire is trouble," I said this none too proudly. "What are they like; my great aunts, the real muses?" She sat next to me on the bed.

"Oh, depends on which one and who you ask. My mother, Clio," her smile came, "Is the muse of history. It is through her in the form of inspiration that many books came about."

"So she was a muse in the modern sense as well," I offered. She laughed and nodded.

"Still is," she didn't elaborate and I was intrigued. Did her abilities translate to our world? As though reading my mind she added, "There is a famous painting of a woman who looks as though she's keeping a secret." She winked.

"Wow, really?"

"My aunt Calliope, whom you are named after, is the muse of epic poetry. She is extremely strong willed like someone else I know and a fabulous singer. She visited our world a lot, especially during the 60's."

"What about Thalia?" I had noted the two muses of similar namesakes before during my studying. Looks like we got our trip to Greece after all!

"Thalia; the muse of comedy and quite the performer," she waved her hand with a flourish.

"Looks like your name fits as well," I winked at her.

"It did," the smile fell from her face, "perhaps someday it will again." I couldn't let the night end on such a low note. I slid out of bed, grabbed her hands and pulled her out onto an invisible dance floor.

"Terpsichore," I proceeded to move in a waltz like fashion. I say waltz like as I was forced to free style. "We can't forget her." She eventually caved and twirled a couple times before calling it a night. She looked lighter than before, so better. I knew she had a long road ahead of her with the battles and searching for a cure for Pops so she deserved to smile now. She kissed me goodnight and headed toward the tent entrance.

She decided for comfort reasons she would bunk with Ophira instead of me. I believed it was more for her comfort than mine. I wasn't the most restful sleeper.

"Catherine and Eleanor," I called to her as she was stepping through. I had been puzzled over the normalness of my aunt and mother's own names. She turned her head and shrugged.

"I'm a big Jane Austen fan." She smiled warmly then left. The glow of her visit hung in the air. I fell into bed; the overwhelming exhaustion I had held at bay for so long had finally caught up with me.

However, my head was so full of thoughts pushing and shoving to get my attention that I didn't think I'd ever get to sleep. I spent a lot of time thinking about Hades, worrying about Hades and worse yet, longing for Hades. It was difficult to separate the fear from the passion and love; yes, there was still that annoying bit, too. I couldn't wait to get home so I could sort everything out in peace or at least in an environment where someone wasn't trying to kill me.

The main matter of course was the baby; there was no running from that. I hadn't prepared myself for children and now I had to deal not only with a new and overwhelming responsibility but the fact that her father was a god who ruled over the underworld. How terrifying would Career Day at preschool be for that kid? How terrifying was it going to be for me?

He had managed to pop into my bedroom, I wasn't sure if it was because we were married or something else that I did to allow it that would have to be undone. Would Nana know? He would demand visitation, in the very least, if not full and total custody. I wondered if I would stand any chance in 'court' with Zeus. Would he, could he abduct the baby and take her away from me? I would of course go after them and bring her back but there had to be a way to manage this all in a saner and safer fashion. Perhaps there was an Olympic version of 'witness protection' we could subscribe to.

The strangest thing was this vision of us as a family kept popping into my head. It was always the same; me sitting in a high back chair, our child, wrapped up in a plush blanket, in my arms and Hades, the adoring father leaning over us both.

The whole thing had a warm and fuzzy glow about it that was quickly diffused once I shuttled him forcefully out the scene.

It was exhausting hating him, fearing him. I longed for the idyllic days of wine and roses and lovemaking and feeling adored and cared for. It was immature, reckless and irresponsible but I longed just the same. When I finally fell asleep my lullaby was playing from a memory. I was still half asleep when I made my way out of the tent and stumbled to the outhouse located near the trees. Morakee was using my bladder as her personal punching bag.

I heard shouting and loud bangs and felt tremors, for a brief moment I suspected I was still dreaming about the attack from earlier. The little structure shook and I hurried out to find Thor glaring at a dark haired visitor.

"Be gone monster," he shouted. Gripping a large hammer, he swung it so fast it was a blur. Thunder bolts crackled and shot out striking the other man. He staggered a little but held his ground. Then he began to warp it. It shifted and cracked creating fissures in lines forcing Thor to retreat into the trees. A large elm, uprooted, toppled heavily down on him, though he threw it off of him like it was a twig.

"What's happening now?" I yelled. I was tired, grouchy and raring for a fight. Not the smartest idea in the world considering I was a mere mortal but I was getting a little pissed that I hadn't had a peaceful night's sleep in weeks. My belly jumped excitedly as the dark man turned. "Hades?" My urge to run into his arms was overridden by my overwhelming fear. "You can't take her." I ran towards my grandmother's tent.

"Wait, I'm only here because you called me." Something in his voice tugged at me and I stopped poised at the entrance of the tent.

"I need to learn to keep my mouth shut." I said through clenched teeth.

"Is this true that you summoned him?" Thor asked a little too possessively for my tastes. "This dropping of Jormungand," he spat at the ground. His eyes were unrecognizable, electricity sparked within. I was suddenly overcome with a newfound respect for his power and appreciation that I was on his good side and hopefully remained there.

"I don't know, maybe." My voice was meek as a child's.

"I couldn't be here otherwise, that's how the oath works, reenacted since our separation." I couldn't argue as I felt the truth in his words. I also felt the sting of his resentment. Nana and Ophira hurried over. Nana look worried, Ophira appeared star struck. I guessed she didn't see many gods or goddesses in her day to day. Boy wasn't I the lucky one?

"Was that before or after you sent a dragon to kill me? Or the bounty for me dead or alive?" The words felt false as they fell out of my mouth. Hades face went from anger to pain.

"You were attacked? Are you okay? What about the baby? You said her, it's a girl?" he stepped towards me and Thor slammed him to the ground.

"Wait," I yelled at Thor, "I need to know." Hades moved to sitting but remained on the ground. Thor glared at me like a child that had been refused his favorite cookies.

"He's lying."

"He's not, at least not about this."

"How do you know? You are just a mortal." The way he said 'mortal' nearly shifted my focus off Hades. I swallowed my anger and softened my voice.

"I don't know how but I do."

"So you trust this slime?"

"I didn't say trust but I don't believe he sent the dragon. It's not his style." Hades gave me a look that was a mix of appreciation and annoyance. "Yes, someone sent a dragon here to kill me and Thor killed it and rescued me and the baby." Thor winked at Hades.

"I appreciate you coming to the aid of my wife and child." Hades forced out his gratitude with a scowl. "But I'm here now so you can go."

"Ex," Thor corrected. "She's, how do they say? With me now."

"Whoa," I turned on Thor. "You're both wrong and I'm not some property to be traded back and forth."

"I don't like him," Thor seethed. Hades glared and jumped to his feet. He began growing taller and taller until he was matching the trees. I had never personally seen this side of him before but remembered the gods and goddesses in Olympus were towering giants.

"You don't want to mess with me lad," Hades sneered. Thor shrugged and followed suit. I felt so tiny and insignificant like a flea trying to calm two dogs raring to fight. I wondered if I could develop a better talent to inspire than violence. They were even with the trees and had started grappling, their feet missing tents, possibly with people in them by sheer luck. We had to stop this before anyone, well anyone mortal, got hurt. My grandmother made to speak and I stopped her.

"My problem, I've got this," I turned to the men and whistled. They paused and stared. "Down here please," surprisingly they became a relatable size though neither released the grip on the other.

"Hades, how do I know that you won't hurt me," I quickly added, "or us if I let you stay?" He released Thor and threw me a wounded look.

"I do not wish to ever hurt you," he shrank a little from my glare, "but you can be sure that the oath prevents me." He kneeled on the ground and gazed upward, "as Zeus is my witness I will do no harm." Good enough for me. "Thor, thank you for looking out for me I appreciate it," He grinned and made his way towards me, I pointed in the direction of the soldier's tents. "Goodnight." He skulked all the way glancing behind him. Before Nana could speak I turned to her, my voice still carrying its false authority, "I'll be fine, go back to your tent."

I realized I was going too far, ordering her around but she didn't argue. I motioned to Hades to follow me. If I wasn't going to get sleep, I was going to get some answers.

"Come in." I sat on my grandmother's bed. In a flash he had pulled me in his arms and was kissing me so passionately I thought I'd pass out. Then he pulled away, kneeled on the floor and kissed my belly.

"I'm sorry," he took my left hand and kissed it softly. "I will kill him for this and for daring to even think about our child and then I will torture him for eternity."

"Can you find him?" I was surprisingly okay with the whole torture scenario.

"I already have but I wanted to make sure you were safe first." I shrugged, having been forced to redefine my previous definition; I wasn't being tortured or killed at the moment so I guess I was safe.

"I'm very confused; I don't know what to believe. I've heard some very disturbing things concerning you." He gave me a guarded look. "I'm not talking about the stories," I added quickly. I had made my peace with the mythologies surrounding him after our first 'dates'. I knew how twisted and biased they could be, especially against someone in charge of ruling over the dead.

Of course that was back when I adored him, fine, that was back when I was head over heels in love. Perhaps some reevaluation was in order, after all.

"Ask me anything," he implored. I indicated the nearby chair and he sat reluctantly. "I am bound by the oath."

"You keep saying that. What is it and how does it work?"

"The oath is a powerful force of magic. It prevents me from coming to you, hurting you, taking you by force or lying to you, without your permission."

"I find that hard to believe after..." I swallowed hard unable to form the words to describe my pain and dejection. I fought against the tears that threatened to spill. He looked conflicted, not exactly a hopeful sign.

"It's complicated to explain," he implored me with his eyes to drop it.

"Well you better try," I didn't want to hear his explanation but I needed to. There was no going further until then.

"I upheld the oath, even after the marriage vows took hold and I wasn't expected to," he was undoubtedly referring to the misogynistic laws that gave women little freedom, he was saying he did something unexpected and respectful, "but after you tried that dangerous escape from Olympus and then your behavior after well I just lost it." He stared at his hands. "I want you to know that I have regretted that grievous act and have punished myself every day since." I snorted.

"A lot of good that did me," he flinched as though I had slapped him, I desperately wanted to. I also wanted to grab him and kiss him and do things with him I shouldn't be thinking about at the moment. Maybe it was my hormones. "How do I know you're not lying?"

"Ask your grandmother, she was present when the oath was taken. She was the facilitator actually." My grandmother had enacted the oath at my parent's or maybe just my mother's request.

"Because you tried to kidnap me; I'm still having trouble wrapping my head around that." There was always something.

"I have regretted that situation for many years but I promise my intentions have always been honorable." I pondered what his definition of honor was. I closed my eyes and yawned, exhaustion tugging me back into my comfy uncomplicated bed. I forced myself to think. Everything could be validated, refuted or if unknown, then investigated by Nana, right?

"You know my grandmother will tell me if anything you told me is false," I stared at the wall as I spoke, unable to bear his gaze. I felt myself weakening around him.

"Yes," he said without hesitation, "You may call her in now if you like." I risked a quick glance at him and shook my head.

"No, it's late and I'm exhausted. I have to be up early for the trip back home."

"You're leaving?" He was beside me in an instant. His arms wrapped around me tight. I pushed him off. He let go but stayed sitting so close I could feel his body heat.

"Yes, I'm going home; to my world. I mean, we're going home."

"I wish you would come home with me." He said this wistfully, there was no trace of expectation there. I was glad. He seemed to be keeping his attitude in check.

"I've been hearing that a lot but I'm done with blindly following people, it hasn't been working out for me. From now on I'm making calculated decisions based on what I think is the right thing."

"I fear my arrogance has caused me to lose you." I was surprised by his response. It sounded like a white flag. I knew he had rights as a father and especially as a god. He didn't need my permission, he could take both the baby and I if he wanted. I'm sure once we were back in the Underworld he could arrange it so we never left. I shuddered violently at that thought. A part of me thought I should be more gracious of his compliance but the wounded prideful part refused to let him off the hook. "You were happy once, do you remember," his voice sounded of fresh tears and breaking hearts, "I think we could be happy again."

"I can't even begin to think about us in any capacity yet, if ever." I spoke to the floor. It was cowardly, inflicting the wound while not meeting his gaze. It was no more honorable than a knife to the back but I couldn't bear those eyes of his, they did things to me, made me want to give in and forget. I was done with forgetting.

"I don't want to be without you, either of you." He didn't bother to hide the pain in his voice, bathing me with its essence. My skin grew cold and I rubbed my arms to warm them.

"It's not about what you want. I don't even know you and I dare say you don't know me either. Obviously we will have contact because of the baby. That is how we do it in my world. We will be fair for her sake and put her above ourselves and our wishes. I need to talk to my grandmother and then I promise I will talk to you before we leave." My voice was quiet and I kept my back to him but he heard my words. "Goodnight," I added, holding my breath until I knew he was truly gone. I half way had expected him to carry me away. A small part of me was sorry he didn't.

Shortly after daylight, the three of us women gathered in my grandmother's tent. Due to the events of the previous night the trip home was being rescheduled.

"I want to understand some things before I make any decisions for me and the baby. Hades told me about the oath; that he can't force me and can't lie to me. Is that true?" My grandmother sat at her desk, sullen and displaced. She had not been pleased with his visit but couldn't blame him because I had inadvertently invited him. This meant she was very displeased with me. I held my ground surprisingly well.

"Yes. If the oath is unbroken then that's how it works."

"How can you tell if the oath is broken?"

"Send him away."

"Then," I had expected something much less simplistic. "He has to obey you."

"Okay. Hades," I called out and he was in the doorway in a flash. "I need you to leave; go home." He looked at me with shock and at my grandmother with revulsion.

"As you wish," he disappeared like mist. My grandmother looked troubled.

"Hades, you can come back now." He appeared in the doorway. I thought he might be upset or at least annoyed but he looked pleased. "Sorry but I had to test the oath."

"Understood," he said with a bow. I noticed the edges of his mouth lifted slightly. "Can you give me a moment to speak to my grandmother please?" He stepped outside. "Listen, whatever I decide is going to be based on my feelings and what I think is best. I understand you have reservations but I owe it to my baby to make sure I'm not banishing her father without absolute reason."

"We just wanted to keep you safe." This sounded more like an apology than a statement.

"I know Nana, believe me I don't doubt that for a minute. I am not saying that what he did in the past was acceptable or possibly even forgivable but I have to look at the now and the future. It would be nice to have his protection; don't you think?"

"Yes. I don't like it but I can't argue the intelligence of it. But he's a god, he's powerful you get that?"

"He's letting us leave." This whispered statement was weighty.

"That worries me," she responded. I nodded though I wasn't entirely sure what she meant.

"Does the oath work in our world, too?" I hadn't thought to ask him before. Of course my mind was clearer without his presence.

"Yes," she nodded her head slowly, "it works on the people involved. It's not hindered by location." Her eyes searched mine, begging me to answer a question she couldn't quite ask. She didn't speak and I didn't press.

"Okay, I haven't decided the extent that he will be involved but I think it will be okay. I can always send him away if it doesn't work out."

"Just be careful with your permission, he's crafty." Like she had to tell me!

"Oh believe me I will."

We decided that we would leave at twilight, the following day. I was relieved because I was exhausted and still hadn't worked the plan out in my head completely. I remained inside for the remainder of the day.

"May I come in?" Hades voice sounded from the other side of the tent. I shifted on my bed; my belly was barely rounding but already uncomfortable.

"Sure," I laughed as my belly jumped. Somebody really liked having him around. I wish I could say the same but I still had very big reservations. However, it was easier hating him when he wasn't close enough to see or touch.

"I wanted to bring you some gifts." He sat beside me on the bed and held out a small wrapped box. "It was a wedding gift from me to you." I pulled the ribbon, removed the silk wrapping and opened the lid. Inside was the familiar orb.

"Where?" I stammered, my guilt tripping up my words.

"You dropped this the day of the picnic." His words were calm and free of accusation. I had stolen his property; he had every right to be angry. Was this another trick?

"I don't know what to say," I was stumped. Here was the evidence I had wanted, that I had taken and he was giving it to me freely.

"I was going to use this to get out of the marriage." Now he looked stumped.

"I don't understand," he waited for me to elaborate.

"I guess I don't either, these are your memories right?" He nodded deep in thought.

"Yes, my memories of you."

"Why are you giving them to me now? Is it because it doesn't matter now that we're divorced?" He took my hand and gazed into my eyes with such intensity my head began spinning.

"Oh no, now they matter the most and I think you are ready."

"I have my own memories," I reminded him, "they're not real clear, kind of fuzzy but I can remember how scared my family was." The one memory of my youth that stood out the most was the image of my parents; my mother crying, my father consoling her and my grandmother angry. My grandfather had already passed away or rather had already been turned into a tree.

"I regret that I can't go back and change that, I am not asking for forgiveness or even understanding. You deserve to see me in my entirety, I couldn't ask for you to come back without you knowing who I am. Every memory is in there; I am not hiding anything from you anymore."

"Fine, I'll look at it. How does it work?" He held the globe and gently placed my hand on top. It felt warm and slowly the wall before me was illuminated with blue sky, purple mountains and green trees. A murmuring could be heard then the distinct voices of people. I jerked my hand away, not wanting to see more. "I'll watch it later."

"Thank you. That is more than I deserve." He slumped a little on the bed. He had never looked less like a god.

"Hades, if I ask you a question you have to tell the truth, don't you?"

"Yes, though I would anyways."

"Did you want me because of a prophecy so you could use me as a weapon and take over Olympus?" Fire burned in his eyes and he looked wounded and angry. I shrunk back a little and he relaxed.

"No. I can't explain all my feelings for you but I assure you my interest had nothing to do with any ridiculous foretelling. I have no desire for war. In fact, I would like to keep you as far away from any danger as possible."

"Well, thank you for that," I hoped I had correctly heard sincerity in his words.

"Might I make a request of you?" I nodded my head in response without thinking. I waited with bated breath.

"Would it be alright if I held you and sang your lullaby?"

"Yes," I surprised myself with the quick response. I didn't know if it was the baby or me or a little of both. He climbed behind me and wrapped his arms loosely around my belly and began humming. I melted into him, unaware of how much I had missed him until now. My defenses crumbled and I found myself desperately trying to hold the walls up. I couldn't trust myself with him but it pained me to send him away.

"You promise to not trick me into giving you permission for anything?"

"Yes," he chuckled. "Well done my love, I'm so proud of you."

"For?"

"Taking precautions and using the oath. You are very clever."

"Aren't you supposed to be offended? I'm essentially saying I don't trust you."

"You are carrying our child and I have not given you reason to trust me so no I am not offended. I am glad you are being cautious."

"Wow,"

"What?"

"You surprise me still."

"Pleasantly I hope."

"Perhaps."

"Then I hope to continue." He squeezed me and continued humming. I examined my missing finger feeling more than a little hypocritical.

"I haven't been cautious. Had I only stayed in Olympus then none of this would have happened. I know I was scared of Demeter but I could have talked to my grandmother instead of running off with David."

"You met Demeter?"

"Yes," I shuddered, "I was wandering the halls and she offered me some food and water. Then she tried to poison me."

"Poison? How?"

"She offered me ambrosia." I waited for his shocked reaction.

"Oh." He was surprised but not horrified as was appropriate.

"Oh?"

"She wasn't trying to kill you; she was trying to make you immortal."

"What do you mean?"

"Ambrosia gives mortals immortality. It almost never happens because it's only available at Olympus or in the Underworld. He told you that so you wouldn't drink it."

"He told me she wanted me dead because her daughter was married to you and I was the 'other woman'. Why would she want me to be immortal?"

"Perhaps she believed that it would help solidify our relationship. She never liked me as a son-in-law."

"Oh, okay." Not the most intelligent response but my brain hurt from all the information being crammed inside so quickly.

"Are you alright?"

"Yes, I'm kind of torn between regret and relief." Being immortal would have protected me from all the horrors I had endured since Olympus but then I would never be mortal. I doubted there was a cure for that. Most would wish for the gift, not the power to take it away.

"She was wrong to offer it without explaining." He offered.

"Yes it is a big decision." I sighed and snuggled into his arms, a force of habit I should control but before I could beat myself up about it a voice in my head said, 'hey we deserve a little TLC we've been through a lot.' So I allowed myself to enjoy it and sank into a temporary bliss while he sang my favorite song.

"This is a nice gift."

"What my love?" He paused.

"My lullaby," I whispered weakly.

"No, this gift is for me. I live for holding you and comforting you. My other gift I haven't given you yet. You will have it by morning." He stroked my hair softly.

"Ok." I yawned.

"I will go and let you sleep." He was pushing the whole Mr. Nice Guy to new limits. The lord of the Underworld was performing some serious ass kissing.

"Could I ask you a favor," I was feeling beyond reckless.

"You control me remember, just command me and I will obey."

"I don't want to abuse the oath." I honestly didn't. I had no desire to punish him. Regardless of his motivation or intentions, my love for him had been real and honest.

"It's not the oath, it's me. I told you that you own my heart. Please, what is your request?" That remained to be seen but I carried onward.

"Could you stay with me until I fall asleep?" Said the mouse to the cat!

"Yes. Would you like me to stay all night?" My reflexive answer was 'yes!' but I had to reign in my twisted emotions.

"I don't think my grandmother would like that." Which was so true but not entirely my reasoning; I had read before that you had to be clear with your boundaries with men; I assumed this meant mortal or otherwise, and you had to stick to them.

"Anything for you," he kissed the top of my head. "Enjoy your second gift." I mumbled thanks as I fell into a deep slumber. For once there was no trouble; real or imagined to wake me.

"It doesn't hurt?" Ophira tugged lightly on my left ring finger. I shook my head. It was revealing of my habit of rubbing the nubby spot of its vacancy that I had noticed its return so quickly. I hadn't even left my bed.

"No it feels normal," I could almost forget that it was ever removed, except for a dark pink shiny scar that circled the base. That would have been covered by my wedding ring but Hades hadn't replaced it. We weren't married anymore. Perhaps he wanted me to ask for its return. It was a considerate gesture but I caught myself missing the band of gold.

"Very good," was the extent of my grandmother's commentary, she looked pleased but wary. She had been acting unusual since the day before. Okay unusual for her considering the very dramatic events. "Ophira, can I have a moment with my granddaughter please?"

"What's wrong Nana," I asked after the tent was empty. "Something's bothering you and I suspect it's not just the Hades stuff." She nodded and waved her hand as though to say keep it hushed. "Someone here is on the wrong side, aren't they?" I whispered. "Ophira," my question sounded more like a plea. I had really become attached to her it would break my heart if she was involved. I didn't realize I had been holding my breath until my grandmother shook her head 'no'.

"I told you it would have to be big magic for anything to get in here," she reminded me.

"That dragon was pretty big," I reminded her.

"No, I mean like Olympic big; that dragon was Python. It had been sent after my grandmother to prevent her giving birth to my father and his sister Artemis." My eyes darted to my repaired finger; great, another trusted person. "No, I don't think it was Hades. I hate to say it but he has taken the best care of you." To her knowledge anyhow, "I still don't like your decision and your mother and father are going to flip." I had to suppress a giggle imagining my parents 'flipping out'.

If you looked up mild mannered in a dictionary their photos would be prominently displayed.

"None of the gods are taking credit, which doesn't mean anything but their involvement would be unusual. I suspect that we might have a traitor in our camps, someone who knew how to cancel the enchantments without raising suspicion."

"How many people can do that?" I knew the camp contained close to 200 men and 50 women.

"Not many but too many to sort out now. Listen, I'm going to assemble a party to accompany you and Ophira just outside the border of the camp tomorrow morning. With our reinforced safety precautions, it makes sense."

"So were staying another night?"

"No, you and Ophira are leaving now."

"Wait, what?"

"I don't want to say more, just trust me. Oh and I've arranged for an escort."

"No, I don't trust him," Hades was scowling at my grandmother's suggestion that Thor accompany Ophira and me to the other side. "He's a scoundrel." She raised her eyebrows at him as if to convey 'you're no boy scout yourself.'

"He saved her life." My grandmother didn't need to whisper as she had Hades shield the tent from eavesdroppers. It didn't make it silent, as that would draw suspicion but rather muffled and indiscernible. Thor puckered his lips and probably would have been driven into the ground if I hadn't invoked the oath on Hades, though I was seriously considering rescinding it.

"Thor, I appreciate your help but if you are going to create problems you can just stay here." His arrogant look in response was haughty. Why were all the gods such snobs? "Fine, you won't have to stay here but you won't be going with us." He skulked back and forth and I feared he would leave but I had to put my foot down now or who knew what problems would develop later.

"Alright but I don't like him either," he pouted like a 3 yr. old. Great, I thought I had given up babysitting in the 12th grade.

"Noted and moving on. Hades," My look challenged him to give me problems.

"Only because it is for your safety, but he better not fail." He glowered at Thor; if looks could kill.

"Thank you." I left them in the conference room of the tent to gather the last of my things from the bedroom. I didn't hear him slide up behind me and embrace me. His breath tickled my neck and awakened senses that embarrassed me in the presence of our unborn child. I pulled away and surprised him and myself by turning around and hugging him.

Eventually our lips found each other and would have stayed there if we hadn't heard the discrete throat clearing from the other room.

"Does this mean you forgive me and will reconsider our marriage and moving back home," he whispered hopefully into my hair.

"No, I'm sorry I haven't decided anything yet. I just needed some familiar comfort. Is that okay?" I felt guilty for leading him on, wow I was a tough adversary.

"Of course, take your time."

"Thank you for fixing my hand," I smiled at the change of subject.

"Don't, that was my doing. I can't take back that horrible event but I can take away the memory if you like." I was taken aback by this offer and intrigued. Could he erase all my bad memories? I entertained a blissfully ignorant union between Hades, me and our baby. It was appealing but it would be false.

"No, as much as I would love to forget my time with David here it's what keeps me on guard. As long as I remember what he is capable of I won't let him try anything again."

"Speaking of memories, you did not like your gift?" There had been very little time and even less enthusiasm to view the orb. I attributed part of this feeling to the fact it was gifted and therefore not a threat to him which made me suspicious and yet a more deeply hidden feeling was afraid of what I would learn. I tried to coax it out into the open but it scuttled into the dark recesses until I had finally relented. "How did you know?" Did he have some sort of surveillance on me? The orb itself, perhaps? I eyed him suspiciously and he smiled.

"Don't worry, I haven't been spying. I know because you would have a lot to discuss with me if you had."

"Oh no, it's not that, I'm waiting until I get home. So I can get comfortable, maybe pop some popcorn, make it a movie night." He looked perplexed. "I'll watch it when I have some quiet time alone."

"Okay, travel safe and call me if you need me. You only need ask and I will be there." His voice was insistent and worried.

"I will," I promised and he relaxed slightly, "but only if absolutely necessary. I want you to concentrate on finding him."

"Méchri na xanasynantithoúme; until we meet again." He kissed me softly and then we joined the others.

"Stay safe," my grandmother kissed me on my cheek. "Oh and one last thing, Calli I need the key." I instinctively reached up to my bare neck.

"I'm sorry Nana, I don't have it," she looked at me skeptically, "I left it in the Underworld." She searched my eyes and decided I was telling the truth. She turned towards Hades but he had already vanished. "You'll be safer without it," she warned me.

"How will I return then?" "You won't." Her face has hard but her eyes were caring. I was sure my mother was pressuring her to get me home, which I appreciated and strand me there, which I did not appreciate. I was going to be a mother myself and was still being told what to do.

"I believe this is yours," Hades had returned and was holding the key necklace. I smiled expectantly. He walked over and placed it in my grandmother's hands. My smiled faded. My grandmother looked pleased. He may have scored major brownie points with her but had lost even more with me. Before I could respond my grandmother motioned us to our spot.

"Hades please," She asked a little nicer than she would have. He created a shimmering portal with a wave of his hand. Thor's face shown with anticipation, Ophira looked nervous and reluctant. He gripped her left hand and smiled down at her. She would walk through fire now without hesitation.

I rolled my eyes and sighed, we were the supernatural Three's Company; me, the pregnant muse, Ophira, the fresh maiden and Thor, god of awesome. He gripped my right and we slowly stepped through and into the familiar kitchen of the farmhouse; home sweet home.

Acknowledgements

I wouldn't be writing acknowledgements for a book if there wasn't a book to write them for and that wouldn't be a reality if not for my dear friend and great author John Harrison. Thank you for making my childhood dream come true! I hope to make you proud and yes, I owe you barrels of whiskey; the good kind of course, not that swill mere mortals drink!

Amanda, wow you are such an inspiring an amazing artist, look forward to you breathing life into these 2

Kris, you are so inspiring with not only your words but your actions; so blessed to have you as my friend all these years. Namaste

Richard, you've been my motivator for so many years and I wouldn't be where I am now without you. Thank you cannot sufficiently express my appreciation.

Tami, thanks for all the encouragement and motivation be it inspiring words or a kick in the butt. You da best! Much love!

Rich, I hope you enjoy the shout out. Haven Acres is such a magical place that I had to throw it in and will be revisiting in later books. And you're pretty swell yourself, too, though you still owe me a song!

Last, but not least; Scotty. I don't know where I'd be without my adorable puzzle piece. You inspire me to be a better person and brought much needed joy into my life. I look forward to many more adventures with you and the day you finally read this book!

About The Author

Karma is a lovable oddball existing amongst the normal people in a region of California that has incited much debate between her and fellow author and friend; John Harrison. He says they live in the Central Valley, she agrees but prefers the term NorCal because let's face it, it's the northern part of California and it just sounds way cooler.

Her three awesome children are grown but still an inspiration for her writing and near enough to pitch her crazy book ideas.

She is a dj, though not the cool 80's vinyl type but the laptop variety (yawn) and a karaoke host and she loves to sing. She also loves encouraging people to follow their dreams. Her dream is to discuss Project Muse on the Ellen show.

You can learn more about her and hit her up, well not literally but figuratively speaking. She's not really into that! She does love to hear from fans and potential fans and is pretty good at responding, regardless of what her mom says!

www.KarmaMarie.Com